TV is a form of "entertainment" tantamount to torture for contestants. A thought-provoking, twisty and genuinely terrifying novel in which the reader has to try and work out who the killer is among those who are just pretending, in a high stakes game of bluff, in which you lie well or die hard.'
Bryony Pearce, author of *Raising Hell*

'*Lie or Die* pulls back the curtain on reality TV and exposes the dark side of society's fixation on the cult of celebrity. Sharp, pacy and thought-provoking, this brilliant thriller will keep you on the edge of your seat until the very last page with twists that you'll never see coming.'
C L Miller, author of *The Antique Hunter's Guide to Murder*

'*Lie or Die* is a can't-look-away thrill fest, complete with a bristling cast and an electric plot, and written with razor-like insight into the reality TV industry. It's punchy and fast, sharp and satirical. It'll make your head spin and leave you hungry for more.'
Luke Palmer, author of *Grow*

'An edge of your seat thriller that will have you gasping as the tension mounts. I tore through this brilliant locked-room mystery as it hurtles along at breakneck speed and leaves you feeling like you can't trust anyone!'
Tess James-Mackey, author of *You Wouldn't Catch Me Dead*

LIE OR DIE

Firefly

First published in 2024
by Firefly Press
25 Gabalfa Road, Llandaff North, Cardiff, CF14 2JJ
www.fireflypress.co.uk

© Alison J. Clack 2024

A CIP catalogue record of this book is available from
the British Library.

print ISBN 978-1-915444-41-7
ebook ISBN 978-1-915444-42-4

This book has been published with the support of
the Welsh Books Council.

Typeset by Elaine Sharples

Printed and bound by CPI Group UK

FSC
www.fsc.org
MIX
Paper | Supporting
responsible forestry
FSC® C171272

For Tim, always x

Things I've learned about reality TV

*There are three parts: Pre-production,
Production and Post-production.*

Hot head cameras, lights and action.

A million Insta followers.

All that glamour and glitz.

At no point did anyone mention murder.

LIE OR DIE

Objective

Players must identify and eliminate both Agents before the Agents eliminate all Players in order to deactivate the Ticking Time Bomb and release the prize money.

Cast

Narrator/Judge – Not a participant in the gameplay but acts as a guide and moderator.

Contestants are given one of the following confidential statuses:

Players – Eight Players must uncover the Agents hidden among them, accuse and vote them out.
Agents – Disguised as Players, the two Agents must work together to eliminate Players. Players are killed by placing an Agent card on them.
Detective – A Player with special abilities. They have the power to find out the status of one contestant of their choosing each night.

Glossary of Terms

Accusation Window – A passage of time in which the Players must accuse a contestant of being an Agent. Up to two contestants can be accused and nominated per round.

Courtroom – The accused are brought to the Courtroom to defend their innocence. If found guilty by the remaining contestants, they are eliminated from the game. Only one contestant can be eliminated per session.

Kill Window – A passage of time in which the Agents can select a Player to murder. The Detective may go to Confessional and have one contestant's status uncovered during this time.

Ticking Time Bomb – When an Agent is eliminated a code will be released. Both codes combine to deactivate the Ticking Time Bomb and release the cash prize. Codes can be used by either the surviving Players or the surviving Agents. The Ticking Time Bomb must be deactivated within the time limit, or the bomb will detonate, and the prize money will be incinerated.

Pink Pony Productions reserves the right to change any or all rules or gameplay without notice or permission.

1

I get it. I'm a crap friend. I violated the girl code. I've apologised till my throat hurts.

Kissing your best friend's ex is a shitty thing to do. I deserve to be punished, hundred per cent. But is it *really* worth killing me over?

Staring into Thea's eyes, I beg her to judge me for the person deep-down she knows I am, not on what she thinks of me right now.

'I'm sorry,' I mouth, my voice catching in my throat.

She throws me a look, her perfectly painted lips pursed in a hard line. *Damn*, if I thought for one second she still fancied JB, I never would have told her. And it was weeks ago, I mean, it's not like I shagged him or anything. It was one stupid kiss.

How many times is she gonna make me pay for it?

My eyes sweep the crowded room, taking in my fellow Citizens' expressions. It's too late, nothing I say is gonna change their minds. No one will look at me. Losers. My head's too mushed to think of any clever words to throw out as a last defence.

I should have seen it coming.

I hold my head up and stick out my chin, channelling strong and defiant.

Thea's first, her polished pink nails reaching up towards the ceiling.

'Guilty,' she says, subtext slapping me round the face. She casts an expectant look around the other Citizens. One by one they vote, raising their hands in a Mexican wave of 'guilty', unanimous in their decision to end my stupid life.

The Narrator clears his throat, and the room falls to an expectant hush.

'Kass Kennedy. You have been found guilty of murder. Your fate is sealed. Death by the electric chair.'

Whatever. Does he have to sound so damn pleased about it? The overcrowded room is suffocatingly stuffy, and the smell of boy BO mingles with Lynx Africa and Domino's. Someone open a window already.

'And as she is dragged kicking and screaming to the electric chair,' the Narrator says, his tone wobbling with anticipation, 'she shouts…'

'Innocent.' I look straight at Thea. 'I'm a Citizen.'

'Bollocks.' Thea humphs. Ignoring me, she turns to the others. 'I was certain Kass was the Mafia.'

The living room fills with chatter as the remaining Citizens talk excitedly. This is so sad. A bunch of teenagers squeezed into one small lounge on a scorching hot evening playing a stupid game. Okay, maybe not stupid. Mafia is the craze of the summer and I love it. Ever since my brother came back from uni and introduced the game to us, we've been playing pretty much nonstop. It's all anyone can talk about.

The thing about this game is that even those you trust

will throw you under the bus, aka the electric chair, with a smile and a *Love you!*

Toby MacPhee is staring at me, a stupid grin plastered all over his equally stupid face. Knob. He is so Mafia, I can tell by the way he keeps double blinking every time he says he's a Citizen.

The Narrator begins again, intoning with a deep, half-wasted vibe. 'Night falls.'

The remaining players shuffle back into the circle. At the Narrator's command they fall quiet and close their eyes. I've totally lost track of his story, something about a spaceship and an alien axe murderer – it's all got very *Among Us*.

I can't be bothered to see how this plays out. I attempt to get up off the floor in one graceful movement. It doesn't work. Halfway up I lose my balance and fall sideways, just missing the side table. Ignoring Toby MacPhee's snorting, I head into the kitchen, helping myself to a Fanta.

Lewis is perched on the kitchen counter, some weird-coloured drink in his hand. He raises his glass. 'My own creation. Vodka, green Sourz and some dubious-smelling pineapple juice I found in the fridge. I've had three. Want one?'

'Big no.' After the JB incident I am *never* drinking again. My end of Year Twelve celebrations are definitely over.

Lewis swirls his drink like a pro. 'Not gonna lie, Mafia and Vodka. Baaad combo. One of the many reasons I can't stand the game. Too brutal.'

I lean against the countertop. 'That's the best bit. You get to hide who you really are and mess with people's heads.'

Lewis grins mischievously. 'No wonder you're so good at it.'

Ouch. I deserved that.

'Why do they keep killing you? You're never Mafia.'

'I guess I have a guilty face,' I mutter.

'Duh, not just your face that's guilty,' he says, waving his finger in circles in front of me. 'You are beyond the doghouse; you're like past the house and way down the garden; you are neck deep in shi…'

'Okay.' I interrupt. I really don't need the graphic description of where my friendship with Thea is right now.

Lewis' thickly lined eyes study me, serious and stern.

'What?' I say frowning. 'I've apologised. I've said it was nothing and she still won't talk to me. She hates me.'

'Stop it,' Lewis says. 'She totally loves you, she's just mad at you right now. Remember the time your mum found weed in your bag and Thea totally owned it so you wouldn't get grounded? And who called out Holly Mortimer on that slapper-story rumour? Or the time that…'

My hand signals for him to stop. 'I get it.' Thea and I have been friends for so long I can't remember a time without her. She and Lewis are my rocks, they're my

4

armour in this crazy world. That one stupid kiss has totally messed everything up and I have no clue how to make it right. 'I just wish she would forgive me already.'

Lewis frowns. 'Then maybe you should prove to her that she can trust you again.'

'Easy. And while I'm at it I'll have a go at solving world peace.'

'Good,' he grins, 'because I love you both and the middle is not a fun place to be. What would Taylor say?'

'Mind your own business?' I grumble. Do I look like I need a Swift-ism right now?

'*It's Time to Go.*' Lewis gives me his dreamy Swiftie look. '*Evermore*, bonus track.'

'Uh, *We Are Never Ever Getting Back Together*,' I say, not sing. 'That was me being Thea, by the way.'

'*You Need to Calm Down*,' Lewis says, wagging a finger. 'Before there's *Bad Blood*.'

'And I'm the sad one,' I say.

A scream of delight comes from the lounge. I jump like a guilty person.

'Sounds like Thea's caught the Mafia,' Lewis says. 'And we can go, fi-nally.' He jumps down from the counter with a slight wobble. 'Whoops, those drinks are strong.'

Thea appears in the doorway. 'We won!' She does an excited 'Yay' dance with Lewis. 'When I say *we*, it was totally me. They had no clue who was Mafia.'

'Toby MacPhee?' I say. I might as well be invisible.

Taking out her phone, she poses for a selfie, lips

pursed, fingers held up in a victory sign – one triumphant Insta posted. She points her phone in my face.

'You'd better not be filming,' I say, pushing my palm over the camera.

'Stroppeee,' Lewis sings, nudging me quiet.

I hate being filmed and Thea knows it. 'Why would anyone care?'

'It's not about caring, it's about sharing,' Thea says. 'The key to staying relevant is to keep sharing.' She turns the camera back to her. 'How did you know Toby was the Mafia?'

'Just a hunch.' I have this weird ability to see through lies. I could be the queen of this game if I was actually good at lying myself. Can't do it. I get all twisted up and tongue-tied. Then I do stupid things, like full on admit to my best friend that I kissed her ex when it wasn't a big deal and I should have just shut the hell up.

Lewis ushers us out of the front door and into the street, shouting our goodbyes over his shoulder. Thea's head remains buried in her phone, her fingers dancing over the screen, her face hidden by a glossy curtain of silver hair.

'What the actual?' She stops so abruptly I almost walk into her. Her head flips up in one sudden move. She pushes her screen into my face. It's a picture, from tonight, before the game started and it's of me. JB is in the background, top off, striking a pose and showing off his six pack. And I am staring. Understatement. The wistful look of adoration plastered all over my face is in direct opposition to my loud appeals of indifference. My mind goes blank as panic overrides logic.

'I … I…' I stutter.

'You told me it was nothing,' she hisses, her lovely deep-dark eyes narrowed.

'JB wasted and showing off his abs, nothing new there.' Lewis leans in further. 'Oh, I see.' He whistles slow and loud. 'Game over, hun.'

'No,' I say, desperately trying to find a coherent thought. 'It's not what it looks like.' My stammering is not helping to prove my innocence. 'I didn't even see JB.'

'To be fair he didn't stay long,' Lewis says in my defence.

'It's just the angle.' I point to the phone. 'The picture is wrong.'

'The picture is wrong?' Thea says. 'That's your defence?'

'Why would anyone take a picture of that?'

'Uh, hello?' Lewis says. 'This is Boredomville. This is literally the only thing that's happened all week.' He holds up his palm. 'And no, it wasn't me, anyone in the room could have posted it.'

I bet it was Toby MacPhee, no wonder he was sniggering.

'But it's a lie…'

'Doesn't matter, it's out there. People see what they want to see.' Thea crosses her arms across her chest. 'Lies are the new truth, everyone knows that.'

My words are tripping over each other. 'It's nothing, I swear.'

'You said that last time, remember? When you were

too busy to make conversation because your lips were stuck to his?' Lewis is behind her miming slitting his throat. 'This looks pretty obvious to me.'

Lewis is right, she really doesn't trust me. I turn on my heel in frustration and head for the high street. It's late, ribbons of red streak across the sky like a fanfare, celebrating the promise of a sunny tomorrow.

Thea follows, her heels clipping on the pavement as she hurries to catch up.

'I don't know what else to say,' I say, striding past the shops.

'You got off with him,' she says.

'I kissed him. Once. And it was weeks ago.'

'Tongues?' Lewis says. 'The definition of getting off is the use of tongues.'

He really isn't helping.

'Admit it. You fancy him,' Thea says, waving her phone in the air.

'No. Yes.' She's confusing me. I turn to face her. 'Does it matter?'

'Ooh, Rocks is still open.' Lewis points at the chippie ahead. 'Chips?'

We ignore him.

'This is stupid,' I say.

'Oh, I'm sorry. You perving over my boyfriend is stupid, is it?'

'He's not your boyfriend,' I shout in frustration. 'You finished with him.'

'Doesn't mean I've *finished* with him,' she shouts back. 'Doesn't give you the right to full on flirt with him … again.'

'I wasn't.'

'Oh, so your face always looks like that?'

'I have no idea what I was looking at, but it wasn't JB.'

'You're lying.'

'I am not, I swear.'

'Why should I believe a word you say? You're a liar and a cheat and a crap best friend.'

'Enough.' Lewis is standing in a dramatic pose, arm draped over his eyes. 'I can't take any more of this.' He points to me. 'Kass, you messed up, BIG time, own it and Thea, you need to let this go. This picture says more about slime ball JB than Kass. Find a way to forgive already. Being stuck in this dump is bad enough, but what I don't need this summer is you two ruining my holidays boy-bickering. *Chicks before dicks*, remember? Our friendship is so much bigger than this and I refuse to have it defined by a boy.' He takes a dramatic breath. 'Now I have had way too much to drink and need some chips and curry sauce.' He opens the door of Rocks. 'When I come out, I expect you to have found a workable solution to this problem and to have remembered why you are best friends … forever.' He flicks his blue fringe from his eyes in one easy movement. 'You are welcome.'

Lewis disappears inside the chip shop.

Thea crosses her arms, two angry red dots colouring her cheeks, looking anywhere but at me.

9

Not sure what else to say, I stare at my feet and keep my mouth shut while the silence bangs at my temples.

I shuffle on the pavement. 'You want chips?'

'No.'

More silence. I chew on my fingernails and will Lewis out of the shop. How long does it take to get a bag of chips?

'I really am sorry,' I say. 'I never meant to hurt you.'

Thea frowns. 'Well, you did. Big time. You never think. You totally take us for granted.'

The accusation stings sharper than a bee.

'I would never put a boy before you.'

Thea's not even looking at me, staring at her phone – she's way more interested in whatever is going on in the world of social media.

I try again. 'You're my best friend.'

'What am I then? Apart from delish eye candy.' Lewis steps out of the shop, bag of chips in hand.

He wraps his arms around Thea, smothering her within his gangly frame.

'Urghh, get those chips away from me,' she says, wrinkling her nose.

Thea was just like me until Year Eight. Then she hit puberty and like the predictable cocoon-butterfly analogy, spread her dazzling wings and flew into the sun, leaving caterpillar-me alone with no clue how to build a cocoon. I'm still waiting for my metamorphosis. I'm starting to wonder if this is it.

Our phones ping.

'Check your phones,' Thea says cryptically. I do as I'm told, zooming in on Thea's message.

Casting Call

Big Brother meets Mafia

We are looking for CONFIDENT, COMPETITIVE & INVESTIGATIVE contestants (17–18) to take part in this EXCITING NEW reality TV game show.

BIG CASH PRIZE.

Do YOU have what it takes to survive?

Email: casting@pinkponytv.com

'What am I looking at?' Lewis pulls his phone right up to his face.

'*Big Brother* meets Mafia? I was totally born for this,' Thea says, hopping from foot to foot.

'I'm glad you said *I*, 'cause hell would have to freeze over before I go in front of the camera,' Lewis says.

'Me too,' I say. Let Thea have her crazy ideas. As long as I don't have to join in, I can be supportive and crutch-like. 'Besides it's what's on the inside that counts, not who you are on the outside.'

Thea tuts. 'No one cares about what's on the inside. It's all about what you can show in fifteen seconds.' She taps her phone screen. 'It's alright for you two with your brains and your books. I don't want to be left behind with some crappy job. This is my way out of mediocrity. I want more. I want KSI more.'

'There are loads of careers you can do,' I say, trying to be helpful.

'I don't want a career; I want to be famous.' She straightens up with determination, pushing her chest out, boobs like weapons. 'So, I'm doing this. And I want to win, so you're helping me. You're so good at reading people. You *owe* me.'

'Sorry?'

'You just said you wanted to earn my trust back.' She holds up her phone, making me cringe all over again. 'Prove it. Put *me* first. Help me win.'

'Oh, nice move,' Lewis says.

I've been totally played. And it worked. I'll do whatever it takes to get us back to normal.

'Fine,' I say. 'I'll do it. I'll apply for your stupid show.'

Thea guilty grins. 'Okay, so I already filled in the online form weeks ago, for both of us.'

'Oh no, you didn't?' Lewis shrieks.

'When were you going to tell me?' I gasp.

'I'm telling you now,' she giggles.

Lewis skips up the road, singing. 'My girls are gonna be famous, my girls are gonna be…'

I ignore the frenzied rhythm of my heart. I'm no Thea. I don't belong in front of a camera. I can't even do an assembly. I choke, every time – it's a whole embarrassment of stammering gibberish. But it's one application in thousands, there's no way I'm getting through… Right?

2

'You are not wearing that.' Lewis is standing in my bedroom, looking totally unimpressed at my TV audition outfit.

'Why not?'

'Because you look like you're auditioning for the school chess club.'

Turns out there *is* something worse than applying for a reality TV show. If your application is accepted, there's a next step. A round of auditions, via Zoom with an actual, proper Executive Producer.

I start to pull my comfy hoodie over my head. 'Thought I was supposed to be natural and show who I am.'

'The world is not ready for a hundred per cent you.' Lewis snatches the hoodie from me, dropping it on the floor like it's radioactive. He steps back, his perfectly painted eyes running up and down me as I squirm under his critical gaze.

'Better,' he says. 'You know you have a shit-hot body, girl; you should show it off.'

'Whatever.' I snort. 'No way I'm going to objectify myself for some ridiculous reality show.'

'Fair play.' Lewis adjusts my laptop on my desk. 'But we are trying to get you on it, so some effort is necessary. Nice face, by the way.'

'Thanks.' I roll my eyes self-consciously.

The sun is blazing through the window. My newly applied make-up is in danger of running all down my face. I flop onto the bed.

'Why did I agree to this "In It to Win It" thing?'

'A Minute to Win It.' Lewis closes my curtains to block out the glare. 'And you know why. Actions have consequences and your roving eyes got you into a whole heap of trouble. This is your chance to redeem yourself, don't mess it up.'

Cringing, the now-familiar guilt heats my cheeks. I'm just keeping my mouth shut and going along with it, at least then I can't be accused of not trying. Thea had her audition earlier. It went really well.

So here I am, about to be interviewed by the Executive Producer: Pippa something. I have to appear witty and entertaining and like I am totally into this whole stupid idea and not being coerced by Thea who wants me to prove she can trust me by doing something so far outside my comfort zone I might as well be on another planet. And I have to convince her of all that in just one minute.

'Just be yourself,' Lewis says. 'Second thoughts, maybe try a little. Ask yourself, what would Rebel Wilson do? No, *be* Rebel Wilson.'

'Bog off.'

Lewis chuckles. 'My work here is done.'

He clicks the Zoom link. I panic.

'Ready?' He steps behind the laptop and makes a heart with his hands.

15

Here goes nothing. Checking myself in the mirror, I take a breath as the words 'Lie or Die Audition' come up in the box next to mine. I hit unmute and a youngish woman appears on the screen, bobbed red hair and an overly perky manner, beaming from ear to ear like an American chat show host.

'Hi Kass. I'm Pippa, the Executive Producer for *Lie or Die*. I'm gonna ask you some questions so we can get to know you better, if that's okay?'

I nod, immediately awkward.

'First off, can I get you to stand? I want to get an idea of all of you.'

I stand, wiping my hands down my jeans.

'Ready?' If possible, her smile's got even wider.

I clear my throat. I am *so* not ready.

'We'll start easy. If you could tell me your name, age, and a little bit about yourself.'

Lewis is mouthing SMILE over the laptop. Pushing my shoulders back, I try to channel my inner Rebel.

'I'm Kass Kennedy and I'm seventeen years old. I live at home with my parents. I have two brothers and a dog.' Lewis is miming a yawn. I smile quickly and unfold my arms, letting them swing awkwardly at my sides.

Pippa's nodding encouragingly through the screen. 'Great. Kass, can you describe yourself to me in three words?'

'Umm.'

Lewis is frowning. I tug at my top with my fidgety hands.

16

'Friendly.' The pressure is epic. 'Friendly.' *I just said that.* 'Forgettable.' *Cringe.* 'Boring.'

'Boring?'

I nod. *Bet you're gonna forget about this in less than a minute.*

'Why do you think you're forgettable and boring?'

Lewis is shaking his head.

'I'm normal.' I can't stop making big hand gestures when I speak, what's that all about? 'You know? Ordinary. I'm not like loud or zany or mad-witty. I'm just me.'

Pippa smiles. 'Pronouns?'

'She, her.'

'Sexuality?'

'Straight.' *See? Boring and predictable.*

'Name one thing you do that's a lie.'

'Sometimes I wear my earbuds and pretend to listen to music, so I don't have to speak to people.'

Lewis is rolling his eyes.

Pippa laughs. 'Me too.'

I relax a little.

'Kass, if you were a Disney princess which one would you be?'

I gawp at the screen. I can feel Lewis' eyes on me.

'Uh, none of them?' I say. 'I don't need rescuing by a privileged white boy with too much time on his hands.'

Lewis stuffs his fist into his mouth.

'If you were a biscuit?'

'Bourbon? It's classic and it is what it is.' I shrug. 'A

Bourbon doesn't pretend to be anything else. It's a chocolate biscuit, end of.'

Pippa nods. 'I do love a Bourbon,' she says, reading her notes. 'So, Kass what Marvel superpower would you say you had, if any?'

I don't have a superpower on account of them not being real. I picture Thea answering these questions without pause, making witty banter and impressing Pippa in a second. Ooh, hang on, I'm having a thought.

'I can read minds,' I say. 'Not for real,' I add hastily, 'but I can tell when people are lying. Like read them.'

Pippa's eyes fly up from her notes. 'Like telling their tics?'

'Exactly.' I point to the screen. 'That.'

'This show is ultimately about lying to win. How far would you go to win, Kass?'

Lewis is miming behind the camera like a sad Christmas charade. Hand clamped above his eyes he's gazing into the future.

'Far?'

'Ever been in love?'

'No?' I thought this was a murder-mystery show?

'Have you ever fallen out with a friend over a boy?'

'God no,' I say, more reaction than thought.

'Reeeaally?' she says. 'You sure about that, Kass?'

'Yeah?'

'In your application you say, and I quote: "I screwed over my best friend for a boy I liked even though she had only just finished with him".'

18

Oh. My. God. I am going to die. Way to have my back, Thea. Pippa's stopped scribbling and is staring at me. My cheeks were burning before, now they're an inferno.

'I … um… No.' I send a full-on SOS to Lewis. This is bullshit. 'I guess I did say that, didn't I?' I glare at Lewis. 'What I meant was I fanci…' My words are sticking in my throat making it hard to talk. '*Liked* my best friend's ex.'

'And did you go out with him?'

'No,' I say. 'I did not.'

'Then how exactly did you…' Pippa reads slowly, '… screw her over?'

Well done, Thea, you have just right royally pissed me off, as I stand in my bedroom being judged by a total stranger for things I didn't do.

Pippa leans into the laptop. 'There are no right or wrong answers, Kass. I'm just trying to get a steer on who you are and whether you would be right for this show.' She takes a beat. 'So, if you had to choose between betraying a friend or losing the game which would you do?'

This is it. This is my out. All I need to do is answer the question honestly and all this will go away – no comeback. Of course, I would never betray my friends to win some crappy reality show – for what? I open my mouth to give my final answer, but my competitiveness has befriended my anger and the words Thea put into my mouth have left a sour taste. I take a step closer to the laptop. If Thea wants me on this show, then she's asked for it.

'I love playing Mafia and I am *ruthless*.' The anger and embarrassment flooding through my veins right now are holding me up like a scaffold. 'I would be fantastic on your show.'

'So, coming back to my earlier question, Kass, how far would you go to win?'

'All the way.' My mouth's not connected to my brain; I can't control it. 'Who needs friends when you have money and fame?'

Where the hell did that come from? I don't recognise myself. My anger dissipates as quickly as it came.

'You go, girl,' Lewis shouts, then clamps his hand over his mouth, his wide eyes gleaming with laughter.

'And we are done.' Pippa puts down her pen. 'Thank you, Kass, that was great. Do you have any questions for me?'

'Um, no.' My voice has lost all its power, less warrior, more mouse. I slump into my chair.

'One more thing,' Pippa says. 'Is there someone with you today?'

Lewis is doing wild 'No' hand gestures at me.

'My friend Lewis is here,' I say.

'Ahhh, hi, Lewis,' Pippa says. There's an expectant tone to her voice which tells me she is used to getting her own way.

Lewis walks behind me, saluting the camera with a cheery hello.

'Nice to meet you,' Pippa says. 'I'm guessing you were there the whole time?'

'Guilty,' Lewis says. His thick cuff rings sparkle silver as he waves his hands in the air, jazz-like. His hair is particularly floppy this afternoon and the sun streaming through the crack in the curtains is really catching the blue. His ripped skinny jeans and oversized black T splashed with bright orange and yellow flowers complete his *way too cool for this town* look.

'Didn't my girl do good?' His arm curls around my shoulder.

'She did. Love your look,' Pippa says.

'Why thank you, Pippa.' Lewis does a little twirl. 'Look like Yungblud, live like Taylor.'

'Totally,' Pippa laughs. So not fair. It's taken a second for her to fall under his spell. I couldn't do that in a minute!

'So, I don't see your name on my list?'

'Nah.' Lewis pouts. 'All this reality stuff's not for me.'

'Sure about that?' she asks.

'Hundred per cent.'

'You would be so good,' Pippa says. 'You were made for telly.'

Lewis pulls a face. 'I aspire to be on the other side of the lens. The one calling the shots. I don't want to be the stereotype, Pippa. I want to change the stereotype.'

'Too bad,' she says. 'If you change your mind, Lewis, you have my number. Gotta go, I've another audition. It was really nice to meet you Lewis, and Kass, well done. We'll be in touch.'

I close my laptop.

'Woohoo!' Lewis bounces up and down. 'Where did *that* girl come from?'

'You know I didn't mean it, right?' I say, still cringing.

'Totally.' He's bouncing from foot to foot. 'You nailed it.' I love that despite what Pippa said to him he still gives me the credit first. 'Wait,' he grabs his phone. 'We need Thea.'

3

Dear Kass,

It was good to 'meet' you last week. We thought your audition was great. We had an unprecedented number of applicants, and the competition was very intense. Unfortunately, on this occasion, we have decided not to proceed with your application any further.

Wishing you the best of luck for the future.

Kind regards,

Pippa Barkley

Executive Producer

Pink Pony Productions

I didn't get in.

It's been two weeks since my rejection. And it sucks.

Knowing I didn't get a place on the show has pissed me off. Knowing Thea has, has pissed me off more.

It's not the being on TV bit that's bothered me: that I don't have to be filmed on live TV 24/7 is a huge relief. It's the nagging voice in my head telling me (in the voice of Pippa Barkley, Executive Producer) that I'm not good enough.

But Thea is.

And I'm still the one who puts *dicks before chicks* despite going through with the application – how's that even fair? So now I'm not only a terrible best friend because I kissed her ex but I'm also a bad person 'cause I'm totally jealous that she's considered shiny and good enough while I've been judged boring and dull.

To overcompensate for my inadequacies as a friend, I've become the most super-supportive bestie ever and agreed to drive her to Wembley with Lewis for the start of the show.

The reception of Central Studios is cool, literally. I'm sat under the aircon, and the constant blow of freezing air is making my skin buzz. Simon Cowell's laughing at me, staring down from a huge picture, his eyes following me like one of those portraits in a haunted house.

Towering palms are positioned in the corners of the room, with fresh flowers in grand displays near the doors. I'm the only one here. Me and the receptionist. She's sat behind reception looking fabulous as I chew on my fingernails. Lewis was with me for about a gazillionth of a second before being whisked away by Pippa. I swear she remembered him *way* more than me and was eager to show him behind the scenes. To be fair, I was invited too, but it was too embarrassing after the whole loser rejection letter, so I made some lame excuse and stayed put.

Sitting here alone, totally awkward, it's like my friends have literally left me behind.

I keep crossing and uncrossing my legs, wishing I hadn't worn jeans, and feeling young and very stupid in my cute sushi T.

I shouldn't have come. I'd hoped that by being

supportive and agreeing to drive here with them, Thea would finally realise how sorry I was, but she's way too caught up in all the excitement of potential celebrity while I'm in danger of sounding like a stuck record. She and Lewis have been thick as thieves with all the TV stuff.

And I miss them.

Above reception hangs a large flatscreen. The top half of the screen is labelled STUDIO LIVE. It's blank. Underneath is a message board, like a fancy paging system for important people or celebrities. A small security camera hangs in the corner, making me self-conscious.

So bored.

The main glass door swooshes open and a rush of August heat hits me before the thick glass slides back, locking out the summer with an efficient clunk. A boy strides in with the lazy confidence of a champion. He pushes his sunglasses up on his head, where they rest casually on his twisted locs swept up neatly in a high bun. He's wearing jeans, but unlike me, he looks fresh and calm. He's beautiful. I mean BEAUTIFUL. He's tall, well over six foot, his tight jeans ripped in several places showing tantalising glimpses of skin beneath. His arms bulge, skin pinging beneath the vest that clings to his contoured chest, in a hot, but not sweaty way. His cheek bones are equally sharp, his face looks airbrushed – no imperfections in sight. And he smells deee-vine. A musky male scent, not too strong, wafts over the heavy scent of flowers.

He heads straight for reception.

'Tayo Asaju.' His voice matches his look.

'Which production?'

'*Lie or Die*. Pink Pony Productions.'

'One moment.' The receptionist taps at her keyboard. 'I have Tayo Asaju in reception.' She nods. 'Sure.'

Looking up through long flirty lashes, she taps a pretty nail on the counter.

'Sign in here, please.'

Before Tayo's finished scribbling, Pippa appears through the double doors.

'Taeee-yooo,' she purrs. 'Great to see you again.'

Tayo shrugs his rucksack off his shoulders. I fold my body into the tub chair. How could I think for one minute I could compete with people like this? They're another league – the shiny people. Thea has *it*, Lewis too. I'd totally buy whatever they were selling.

I guess that's what Pippa Barkley, Executive Producer, saw in them and not me.

Tayo heads through the door towards his dazzling future. I smile, but he doesn't notice.

The need to be out of this artificial, glossy place with its weird foliage and perfect people is overwhelming. Jumping up, I stand in front of the door. Nothing happens. I wave my arms in the air but the door remains shut.

'It's locked,' the receptionist says in a bored voice. 'Use your lanyard. You need to swipe the pad on the left.'

Wow. I bend forward, stretching the lanyard around my neck until it hits the pad. There's more security than Area 51.

26

Is it to keep the celebrities in or the ordinary out? The glass door swooshes open, and I propel myself up the studio drive quicker than you can say 'The Real Loser of Wembley Park'.

Standing on a busy crossroads, with its noisy traffic and dirty pavements, I'm much more at home. Across the road is a cafe. My stomach groans. Lewis will message when he's done. I dash across the street.

Five minutes later, I'm tucking into a sausage sandwich on thick white, licking grease from my fingertips, giving a metaphorical two fingers to beautiful Tayo Asaju and all the shiny people.

The cafe's tiny. After the sterile perfection of Central Studios, I'm happy to sit in the corner squashed up against the window. From here I have a great view. Central Studios sits on a crossroads, stretching far back along the road. When the sleek building ends, the high security fences topped with barbed wire rolls still run on for as long as I can see, enclosing the grounds like a secret garden. It's massive and totally out of place in this otherwise normal high street. Mirrored windows cover the exterior, gleaming and sparkling like the stars inside, reflecting Wembley back on itself, never allowing the outsider a glimpse of the secret world within.

'Is this seat taken?'

A soft voice shatters my calm. I look up with a guarded huff, into a pair of dazzling blue eyes, half hidden under a messy fringe of bleached, white hair.

I pull my mug of tea unnecessarily close. The table

tips as he sits, dumping a large holdall on the floor under the table. Putting his mug down he reaches for the sugar. I disappear into my phone.

'Waiting for your psych test?'

'Sorry?' I say.

'*Lie or Die.*' He leans in, whispering through a cheeky grin. 'You don't look like one of the locals.'

Glancing around I swallow a giggle: everyone's really old. 'My friend's testing. Tested. She's not come out so I s'pose she passed and she's in the show and everything. I came with her. To support.' *What am I waffling on about?* 'My other friend's being shown around.' I stammer in a desperate attempt to not look like a huge fangirl stalker. 'He's taking me home. Driving.' *Shut. UP. Kennedy.* 'You?' I try to deflect from the car crash that is me.

'Yeah, waiting for the test,' he says. Of course he is. He has that look, that already filtered, 'Tayo' look. Perfectly dressed in jeans, casual long T and Airforce Ones, he's ready to walk onto the set of *Love Island*. His snow-white hair flops over his eyes which he flicks casually with his hand. He has a small tattoo on the inside of his wrist, but I can't catch what it is.

'I wonder how many people fail these tests; you never hear, do you? I wonder what they're looking for.' He plays with the sugar. 'Sorry, I gabble when I'm nervous.' He rests one hand over the other as if willing himself calm. 'To be honest, I'm not sure what I've got myself into.'

'You don't play then?' I ask. His smile is infectious and I full-on grin back.

'Mafia? God yeah. Love it. But it's one thing to sit in your mate's house, wasted, and quite another to play with complete strangers while live streaming.' He stirs a shitload of sugar into his tea.

'Why are you playing then?'

'I kinda did it as a dare.' He holds his hands up. 'Okay that sounds lame.' He gazes out of the window and his face turns serious. 'I guess I wanted to show the world I could win.' He turns back to me, grin back in place. 'That's the beauty of this game, even the quiet ones can have a voice.'

'I'm sure you'll be fine.'

He shrugs. 'So, why not you?'

My turn to shrug. 'Not my thing.' I'm not about to get into it with a stranger.

'I get it. I wouldn't be here if my mates hadn't applied for me.'

'Me too!' I say. He looks at me with curious eyes. 'My friend applied for me.'

'So, what biscuit are you? I was a Jaffa Cake.'

I grin. 'Bourbon. Solid and dependable.'

His eyes are dancing. 'You always know what you're gonna get with a Bourbon.'

'Jaffa Cake, though?' I'm enjoying this. 'Cake or biscuit?'

'Exactly. It's the unanswerable mystery of the biscuit world. Who, or rather, what is Jaffa Cake?'

'Interesting,' I say.

'So, what happened?' he says.

'She got through. I didn't.'

'Well, that sucks,' he says.

He's got that easy to talk to vibe. 'She deserves it. She's a natural at this reality stuff.'

'And you're not?' he says.

'Clearly not. Boring to the core.'

His look changes. 'Bourbons could never be boring.'

Oh god, my cheeks are heating up.

'Maybe not boring. Normal. Well not TV, that's for sure.'

'Is that your fear? To be seen as normal?'

'My fear?'

'Yeah, you know, they always ask what your biggest fear is. Do you have some deep dark fear of being boring?'

'Not really. I guess I always feel out of my depth. My friends know exactly who they are and aren't ashamed to show it. I've no clue about any of it.'

He gives me a questioning look.

'I guess I'm scared of being ordinary.' *Oh crap, too much.* 'And I can't stand slugs. I stepped on one once – barefoot. Disgusting.'

He sips his tea. 'Agreed. And for what it's worth, there's nothing wrong with being ordinary.'

'Tell that to the exec of *Lie or Die*.'

He leans on his elbows. 'Maybe they didn't see the real

you.' I squirm under his crystal-blue stare. 'Don't for a second think you're not good enough. None of it is real, it's all just one big lie.'

A shrieking siren catches our attention before the flashing blue comes into view. An ambulance is hurtling down the street, pushing cars onto the curb in its hurry to pass. It turns left at the traffic lights, straight into the studio car park.

Jaffa Cake boy jumps up and grabs his bag. 'Need to go.'

His reaction surprises me, why the rush? Should I go too? Checking my phone, I stay seated. Someone will call me if it's an emergency, right?

'Good luck,' I say. The next time I see this guy he could be famous, how random is that?

'Thanks.' He takes a last sip of tea. 'I'm Noah by the way. Noah Winston.'

'Kass Kennedy.' Unsure whether to get up, I shuffle in my chair. 'Hope everything's okay.'

Noah's staring out the window. 'Yeah, I'm sure it will be.' He tears his eyes from the window to smile a *not bothered* at me.

His mouth twitches on one side and he pushes his hair from his eyes. He's lying, he's totally bothered. Maybe he's worried the show will be cancelled and his big chance will disappear. I smile reassuringly back. 'Look after my friend, Thea, for me.'

'I will.' A strange expression clouds over his face. My

superpower read on people tells me he's sad. A split second and the moment's gone, his face returns to friendly. 'Nice to meet you Kass totally-not-boring-Bourbon Kennedy.'

The minute he leaves, his phone becomes glued to his ear. He runs across the road and disappears behind the ambulance, me and our short conversation forgotten. So much for Bourbons not being boring – more like instantly forgettable. I should have been a Wagon Wheel, or something exotic like a Viennese Whirl.

The sight of the ambulance is making me uneasy. I text Lewis.

U ok?

He texts straight back.

> **DW, we good.**
> **Someone's had an accident.**
> **Looks bad.**

Oh.

I relax. At least it's not Thea. No point in rushing back, I'll only be in the way and I'm crap in a crisis. So, I sit in the cramped, noisy cafe and watch the drama unfold, like my own personal reality show. Lewis and Thea might as well be miles away, enveloped in a world of glamour and glitz and celebrity, while I'm stuck here, firmly grounded in the real world by a wobbly table, faded lino and a mug of milky tea: sad Mrs No-friends who got left behind.

The paramedics take an empty stretcher bed through the doors. Pippa's red hair bobs about everywhere and

Lewis is hovering at the reception door. Even from across the road I can sense the tension. The stretcher returns, rushed out the doors, the victim shielded by the paramedics running alongside, gesturing urgently to one another. The ambulance screeches into the traffic, sirens screaming as it demands a path down the middle of the road at breakneck speed. I send a silent prayer for whoever's in the back.

With the ambulance gone, the show's pretty much over and I flop back into my chair. Taking my phone, I look up Noah on my socials. Can't find him. Sipping my tea, I try to remember what he said his surname was. I'm sure he said Noah Winston.

Still no one comes up remotely like the boy I just met. I Google him. There's nothing.

Damn, how can I say I know him when he's famous if I can't even get his name right?

My phone buzzes. It's Lewis.

Where are you?

Across the street.

I leave out the bit about trying to stalk an almost celebrity.

Get over here.

Pippa wants to talk to you.

My heart leaps into my mouth and is in danger of being spat onto the table. My phone buzzes again.

Hurry up. You're in 😬 😄.

4

'Where. Have. You. Been?' Lewis is pacing up and down the studio entrance with an almost hopping excitement.

'Um,' I say. 'I was getting a drink and...'

He waves a dismissive hand. 'So much drama. One of the contestants has super-bad shellfish allergies, which was all good until she somehow ate a fucking fishy thing and couldn't find her EpiPen. First aid kit...' Lewis' hands fly into the air. 'Nowhere to be found. Ambulance got here just in time.'

He stops, I wait.

'She's gonna be fine,' he says, without conviction. 'I think.' He shudders. 'To be honest, didn't look good. Totally gross.' I'm cold despite the hot day. 'Pippa went full-on mad at the runner in charge, apparently she'd been told to keep a spare pen in Production – couldn't find it, said she put it in the medical kit and it vanished.'

'Is Thea alright?' I say.

'They have no idea,' he says. 'The contestants. Pippa said to keep quiet, so's not to freak them out. It was an accident.' He doesn't look as convinced as he sounds. 'Weird though, right?

I shrug. 'I guess? Wow, that runner must be feeling awful ... just imagine...'

'Urghh, get to the point, Lewis,' he interrupts. 'So, anyways, this means the show is going live in a few hours

34

and Pippa's looking to fill a space. And I suggested you.' He reads my thoughts. 'Whiiiich was totally unnecessary as she already had your name on her radar and you're here, which makes it easier for everyone … so you're in.' He raises his hands in the air for a quick, 'AHHHH'.

My *AHHH* is just as big, but wholly on the inside.

Ohmybloodygod.

Lewis ushers me through the doors. The freezing gust of air-con blows away any doubt this could be a dream.

Pippa rushes over and envelopes me in a sweetly perfumed hug.

'Kass. I have the best news. We have revisited your audition tape and decided on a change of direction. We would lu-uve you to take the psych test with a view to staying for the live show, as a contestant.'

Ohmybloodygod – I think I've said that already.

No clue what to say, so I just gawp at Pippa, still held within her surprisingly strong grasp, lifting my lips in what I hope is a smile.

It works. She releases me and turns to the mountain of loveliness standing by her side. 'Henry, we need to work fast.'

My confidence nose dives. Even the crew are beautiful. I'm assuming Henry's important as he's carrying an iPad like a clipboard. He's totally unaffected by all the excitement, as if me and all this drama are totally beneath him. He stares down at his iPad with an air of efficiency. I shrug a *this is crazy* look at him. He doesn't smile back.

Pippa's phone pings. Pulling Henry to one side she whispers furiously.

'We said no,' she hisses, grinding her heel into the carpet. 'Concentrate on doing the job I'm paying you for.' I'm getting quite a different picture of Lewis' new friend, she may be small, but she is fierce.

Henry spins on his heel and disappears through the door. Pippa turns to Lewis.

'Leew-wis,' she coos. 'We are on a tight deadline and I'm a runner short now Emily has gone to A&E with…' she stops herself. 'I could use some help. Don't suppose…?'

Lewis beams. 'Whatever you need.'

'I've no money in the budget, but I could use an extra runner? We take work experience people on sometimes and it would look great on your CV.'

I imagine Lewis running around the building doing Pippa's every whim and the image makes me giggle.

Pippa turns to me. 'You'll need parental consent.'

Parents? My face must be mirroring my inner panic.

Pippa cocks her head. 'Problem?'

'They're not exactly fans of reality television.' Understatement.

Pippa shuffles on her designer heels.

'Oh, now?'

She raises her eyebrows.

I hit video without thinking.

'Hey.' Dad looks tired. I remember he's been working

overtime; the car needs a new steering rack. No idea what that is, I just know it's expensive.

'Dad, I … Oh.' Pippa grabs my phone and pushes it into her face, a full on stella sunbeam smile filling her narrow features.

'Mr Kennedy, I'm Pippa Barkley, Executive Producer, Pink Pony Productions. So pleased to meet you.' She's gushing down the phone, a tidal wave of charm designed to drown my dad. 'One of our contestants has been taken ill and Kass has been a superstar and agreed to step in and save the day.' She's totally talking over Dad. 'I know this is very last minute, but I can assure you we take cast wellbeing super seriously to ensure this experience is the very best.'

He shouts over her. 'I've heard horror stories about these shows.'

'We are legally bound by tight, tight welfare laws,' she says. 'All contestants have gone through vigorous screening tests. Your daughter has been selected from the thousands of applicants. It's a great opportunity, Mr Kennedy.'

I feel sorry for Dad as he melts quicker than Olaf in a heatwave under the force that is Pippa. 'Yes, I suppose so…'

Pippa taps at the screen on her iPad.

'On behalf of Pink Pony, I thank you for your cooperation. Sending the info over now. It's a standard contract. I'll need a hard copy, but if you could send your virtual consent over asap.' She hands the iPad to me so I can add Dad's email address. 'You should be very proud. Kass is a special young lady.'

Cringe.

Pippa passes my phone back, but she's hung up. She claps her hands, and I can almost hear the insinuated chop-chop.

'This way.' Henry reappears at the doors. Taking my look as reluctance, he lifts his heavy lids and locks eyes on mine. 'I need to get you to Dr Simon, right now,' he says. 'Psych test.' He raises his palm up. 'No, it's not long. No, I don't know what he'll ask and yes, it's compulsory. Every contestant must pass the psych test. As well as the post-show breakdown and check-ups, even if you are agented, you are contractually obliged to visit Dr Simon,' he mumbles under his breath in one monotonous monologue, 'or any other psychologist Pink Pony Productions see fit to hire, for as long as they deem necessary.'

Lewis takes my elbow and guides me towards the stairs.

'My clothes.' I pull my T down to highlight the cartoon sushi which doesn't seem so cute and funny anymore. 'I can't.'

'I'll sort it,' Lewis says, quietly calm.

'But I...' I choke on my panic.

Lewis wraps his arms around me in a safe Lewis hug. 'I'll sort it.' He rests his chin on the top of my head and squeezes all the self-doubt out. 'You can do this. Think of the prize money. You could actually get that car. Go to uni. You could help your parents.'

He has a point. It would be great to help out at home. And I could finally escape Boredomville.

'And Thea – she's not as tough as she pretends. This is the perfect way to put the whole stupid boy drama behind you. Friend *and* fortune, it's a win-win.'

He's right. For all her talk about being tough and invincible, Thea needs a wing man and the bizarro gods have chosen me. If I can help her win, then she'll realise that I really do have her back and proper forgive me. I need to do this for us.

And who wouldn't jump at the chance of sharing a fortune?

5

Psych test done; I'm rocketed through the building like my life depends on it. Henry's in such a hurry he doesn't notice his black hoodie fall onto the floor. I pick it up.

'Here,' I say.

He grabs it, saying nothing. What makes Henry rock? Maybe he's been working with Pippa too long. Not gonna lie, Pippa is a little scary.

I'm ushered through a long corridor of fame. I recognise the faces: *Britain's Got Talent*, *Friends*… I stop dead, buzzing. I'm walking down the same friggin' carpet as Ross and Rachel. Fun-sucker Henry *tuts* impatiently, herding me into make-up.

'Where's Thea?' I whisper to Lewis as I sit. He glares me a *shhh*.

'Girl Next Door look.' Henry talks to the make-up lady, his voice as bored as his expression. 'No zhuzshing. Her words. Not mine.' Without waiting for a reaction, he walks out, gesturing for Lewis to follow.

'Girl Next Door, banging theme,' a voice says.

'Theme?' I swivel around to find its owner in the seat next to me. Her hair's shaved, undercut over a long onyx-black Pixie cut, one of those daring styles you need bags of personality plus striking features to pull off, emphasised by the bright make-up and ruby-red lips which shouldn't work but really, really do.

'Everyone has a theme.' She spins on her chair.

'Isn't Girl Next Door code for boring?' I say.

'Nah. Everyone loves the Girl Next Door. Makes you well-relatable.'

'Yeah.' I frown at my reflection. 'Normal's a treat.'

She grins. 'I'm Amara.'

'Kass,' I say.

'Kassandra?' Amara says, still spinning. 'Like the Trojan princess? Wasn't she the one with the prophecies?'

'Doomed never to be believed.'

Amara slaps her head with her palm. 'Soz, too much. Bit nervous, not gonna lie. Bore on, Amara.'

I laugh. What's her theme? Fierce with a side of kick ass?

Henry sidles back in. 'You should be in your dressing room.'

Hopping off the chair, she salutes Henry.

'Funny,' Henry says, his face unchanging from the now normal scowl.

She winks at me. 'See you in the game, friend.'

'Come with me,' Lewis says, giving me a look of approval.

We stop outside the loo. 'I'm good… Hey.' He pushes me into the tiny space, squeezing in behind me. 'Thea?'

She looks cute in ripped denim cut-offs and a powder-pink T. Her silver hair's dipped to a subtle purple at the end and her make-up's flawless. She's perfect, equally as stunning as Amara the Fierce.

'You're really in!' She hugs me. 'I nearly died when I heard. Shit, I shouldn't say that, y'know, 'cause of Allergy girl. Lewis told me. Is it bad I don't feel bad? I mean, I do, but it got you in, right? And you look hot.' She rolls her eyes. 'I'm such a bitch.'

'Girl Next Door,' I say, glowing from her greeting. It's the warmest Thea has been since the whole JB thing.

'I don't know where you're living but I'm moo-ving,' Lewis says, playing with a lanyard around his neck.

Thea grabs it. 'Crew? Since when?'

Lewis jumps up and down. 'Since now. You're looking at Pink Pony Productions new RUN-NER.'

'How mad is this? All three of us here, together.' Thea's eyes dance with excitement. 'We could actually win. We can split the prize money, for all of us.'

Their excitement is contagious. I've missed this so much.

'Not gonna lie, thought there would be more people here.' Thea says. 'I haven't seen anyone even a little bit famous. Where are all the hot single superstars?'

Lewis shrugs.

'It's not how I imagined it,' she says. 'Thought it would be more glam, y'know? It would have been cool to bump into a celeb, even a D-lister.'

'We don't have long,' Lewis says, ignoring her. 'I thought we needed to figure out our game plan.'

Game plan?

Lewis speaks quickly. 'You two don't know each other, right?'

Thea's pouting through beautifully shiny lips. 'Pippa knows we came together.'

Lewis shrugs. 'It's in her interest to keep quiet.'

'Noah,' I yelp.

'Whose Noah?' says Thea.

'Contestant. I just met him. I told him about you.' The panic I'd almost forgotten about is snaking its way back through my body. 'What if he tells?'

Lewis squeezes my shoulder. 'Was he nice?' I nod. 'Shagable?'

'No way am I sexualising myself to win a game,' I say quickly, before Thea thinks I fancy him.

'If he's nice, befriend him. You're gonna need allies, use them to your advantage. If it doesn't work, kill him.'

I concentrate on getting my breathing to a more normal pace.

Lewis nudges Thea. 'Play nice. When you get nervous you channel bitch, so be aware and dial it down.' He turns to me. 'Cut the imposter syndrome, you totally deserve to be here. You are fierce, so dial it up. Own don't moan.'

'Own don't moan?' Thea snorts.

'As the person who knows you best and loves you biggest, I'm just saying,' Lewis says.

The nerves scatter back into my tummy like a circus

of clowns, somersaulting and tumbling and making me feel like I'm gonna puke. Stepping back, I accidently set off the hand dryer.

'*I Knew You Were Trouble.*' Lewis is laughing.

I grin an apology. '*Everything Has Changed*?'

Thea humphs. 'Now is so not the time for your Swift titles crap.'

'Keep your hair on, Buzz Killington,' says Lewis. He squeezes our shoulders. 'Tell no one you're friends. Work together. In there you have each other's backs. Right?' Thea snorts an *of course* and I nod like I mean it, 'cause I really do.

'You can trust me,' I say to Thea.

'I do,' she says, but the slight squint of her eyes and the flush of her cheeks suggests otherwise.

Lewis' head bobs excitedly from one of us to the other. 'Let's forever friends it.'

I place my hand on Thea's held out palm. Lewis places his on mine.

'Strong like mountains,' he says.

'Strong like steel,' Thea says.

'Always,' I say. 'Love you, guys.'

'Love you more,' Thea and Lewis say together.

We hold onto each other, like we did when we were six and scared of Ella 'Bully' Brookes.

'We should go,' Thea says. She rearranges herself in the mirror until she's happy.

Lewis looks at me. 'Ready?'

'Wait,' Thea says. 'Give me your phone. They took mine.' She grabs my phone. 'One for luck.'

We strike a pose. One pre-reality-show selfie taken.

6

At the end of the corridor, double doors block my way. I peer through the glass to an empty canteen. Chairs are stacked on tables, a row of clean serveries run along the wall, their empty stainless-steel shelves sparkling in the light. I tap my lanyard on the pad but the door refuses to open. Strange. Why would it be shut, everybody needs to eat? I spy a vending machine in the corner. I tap again — then again, the need for comfort snacking making me a little hangry. The doors remain stubbornly closed. I humph. And talking of people eating, Thea's right, where is everyone?

'There you are.' Pippa's marching up the corridor, Lewis right behind. She steers me away from the canteen and ushers me through a door, ripping off the name plate with an efficient swipe, but not before I catch the name: BRYONY, *Lie or Die*. I guess that's Allergy girl. My heart does a guilty flip.

The dressing room's small and the Bryony-sized allergy elephant is taking up all the room. She was in here, struggling for help. The thought makes me shudder. I hope she's okay.

'This is yours,' Pippa says over-brightly. 'We launch at eight. Help yourself to snacks.' She gestures to the crisps and chocolate sat on the dressing table.

'Just think,' says Lewis. 'I'll be watching you on my phone. How mad is that?'

'There's two hours of live streaming tonight, then an hour-long show at eight on the next four nights,' says Pippa.

'It's not all live streamed?' Lewis asks.

Pippa shakes her head. 'It's usual practice to record everything and then edit the juicy bits down into an hour-long show. This means we can steer the best storylines to say exactly what we need.' She turns to me. 'Any questions?'

My mind is screaming hundreds, but I say nothing. No one's mentioning Bryony. I guess the show really does go on.

'Great.' She turns to Lewis. 'You're gonna shoot off home for those hard copy consent forms and some clothes, right?' Lewis nods and Pippa beams. 'Thank goodness you two came along today.' She stops in the doorway. 'Almost forgot. Need your phone.' Rummaging in her pocket, she pulls out a small see-through bag. Something drops onto the carpet. I pick it up. It's long like a biro, only thicker.

I pass it quickly to Pippa, glancing at Lewis. He saw it too, the words: 'EpiPen Auto Injector' written clearly on the side in a bright yellow strip.

'Thanks.' Flustered, Pippa pushes the pen into her pocket, avoiding my eye. 'I found it in the fruit bowl when I cleared the room for you. Weird, we searched this room and I swear it wasn't here.' She laughs unconvincingly. 'I guess that's why they call it blind panic.' She stops laughing. 'I gave specific instructions for absolutely no shellfish in the building.'

'Super-scary accident.' The slight wobble in Lewis' voice tells me he's way more uncomfortable than he's letting on.

'I know, right? One sniff of a crustacean and…' Pippa grimaces.

How do you accidently eat shellfish? It's not like you wouldn't notice a prawn on your plate, especially if they made you really, really sick. Plus, the canteen is closed, there *is* no food. So where did she get it from? Who gave it to her? I keep my thoughts to myself and push the weird away, smiling sympathetically.

Pippa's eyes lock onto mine. 'We would rather the other contestants didn't know about Bryony's accident; it won't do for morale just before we go live.'

'Of course.'

She shakes the bag in my face.

I slip my phone into it.

'And the lanyard. You're not a visitor anymore.'

I hand it over.

'Le-wis,' Pippa says, like she's calling her cat. They disappear.

And I can breathe. This is all way too intense.

My eyes settle on my reflection in the mirror. My make-up doesn't look half bad. This girl *could* be the Girl Next Door. I square my shoulders and stick out my tits. This girl might actually be in with a chance. I fidget back to a more comfortable stance. The girl in the mirror is in danger of losing herself in all the hype. The real Kass is

48

here to help Thea, that's all. I refuse to let this experience change me. In the here and now, I vow to keep it real – proper real not reality real.

I help myself to a KitKat, stuffing it down my gob in one comfort-eating gulp, and reach for a packet of ready salted.

Henry appears, startling me, sending crisps flying everywhere. *Would it have hurt to knock?* There's not even a shadow of a smile threatening his lips. I thought you had to be sociable and witty and very Lewis-like to work in TV?

'You're needed for the intros,' he says. 'We're behind schedule so hurry up. Time is money.'

I fight the urge to take the piss out of his *time is money* cliché.

'Intros?' I fall into step by his side.

'VT bites.'

I don't know what *VT bites* mean either, but I don't think Henry's up for sharing.

'You'll love it – one-on-one time with the camera.'

Well, Henry's got the wrong girl.

'Like when a contestant kisses the love heart on that cheesy dating show, *Dump or Date*?' I fake laugh, attempting to bond. 'So cringe.'

'I worked on that show.' Henry's eyes darken.

CRAP. End of bonding.

Henry leads me up the corridor and through a heavy door marked STUDIO. We're in a small space between two sets of doors, washed in red light.

'When I open this door, stay quiet,' he says. 'The red light means they're recording.'

The word 'recording' makes my insides flip. The nerves are back, worming through my veins. I adopt my most serious face and give myself a little talking to. *Remember why you're doing this. Show Thea she can trust you and don't screw it up.* As Henry pulls open the door and gestures for me to walk into the darkness, my heart catapults right into my mouth.

7

I'm standing in a television studio. It's massive, like two football pitches massive and graveyard quiet. An eerie, empty stillness hangs in the air. The cold grips hold of my shoulders, its gnarly fingers pinching through the sleeves of my T, making little bumps bubble on my arms. And it's dark. Really, really dark.

Henry marches into the black. A sea of cables snake along the floor in all directions, secured into place with yellow hazard tape. As my eyes adjust, I take in the brick walls painted black. A metal staircase in the corner leads up to a gangway which runs the length of the studio. My eyes follow the shiny metal as it disappears behind a thick black curtain, concertinaed against the wall like a towering shadow. There's a sink in the corner and the biggest broom I've ever seen. A big hazard sign sits above it with rolls of cable hooked up on the wall like giant liquorice doughnuts.

In front of me is a large wooden wall, a corner of a giant rectangular box that stretches out in all directions butting up to the huge hangar doors at the end of the studio. There are no windows or doors, just one solid shape dominating the space, a set enclosed within a giant wooden box built within a huge television studio. Like one of those Russian dolls, hiding figure upon figure within its brightly coloured packages.

A lighting rig hangs high above. Shiny metal poles zigzag together, a huge silver web stretching across the entire ceiling. A fragile, thin wooden walkway runs across the abyss. I shudder, you couldn't pay me to go up there.

I hurry after Henry, hopping over the cables, willing myself not to fall. He pulls back a black curtain, blinding me with a flash of bright light and ushers me into a small space.

A girl's perched on a stool. Dead-straight, jet-black hair frames her serious face and perfectly winged black eyeliner sweeps around dark eyes. Her cropped white T has a logo on the front: *Sad, lonely and bad at maths*. Can totally relate. She's rocking a pair of buckled knee-high platform combat boots. They're the type of boot I'd love to wear but don't have the guts.

'Last one,' Henry mutters to a middle-aged man with mad hair and a greying beard.

'You're all done, Cali,' the bearded man says to the girl on the stool. 'Well done, you nailed it.'

Combat-boot Cali jumps down, totally unfazed. A green curtain hangs behind her, the fabric pulled creaseless tight. It hits the floor and carries on, covering the ground with a flawless lime-coloured green.

Henry holds the curtain up for her to leave. As she passes me, she smiles.

'Don't worry,' she says, 'it's a breeze.'

Yeah right. 'Nice boots.'

'Thanks,' she says over her shoulder. 'Keeping it real.'

Henry drops the curtain behind them and disappears.

'It's Kass right?' The bearded guy's squatting down, loading a camera. 'I'm Jeff, the senior cameraman. I'll be doing your MIV today.'

'MIV?' I say, Cali forgotten.

'Master Interview. Henry didn't explain?' He throws an impatient look to a girl angling a bright light on tripod legs.

'I'm Rita,' she says. 'We're going to film a quick introductory interview. Who you are, what you like to do, what your game plan is. Yeah?'

Jeff pulls his hand through his hair. 'You good to go?'

I nod, best to get this over with as quickly as possible.

He gestures to the stool swallowed up in the pool of light. I sit, squinting.

The make-up lady appears from who knows where.

'Relax, love.' She winks as she presses powder into my cheeks, chin and forehead. 'Try not to squint, doesn't look good on camera.'

The curtain moves and Lewis appears. Before I can say *hi*, Jeff hoiks the camera onto a tripod and points the huge lens towards me. Rita holds a microphone on a long stick over my head.

'Hey,' Jeff says to Lewis. 'Move those cable-cutters out of shot.' He gestures to a bright yellow-handled tool lying on the floor, its sharp curved blades glinting in the light as Lewis picks them up. 'Careful, they cost a fortune.'

I try to balance on the stool while not squinting and

try to shift my face into some kind of TV-friendly look while my stomach mutinies and threatens to throw up the recent KitKat.

'When you see this red recording light.' Jeff's pointing to the front of the camera. 'You go…' He waves his hand. 'I'm Kass blah di blah, I'm from blah, I love boys and knitting at the weekends.' He winks. 'That's of course unless you don't?'

'Knit?' I daren't take my eyes off the front of the camera in case the light comes on and I miss it.

He chuckles. 'Let's try it.'

The bright yellow light's shining straight into my eyes, so I can't see the camera recording light.

Smile. Lewis' voice is in my head. I try to look casual and relaxed.

Don't squint, make-up lady's voice is now in my head with Lewis.

'Hi, I'm Kass. I'm seventeen and I'm from Essex. I love Mafia and…' My mouth's open but nothing's coming out. 'I … have nice hair.' My hands grip the side of the stool. *I have nice hair? I have nice hair???* My eyes flit around wildly. I've got nothing. There is literally *nothing* in my head.

'Good start.' Jeff's voice is bouncy and light. 'I know it's daunting but try to be as natural as possible. Try not to look directly into the camera. And remember to blink. Not sure where you were going with the hair…' There's a ripple of laughter.

'Sorry,' I say. 'Totally dried up.'

Jeff smiles. 'Happens to everyone.'

'How about you take a look at one of the others, see how they've done it?' Lewis says, his eyes pleading with me to cooperate. He spins round to Rita and Jeff. 'Is that possible?'

'Sure,' Rita says.

The stool is hard against my bum and I fidget nervously. Jeff clicks a camera card into a laptop and fast forwards through some footage. I glance down at my H&M, twelve quid white trainers, now slightly grey from the London dirt and wish I had shelled out for Airforces when Thea got hers, but money is tight in our house and the need for driving lessons overrode my fashionista instincts. Still, there's always the cash prize if we actually manage to pull this off.

Jeff motions me nearer. On the laptop is a girl. She's perched comfortably on the same stool that's giving me so much trouble, one long leg curled over the other, hands resting on knees. She looks like a model, big wide baby-blue eyes stare out from under a perfect fringe, straight glossy hair the colour of straw falls perfectly to her toned shoulders. She's wearing a yellow floral off-the-shoulder halter, not too daring, just daring enough, which pops against her summer-tanned arms.

The camera loves her.

You have got to be kidding – *this* is supposed to make me more relaxed? I've never felt more like a geek suffocating in the shadow of a beauty. I try to flick the green-eyed monster off my shoulder.

Jeff pushes play.

My new nemesis bursts to life.

'I'm Skye Greenhill and I'm seventeen years old. I'm in my final year of college and hope to study psychology and criminology next year.' *Well, whoopy bloody do, she's clever as well.* 'I'm also a part-time model and have just come back from Milan which was awesome.' *I knew it!* She has that whole Cara Delevingne eyebrow-thing going on. The green-eyed monster climbs right back on my shoulder. 'It's easy to dismiss me as a ditsy blonde.' She tucks a piece of hair behind her ear in one easy move. 'But I want to prove that you can have brains and beauty. I *want* my castmates to underestimate me. I love Mafia and am ready to play my own game.' She smiles cutely at the camera. 'They won't see me coming.'

Well, isn't Skye just great.

All eyes turn to me.

'Easy.' I plonk myself back on the stool. Rita holds up the long microphone thing again.

'It's a boom,' she says, catching me staring.

I duck slightly as it comes dangerously close to my head.

'Oops.' Rita grins an apology.

I relax a little. I'm not the only clumsy one. I can do this.

Here goes nothing.

I lift my chin in a *screw you* to Skye the Great and focus on Lewis, not the lens.

'I'm Kass, I'm seventeen and I'm from Essex. I'm at college right now. No clue what I'm going to do after.' I pull an awkward *eek* face. 'I like playing football, badly, and walking my dog, Harley, but not at the same time obviously.' *Oh please shut up.* I send a silent *help me*.

'How do you feel about being in the game?' Jeff saves me.

It's hard to talk through a smile. 'I love Mafia. All my friends are mad about it, and we play all the time.'

'How would you describe yourself ... as a friend?' Jeff says.

'Loyal...' I blurt the word out then stop. My cheeks burn crimson, convinced that my JB cock-up is plastered all over my face.

Jeff interrupts. 'Always put the question in front of the answer.'

'Oh.' I shake off the guilt. 'I would describe myself as a very protective friend. I'll get aggy if you double-cross me, so watch out.' I wag a finger at the camera but decide it's too cringe and quickly put it down.

Jeff's voice fills the silence. 'What qualities do you think you bring to the game?'

'I have ... sorry. The qualities I bring to the game is, are, a good sense of when someone is lying, so I should be able to tell if someone is messing with me.' I'm babbling, can't stop. 'I am praying I don't go out first. That's the worst, isn't it? To be the first out. And I'd rather be executed than murdered.' I stare into the camera. 'So, send me to the electric chair. Kill me already. Just don't murder me in my sleep.'

I laugh … and then die inside. Who laughs at their own crap jokes? At least it shuts me up.

'Perfect,' says Jeff quickly. 'Let's check it and move on. Well done, Kass.'

'So, is this going out on regular TV?'

'These will be popping up on all social media platforms,' Jeff says. 'As a new show, the company can put it out exactly how they want on live-streaming sites. If it's popular, they'll sell the concept to one of the big players for a small fortune.' There's a hint of bitterness in his tone.

'Hashtag trending murder, baby,' Lewis says.

'If you say so. I'm too old for all this,' Jeff mutters. 'And that's a wrap. Well done,' he says, after a nod from Rita, and I'm forgotten. 'What's next?'

Rita taps on her iPad. 'Remote cameras need checking.'

'Brilliant, let's get these up to *El Capitano*. Won't mention the fact I'm doing her job, in zero time. Experience used to count for something.' Jeff turns his back on us. 'I worked on *Friends*, for god's sake.' He coils the camera cable from arm to hand, in one pissed-off, over-worked motion.

Lewis ushers me out.

'Wow!' I whisper to Lewis as he drops the curtain behind us. 'Jeff is not a happy cameraman.'

'Jeff needs to turn his frown upside down.' Lewis giggles.

I giggle back. 'Who's *El Capitano*?'

'The director,' Lewis says in an awed tone, stopping to tie his shoelace.

Jeff's grumpy voice travels through the curtain. 'Any news on that girl Bryony?' My ears prick up at the sound of Allergy girl's name.

'Nothing new,' Rita says.

'She looked in a bad way when I saw her,' Jeff says.

'It was horrible.' Rita's voice is quieter; I have to lean against the curtain to hear. 'Still no idea how it happened. When I got to her dressing room there was no sign of any food at all. And the panic in her eyes.' I can almost hear her shudder.

Lewis stands and I gesture for him to stay put and be quiet. We listen through the curtain.

'You found her?' Jeff again.

'No, Pippa was already there, and the runner. It was a mess, they did nothing, just froze. It was me who called 999 and sent the runner for the EpiPen, which she couldn't find.'

Lewis mouths a *'Wow'*.

'Shock makes people do strange things,' Jeff says.

There's a brief pause before Rita speaks. 'When did you see her? Thought you'd gone to lunch.'

Jeff snorts angrily. 'Yeah right, had too much to do, just grabbed something from the canteen.'

I pull an *OMG* face at Lewis. No way did Jeff get lunch in the canteen, it looks like it's been shut for weeks.

Jeff is still speaking. 'Saw her getting into the ambulance. Look I'm done here if you need to get on.'

Grabbing Lewis' arm, we leg it back out of the studio. The last thing I need right now is to be caught eavesdropping by a grumpy senior cameraman who has just outright lied to his work colleague.

8

I'm getting mad *déjà vu*. We are standing in the strange half-lit space, staring at the studio doors. There's no red light, nothing is being recorded. It's no man's land, behind us is the real world and in front, the unreal world of Reality.

'Come on.' Henry walks the opposite way from last time, around the corner of the set to stand in front of a large double door in its side. The *Lie or Die* logo is splashed across the front in bright letters. There's a touchpad the shape of an electricity bolt on the wall to the side, glowing electric yellow. This must be the way into the house. *Oh crap, this is it.*

'It's not time yet,' Henry says, as he towers over me. 'This is a dry run. We're late.'

And time is money, I get it. Thanks Henry, great pep talk.

Tapping his lanyard on the glowing pad, the door opens with an efficient click. Henry pushes it wide and bundles me in so fast, I only get the briefest glimpse of the house. He rushes me straight to a bright yellow door labelled COURTROOM, opens it, and pushes me through. His beautiful, but bad-tempered face is the last thing I see before I half fall into the room.

I'm in a courtroom; I guess the clue was on the door. On the wall next to me is a raised area; one long bench runs along each line with a fancy wooden balustrade separating two levels.

All the contestants are lined up on the two rows. They're all TV gorgeous and every one of them is staring right at me.

Oh floor, please swallow me whole. I hurry to a space at the end of the bottom row. Between my seismic discomfort, Henry's pushing and the intensely bright lights shining right in my eyes, I stumble over the step and trip right into the first contestant on my row.

'Whoopsie,' the contestant says, holding out his arms to catch my fall. 'Whoops.'

Despite being beyond nervous, a chuckle coughs its way into my mouth. I'm staring into kind brown eyes defined with thick dark brows drawn together with concern. Mad black hair frames his cute face which he keeps checking nervously with a shaking hand.

A rumbling of giggles fills the rows. I straighten and take a bow to ease the awkward.

'Thanks for the save,' I say, letting go of Whoopsie-whoops boy. I am actually dying. Way to make an entrance, Kass.

I look for Thea. She rolls her eyes.

'Hey, Girl Next Door.' Amara the Fierce from make-up salutes me, grinning wildly. 'Nice entrance.'

I'm laughing on the outside while full-on cringing inside.

Noah from the cafe is stood next to her, his eyebrows

raised in a question. I shake my head in a *tell you later* and he nods. Knowing that he's in here too, a friendly face amongst all these shiny people, eases the embarrassment a little.

'Welcome, contestants.' A bookish woman appears, crossing to stand in front of us. She looks calm and very in control. 'On behalf of Pink Pony Productions, I would like to welcome you to the very first recording of *Lie or Die*. I'm Isla Kelday and I am your director. Even though you are not individually mic'd up, please do not swear.' Isla pauses, she seems nice, less scary than Pippa. The crew are dotted around the set.

I wish that Lewis was here, but he left straight after my MIV to get clothes and consent and won't be back till after the launch. My fingers tense and untense. Whoopsie-whoops boy does the same, a little too enthusiastically and elbows me in the ribs.

'Whoopsie,' he says to me. 'Such an oaf.'

Oaf? I try not to giggle.

'Can't see a thing.' He shuffles on the spot, intermittently pulling his well-worn Storm Trooper T-shirt down over his bum. I smile, immediately comfortable with his less than perfect demeanour. He full-on friend-grins back.

'I'm Max,' he says. 'And I am bricking it.'

'Kass,' I say. 'Also bricking it.'

Isla continues. 'For the duration of the filming I'll be watching you from the main gallery,' Isla says.

I look up to where she's pointing. The main gallery must be hidden behind all those black curtains.

Isla's still speaking. 'We'll view everything using the remote cameras set up around the house and the manned pedestals in the camera-runs.'

Turning back to the front, I spot the camera in the corner. Following the line, I find another in the centre, small and round, attached to the top of the back wall. Red lights sparkle underneath each little round belly. The middle camera is pointed right at me. I immediately stare at my feet. Panic-mixed adrenaline gushes through me. Clasping both hands, I lift my head reluctantly, attempting to look natural and totally at home.

Rita walks up to Isla.

'One moment,' Isla says, holding up her hand. She disappears into a huddle with Rita, cameraman Jeff and some other crew.

I take the opportunity to check out the other contestants. On the other side of Max stands a wiry boy. Also TV-good-looking. He's tall, not quite Tayo tall, with a shaved head. He's wearing skinny jeans and a black vest. But I can't take my eyes off his tats. His arm is covered with a sleeve from wrist to shoulder. He totally catches me gawping. He has the most intense smoky green eyes which, right now, are boring into mine.

I smile, praying he can't tell how intimidated he's making me, and lift my hand in a quick *hi*. He does a weird half-sneer smile before turning back to the front.

Max pulls a *what a wanker* face and I try not to giggle.

On the other side of Tattoo boy stands another boy, impeccably dressed in a blue-and-white striped sailor top and a denim fitted jacket with blue skinny-fit trousers. He's checking out his opponents with a cheeky confidence. He catches my eye. I smile. He looks away.

Rude.

Combat-boot Cali is standing at the other end of my row. On the top row, behind us, beautiful Tayo stands next to Skye the Great, easily recognisable after her MIV. What a perfect-looking couple they make.

The set is small. The walls are panelled wood and match our raised platform. In the centre of the wall opposite is a fancy seat, raised on its own wooden-panelled platform. Above the seat hangs a flag with *LIE OR DIE* in the middle. This must be the Judge's seat. Either side are two smaller platforms, less elaborate. A small wooden barrier runs around the top of each, like a row of prison bars.

Set to the side of us, enclosed in a metal cage and raised high on its own stage, is an electric chair.

I don't linger on it – it's freaking me out. I'd rather be ostrich-like and forget about the most brutal part of the game. I get it, I know it's not real. I've sent many people to the electric chair when we play at home, but seeing it in front of you is different. If you sit in that chair you've lost, you leave with nothing, game over. The chance of fame and fortune is gone in an electric blink. The thought of being responsible for sending someone home and ending their dream fills me with dread. Let's face it, nobody remembers the losers.

Seeing me looking, Max nudges me.

'Do you think it's a real electric chair, like from a prison?' he whispers, a bit too loudly.

'No,' the boy in the sailor suit next to him snorts snarkily. He leans forward to talk around Tattoo boy; his cherub-like face crimpled into a scowl. 'But it's the scariest part of the game.'

'It's not really scary,' Max says. 'It's just a prop.'

Sailor boy tuts. 'You sit on that and you are more than dead.'

'Can you be more than dead?' I whisper.

'I'm not planning on finding out.' Sailor boy pushes his shoulders back confidently. 'You need to reach top three if you're gonna have a chance of making it. Top three: anything below that and no one will care. No one will remember your face. And you'll never get a TV agent, so you're more than dead, you're totally finished.'

'That's cheery,' Max says. 'I'm just here for the game. I'm not bothered about the fame thing.'

'That's a lie,' Amara the Fierce sneers from the back row making her fringe bob over her eyes. 'Anybody who says they don't care about the money or the fame is chatting total BS.'

'Totally,' Sailor boy says, throwing a smile of agreement to Amara.

Amara tilts her chin up, speaking loudly. 'I plan to ride the fame train all the way to Hollywood and I'm not afraid to admit it.'

'Well, I'm totally here for the fame.' I'm not surprised Thea pipes up. 'I'm gonna be an influencer and this show is gonna help me.'

'Good for you,' snarky Sailor boy says. 'Speak your truth, girls.'

Max whispers to me. 'I really am here just for the game.'

I'm not about to admit why I'm here, so I just smile and hope I get forgotten in this ocean of whale-sized personalities. I'm pretty sure no one will remember my face regardless of how well I do, but the competitive imp perched on my shoulder is screaming that I better not be out first, that's one humiliation I don't need, plus if I was one of the first out, I'm pretty sure Thea would kill me. If I can do well *and* help Thea do even better, she will have to forgive me for the whole JB fiasco, and we can finally move on.

That's my plan anyway. Having been given a second chance the pressure is on not to screw it up.

All the walls around the room are covered by black curtains hung floor to ceiling. All except the wall behind the electric chair. This wall is curtain free. Smooth black glass from hip to head height, like the privacy glass you see on posh cars.

Isla's back, standing behind a central lectern, facing us.

'First of all, you need to congratulate yourselves. To get this far is a huge achievement.' We smile a wary well done to each other, someone on the back row hollers; I'm guessing it's Amara the Fierce. 'And I have news. As you know, this is the first full studio production to use only social media for its output. We've been posting show teasers all week on social media forums, and I am so excited to announce that, as of six o'clock, we are trending.'

This time everyone cheers and claps. Isla waits for us to calm down before continuing. 'In a moment my talented sound team will fit your lavalier microphones, or LAVS.' Two of the crew lollop towards us, their hands loaded up with small black boxes and cables.

'Treat these with care,' Isla continues. 'The crew get quite grumpy if they are broken.' She turns serious. 'Now for the basics. You are all familiar with the game of Mafia and the rules are the same: two Agents, one Detective, seven Players, you must defeat your enemy to win.' We all nod.

'The game will last for four nights and four days, starting with Night One which begins tonight with the launch. Day One will be tomorrow. Each night there will be a Kill Window – this is the time for the Agents to murder a victim. The daytime Accusation Window gives the contestants the opportunity to uncover who they think are the Agents. All accusations will be brought here, to the Courtroom, and the accused will be put on trial. If found guilty they will be sent to the electric chair and eliminated from the game. If you are eliminated or are murdered by the Agents, that's it, folks, you go home with nothing. Detective, you can come to the Confessional with one contestant's name each night, and you will be told if they are a Player or an Agent. It's up to you how you use this knowledge. You can share or keep it for yourself. You may reveal your identity at any time but beware, there is nothing to stop an Agent masquerading as the Detective and lying about any contestant's status.'

Panic crashes over me in waves and I'm in danger of drowning. I don't want to be the Detective; it's a role I've never played and is way too much pressure. Every time we play, the Detective is always killed as soon as they're revealed. Why wouldn't they? If an Agent knew that someone could reveal your identity, wouldn't you shut them up?

'What's the one rule of *Lie or Die*?' Isla throws her hands up in the air.

'Trust no one.' Our excited voices ripple around the Courtroom.

Isla holds up a circular card with a letter 'A' on it. 'Agents, you will be given Agent cards. To kill your victim, you must give them a card without attracting attention. Players, as soon as you are carded, you are out. You must immediately come to the Confessional without talking to anyone. It only takes one card to kill.'

The sound men have taken a row each. The younger one is fitting Skye's LAV. She's girly giggling. It's massively irritating.

'Now, Players. We've added some props along the way. Some are clues, some red herrings. All are designed to get your investigative juices working. I urge you to lean into them, have fun, play along with the murder-mystery concept. The more you do, the more entertaining you will be.' Isla glances at her watch. 'We're behind schedule and we need to quickly test the Narrator.'

Max is having his microphone fitted. Every time he moves, he accidently elbows me, followed by a 'Whoopsie-whoops.' It's too funny. I wish Lewis were here to see it.

'Remember, this is an entertainment show. So, folks, *be* entertaining. You will get used to the cameras. If at any point you are uncomfortable, look into a camera and say the safe word: Bumblebee. This tells us what you want to say is confidential and we will be there to help.'

Bumblebee. The word buzzes around my head as I try to park it in my memory. *Safe word – Bumblebee.*

'Anything you say or do within the game can and will be used on the show.' Isla wags a warning finger at us. 'So, people, BE mindful. Do not assume we won't use it; we will! It's no use blaming the editors after the event. If the words come from your mouth, then you only have yourself to blame.'

The sound guy has reached me. He hands me a chain with a small microphone on the end, and I put it over my head. The microphone sits below my collar bone. He clips a small box around my waist and gestures for me to tuck the cable through the neck of my T-shirt and out of the bottom, which I do. He clips the cable into the small box.

'Don't unplug that,' he says.

'Okay.'

Spinning the box around to my back, I hide it under my T-shirt. It sits in the dip of my back. Oh, I could easily forget this is on. He gives me the thumbs up. I do the same. *Cringe.*

I chance a sneaky glimpse at Thea who makes a *this is awesome* face. I'm way too nervous to agree.

Isla claps her hands. 'Kass, right?'

My heart jumps into my mouth. 'Uh, yes.'

'Can we borrow you for this?' Isla beckons me down.

Everyone's staring again. Tattoo boy has a *why you?* look plastered on his face.

I climb into one of the docks, hovering over the chair, and turn to face everyone.

From here I get a perfect view of all of them. Thea's every bit the reality star. Anyone else stood next to Skye the Great would fade into her shadow but Thea's strength shines out like a beacon.

Isla speaks. 'For this practice exercise, Kass is the Accused. The Accused takes their place in the docks. And the Accuser stands here.' Isla walks to the lectern. 'Now contestants, it's time to meet your Judge and Narrator.'

9

A ripple of excitement prickles around the set like static electricity.

Having never met a real-life famous person, I've no clue how I'll react. I hope to be unflappable and take it in my stride, but if KSI walks through that door, I'm gonna lose it.

The lights over the benches dim. The Judge's chair goes dark.

Isla beams. 'We are so excited to introduce to you, for his very first television appearance … the one and only Cohin.'

Eh?

The space above the Judge's chair glows. There's someone, or rather something, in the chair which, two seconds ago, was empty. A human-shaped silhouette. Kudos to production, I did not see anyone walk in. That was nicely done.

The silhouette is hunched over, head covered by a large hood.

He's flickering. I can't help but shiver.

The head moves. Hands pull the hood back to reveal a face. The silence is broken by confused cries.

The person in the chair looks exactly like Thea.

No, wait, Amara.

No, Noah.

What the hell is going on?

'It's a hologram,' Max says on a sharp intake of breath. 'A proper transmorphic hologram.'

A what? Is that even a word?

Now it's Combat-boot Cali. Now it's me. It's seamlessly changing from one of us to another.

Isla steps up to the Judge's seat and *it* turns to her.

'Welcome Cohin,' she says.

The face changes to an exact replica of Skye the Great.

'Thank you, Isla.'

'It's me,' Skye squeaks, confirming the likeness of the voice. An awed mumbling ripples through the stands.

Isla turns to us. 'Contestant Originated Holographic Integrated Narration. We call him Cohin. The first computer-generated television presenter. Anything you do or say can be projected onto Cohin, and replayed in real-time, single person playback.'

Tayo lets out a whistle. 'Impressive.'

Cohin pulls his hood over his face and bows his head.

'Cohin will always tell the truth,' Isla says. 'However, context often plays a vital role, so be aware that what you see and hear may not be exactly how it looks or sounds. Everyone happy?' Assuming we are, she carries on. 'We are just going to run the electrocution sequence with you all.'

I can't help the shivers that sprint down my back at the word *electrocution*.

'Director has left the floor,' Rita says, which prompts the crew to move. She nods at me. I nod back – not exactly doing anything apart from looking guilty. Rita's wearing a headset and appears to be listening intently to someone in her ear.

I remind myself to breathe.

Cohin's head raises, but the hood remains in place, shielding his identity. He appears to be waiting with the rest of us.

My eye catches Thea. Her hands make a heart shape. She drops them quickly.

'When you're found guilty.' Rita talks to all of us. 'Take the hood in front of you and move to the electric chair. When the music starts the chair will buzz. Remember you are being electrocuted, so you can jump around a bit if you want.'

That's just sick.

She turns to me expectantly.

In front of me is a black hood hanging from a hook, the *Lie or Die* logo embroidered on the front. Leaving the dock, I climb up the steps and sit in the electric chair, my face burning. It's uncomfortable. And the cold of the smooth metal quickly seeps through my jeans. I rest my hands on the thick metal arms and smile.

Shit, don't smile, you're about to be fried. I sit in the electric chair, trying to be serious and sombre and suitably sad.

Cohin speaks and I'm grateful for the save. His face is

hidden under the virtual folds of his heavy hood. His voice has changed. No longer like Skye's, he sounds neutral, generic. He must have a default, go-to Cohin voice.

'Kass Kennedy. The Jury has spoken. You have been found guilty. The sentence is death. You must now put on the hood.'

I throw the hood over my head and the world becomes invisible. I'm glad for the break from the glaring lights and the stares.

'May the gods have mercy upon your soul.' Cohin's words fill me with a guilty dread, even though I haven't actually done anything.

Music fills the studio, quietly at first. The chair begins to buzz. I attempt a few jerks and twists but, talk about stupid. I try not to laugh, smiling secretly behind my hood. The music builds menacingly, the buzzing of the chair increases, vibrating beneath my weight. It takes me by surprise, and I squirm. Suddenly I don't feel like laughing. Louder and louder, the buzzing is full-on in my ears and the music booms through my bones as the tension ramps up to completely terrifying.

And that's when I scream.

10

It's a full-on body-shaking, lung-filling, ugly scream of terror, no acting required, as the chair tips backwards and the floor disappears. I'm falling. It all happens so quickly. The studio dark behind my hood is coloured with obsidian black as my body plunges into an abyss. Soft, spongy folds break my fall.

Shiiitting bollocks I did not see that coming.

I guess I'm dead.

I hoik myself onto my elbows and pull off my hood. I'm lying on a thick rubber mattress. It's black-out dark under here, but a small exit sign helps, shining a pitiful amount of light over a crawl-space exit. After the mad hustle of the Courtroom the quiet is unnerving. I dust myself off. I'm right under the electric chair. It's small and cramped. If I stretch out my arms, I can almost touch the walls.

I listen for any indication that someone's coming. There's nothing. It's friggin' freezing down here, claustrophobic and spooky as hell. Climbing off the mattress, I head for the exit, arms waving wildly through the blackness, fingers spread out and tensed.

Oops.

My elbow bangs into something and a heavy shape falls into my path, knocking my shoulder before thudding to the floor. The black drape that once covered it, camouflaging it in the murky darkness, crumples by my feet.

The shocked shriek that leaves my lips is as uninvited as the shape in front of me.

It's a body.

And it's naked.

It's not real. The half-light from the exit sign is just enough to see some detail. My eyes are immediately drawn to the area where the boy bits should be and there is nothing, just like a life-sized Ken doll, but it's good, lifelike. I mean hats off to production, the budget for this show must be well high. As my heart returns to a more normal rhythm, I kick myself for my stereotypical girly scream and prod the body tentatively. It's cold and rubbery. I wonder what it's gonna be used for and am pretty sure I'm not supposed to see it. If Henry catches me man-handling the prop dummy, I'm probably dead. Its hair is bleached snow white. I chuckle, it looks a bit like Noah, or at least the bits of Noah I've seen. Grabbing the cloth, I cover it up again, pushing it back into the corner, hoping it doesn't look like I've disturbed it.

I don't go far before the ceiling lifts and I can stand. I'm in a long, empty tunnel with a small track running down the centre. I head for the door at one end, walking between the railway of metal tracks.

The door's locked. I push hard, but it remains stubbornly closed. There's a sign, white writing glowing in the darkness.

Exit.

Camera-Run One.

Shame I can't actually get out.

I notice that the inside wall next to me has turned to glass. I can see right through to the Courtroom. My first instinct is to duck.

I remember the wall from the other side, black and impenetrable. Straightening up, I peer through the glass. The electric chair is back in place. The guys on the bench are leaving. I wave, which is stupid as I'm behind blackout glass. Pippa and Rita are on the other side of the set, talking. Jeff's standing apart, he doesn't look happy.

The line of contestants dribbles out of the Courtroom. Noah's last. Taking the steps two at a time he jumps down to the floor where Pippa greets him. Everyone else has gone, leaving the two of them alone. I can't hear what they're saying, but they're deep in conversation and judging by their body language it's pretty tense. Noah's facing me, face focused, hands moving madly. Pippa has her back to me. I recognise the green cardi and sharp cut of her red hair. She's shaking her head, a lot. Her body language is a world away from the hyper-efficient Pippa I met earlier. Noah stands straight, his face stern and anxious. Suddenly he reaches out and pulls Pippa towards him in a tight embrace.

Did not see that coming. Surely they barely know each other?

The tunnel fills with light as the camera-run door is

78

opened from the outside. Standing in the doorframe is a silhouetted Henry.

Stepping out, I mumble my thanks. 'It was locked,' I say by way of explanation, conscious of my guilty face as I realise I've been caught watching something private. I glance back to the Courtroom, it's empty. There's no sign of Pippa or Noah.

Henry doesn't notice. 'Only opens from the outside,' he mumbles, closing the door firmly behind me.

'That's not very health and safety.' The joke's lost on him. I can't detect even the smallest twitch on his begrudgingly good-looking face. Part of me wants to mention the prop dummy just to see his reaction but I don't, no point in pissing him off any more than he obviously already is.

The efficient clip-clip of heels coming towards us makes Henry stop and stiffen. Pippa appears around the corner of the set, her face the picture of an Executive Producer.

'There you are,' she says, as if I've been missing for ages and she's finally found me. 'Your dad's sent back your contract. The dry run is over, and you are good to go.' Taking my elbow, she steers me towards the main set door. 'If you're ready?'

I am so not ready. My galloping pulse is a sure sign of my inner freakage while my brain is trying to convince every inch of my body that this is what I want.

'Let's get you into the house, everyone's waiting.'

She taps her lanyard onto the shining lightning bolt pad and pulls the door to the house open wide.

My heart's thudding so loudly it's threatening to break through my chest.

'You're a nice girl, Kass. You remind me of…' She stops, a strange expression on her face. It's gone in an instant. 'Good luck.'

Pippa pushes me gently inside. The door clicks shut behind me, the lock sliding into place with a secure clunk. Spinning around I try the door with both hands. I want to tell her I'm not ready, but it's too late. It won't open without the lanyard. The only way out now is to play the game, for me and Thea, and if we're gonna walk out of these doors together, not crawl out from under the set, I'm gonna have to do my very best to win.

11

We are ten minutes from launch, or at least we were when Pippa sent me in. She called it 'Time to warm up and acclimatise'. I call it 'Time to freak out and reflect on present life choices.' We have no phones or watches, there are no clocks, so there is no way to tell how long we have. Not knowing is making me even jumpier.

We are all milling around in a brightly decorated, open-plan room. There's graffiti-style tagging all over the walls, each one the same: TRUST NO ONE. The room's way smaller than you might think from the television, and *so* bright, the whole ceiling is filled with blinding yellow light.

On the far side is a small kitchen area. There's a door in the back wall, labelled STOREROOM. Tucked into the corner is another door labelled BEDROOM 1.

I'm watching everyone from the sidelines, stressing big time. I try to cement faces in my mind to distract me. Combat-boot girl Cali – small, cute and a little bit emo; Amara the Fierce from make-up – feisty, and loud, rocking a haircut Rihanna would envy; drop-dead gorgeous Tayo from the foyer; snarky Sailor boy – no clue what his name is, must find out; bleach-haired Noah – in it for a dare; Skye the Great – model with a brain; whoopsie-whoops Max with his oversized baggy *Star Wars* T; and Tattoo boy – bad boy, good looking but totally up his own arse. Thea and I make ten.

Easy…

The other nine contestants, all way shinier than me, explore the house with a confidence I would die for.

Amara and Cali are in the kitchen, trying the kettle.

'It's broken,' Cali says.

'No electricity,' says Tattoo boy.

Bored, they move on. Cali pushes the storeroom door, but it doesn't budge.

Max peers through a glass door in the corner of the room. 'There's an outside space,' he says with an admiring whistle. 'Set must go straight through the studio hangar doors. Clever.' He tries the door. 'Totally locked in,' he says. 'Hope no one's claustrophobic.'

On the same side as Max's garden door, separated from the main living area by a huge glass wall is another door labelled BEDROOM 2, also locked. Inside it's black. Noah and Thea are peering through the glass, Noah's bleached-white hair popping against the darkness.

A huge circular table dominates the living room. Two large sofas and a chair make up the rest of the furniture: stylish, expensive. Tattoo boy is lounging, cat-like, totally comfortable in his new surroundings.

On the wall above the sofa is a huge digital display. Two sets of red numbers stare down, set at zero. They're not moving, but it's obvious they're gonna be counting down to something.

'Hi, I'm Skye.'

Totally didn't notice Skye the Great walk up. She's

beaming a smile of friendship my way and, caught off guard, I smile right back.

'Kass,' I say.

'It's all a bit full-on. Thought I'd stay out of it for a bit, get used to it, y'know?'

Skye the Great is shy? No way. Didn't see that coming.

'I keep telling myself not to look at the cameras, but it's all I can think about.' She laughs a sweet Snow White laugh and I half expect to see a couple of blue tits flying round her head. *Idiot. Who's the tit now?* Her eyes rise up to the corner of the room and mine follow. A small round camera sits in the corner, a fierce red light on its bottom, blinking. 'They say you forget they are there, but I can't imagine it.'

'My stomach's rolling so much I may actually puke,' I say.

Skye giggles. 'Me too. I'm desperate for a wee but too friggin' scared to go.' Her head nods towards the camera. 'What if they're watching?'

The nearest camera makes a whirring noise and spins towards us. Skye grabs my arm, mouthing an *OMG* at me.

Who knew? Skye the Great, model with a brain, is actually alright.

'What are you two whispering about? Plotting already?' Snarky Sailor boy is striding towards us. Outwardly confident with shoulders back and head held in a jaunty pose, the tiny beads of sweat puckering his forehead betray his nerves.

'I'm Xander.'

'Kass,' I say. 'And this is Skye.'

'Xander?' she asks.

He holds up his hands. 'I know, tragic. My mum was totally into *Buffy the Vampire Slayer*. Could be worse, could be called Angel.'

'Or Spike.' I giggle.

He pulls a face. Skye laughs. To be fair he totally rocks the name. Deep, dark eyes the colour of smoke peer through long lashes. Dark curls fall to his shoulders, high cheek bones and full, cupid lips give his face a feminine quality. Sailor boy Xander is in the *fit enough to be here* category. Bet he's not quite as innocent as he looks.

'I am crapping my pants,' he says.

'But you seem so together.' I laugh. I'm getting less snarky and more little brother vibes.

'Total act,' he says. 'The outfit cost a fortune, need to do it justice.'

'You are rocking it.' Skye squeezes his arm.

'You're so sweet.' Xander beams.

Skye leans in conspiratorially. 'I don't understand, if we're not live yet then why are we recording?' Her eyes drift up to the nearest camera, its red light blinking as it points towards us.

'To get our reactions,' Xander says, pirouetting towards the camera in a fierce runway move. 'They'll take bits to drop into the show later, it's no big.'

Maybe not for him, Xander's way too comfortable in

front of the camera. I'm glad to have found an ally in Skye, who's just as uncomfortable as me.

I search the room for Thea. She's talking to beautiful Tayo. They must sense me, 'cause they look over at the exact same time, catching me staring. I look away, not having to fake the heat in my cheeks.

'Who wants to check out the Confessional?' Amara bellows.

'Me.' Xander runs over to the two yellow doors by the main entrance, one labelled COURTROOM and the other, now being pulled open by Amara, reads CONFESSIONAL.

'I love your look,' they say in unison, stopping and laughing. 'Jinx.' They disappear – the yellow door closing behind them, Xander's voice still loud and clear through the laughter. 'Let's be besties.'

'Shall we see if the bedrooms are both locked?' Skye the Great is asking *me*? A ripple of confidence surges through me as we set off across the room to what I pray is not a communal bathroom.

As we cross the floor the lights drop and the middle of the table flickers. All conversation stops.

Noah walks towards me.

Cohin appears in the middle of the table. Just his hooded, faceless torso, as though the table has cut him right in half.

'Help me Obi-wan Kenobi, you're my only hope.' Max walks up to him. 'Cohin is so cool.'

'Thank you, Max,' Cohin says.

Max jumps back. 'Woah. Can I call you Yoda?'

'I am a Contestant Originated Holographic Integrated Narration system. Cohin for short.'

'That's a no then?'

'All contestants gather around the table.'

We all stand around the table. Amara and Xander appear from the Confessional, excitement coming off them in turbo-charged waves. Cohin hovers above a domed plate in the middle of the table, which looks exactly like the eye of a fly.

'Contestants, sit.'

'Would a please cost anything?' Amara says, but sits.

The chairs are totally stylish, and we sit stiffly upright, hands down on the glass top. Even sitting, everyone can be seen. It's gonna be hard to hide anything in here. Skye is to my right and Max is to my left, puffing with excitement.

Cohin's face is stuck in an awkward smile. As well as mimicking us he has his own face, shadowed by the hood. Only a pointy chin and thin mouth are visible, a cryptic AI narrator in a game of mystery. We're all watching him expectantly, unsure what to do.

'Has he glitched?' Max leans forward and waves his arm right through him.

The main house doors fly open with a bang, making us jump. Rita scuttles towards the table.

'Don't mind me.' She ducks under the table, uncovers a panel in the central pedestal and fiddles with wires. We all watch through the glass as she ducks back out and stands, talking into her headset. 'Try now.'

Cohin moves and we all cheer in solidarity.

Rita smiles. 'Just needed a jiggle. Going live in two minutes. Good luck everyone.' She runs back out through the main doors, tapping her lanyard on the small pad.

'Contestants, welcome.' Cohin pulls his hood away to reveal the face of Noah.

Noah whistles under his breath.

'Freaks me out,' he says.

Cohin doesn't react. 'We are about to go live. Contestants, do not swear. All contestants must remain seated unless otherwise directed.'

Excitement fizzes round the table. My skin is buzzing from fear-sprinkled anticipation. Thea's a picture of calm, but the slight flush of her cheeks tells me she's bricking it as much as I am. I smile across the table and her eyes widen in reply.

'Good luck,' she mouths.

Cohin counts down from ten.

'Nine.'

At each number the energy gets a little more tense and my pulse races a little quicker.

'Eight,

Seven,

Six.'

My palms are sweaty, I rub them on my thighs.

'Five.'

'Here we go,' Max whispers.

A murmur of good wishes circles the table.

Cohin stops counting at five, his face morphing into numbers that count down in a pulsing beat.

Four,

Three,

Two,

One...

A soundtrack blasts the room, and a sequence of images appear above the dome in the middle of the table, like a three-dimensional television but without the television. The music is loud and catchy, and we watch the opening sequence with wide eyes. A miniature *Lie or Die* house appears, with our faces and names, and we cheer each time a face appears.

The sequence finishes with an audio boom fading into a voiceover:

THERE IS ONLY ONE RULE – TRUST NO ONE.

The loud whirr of the cameras turning fills the room. Cohin appears again, hooded, wearing his anonymous Cohin face. 'Welcome to *Lie or Die*. I am Cohin. The Contestant Originated Holographic Integrated Narration system brought to you by ArtelTechnix. I am the eyes and ears of the game. Both Judge and Narrator, I'm your guide through what is the deadliest reality murder-mystery show ever played, and the first studio-filmed programming to be streamed exclusively on social media.'

Not sure if I'm on camera, I pull an *I'm impressed* face. It's actually really hard to smile when you're this nervous.

'This is not a game of survival of the fittest, but of the cleverest, the most devious and the most despicably deceitful.' Cohin's face morphs into Thea's. 'Only those clever enough to mislead and outmanoeuvre will stand a chance of winning the cash prize and the title of *Lie or Die* Champion.' Thea's face morphs into Cali. The Narrator bot continues to change his face to ours one after another: Thea, Xander, Tattoo boy, me, Cali, Skye, Amara, Max and Tayo, and then back to Noah before looping round again.

'Two murderous Agents, one undercover Detective, seven innocent Players. In a game where everyone is lying, do you have what it takes to survive?'

A drum roll rumbles through the speakers.

'Contestants, you will soon receive your status.'

I am trying to listen but the voice in my head won't stop screaming. Oblivious to my rabbit-in-the-headlights excitement, Cohin continues.

'As well as Agents and Players, there will be one Detective hidden amongst you, playing as a Player, gathering evidence on all contestants. They may reveal their identity when, and if, they choose. To win, Players must uncover both Agents. Agents you must eliminate all Players and remain undetected. How many of you claim victory is up to you. You can work together and share the prize or wait for your fellow contestants to kill off your competition and claim it all for yourself.'

Thea dares an excited glance at me.

A drumroll starts low and builds.

'And what is the prize for which you are all willing to kill? The winner or winners of *Lie or Die* will claim a share of a £50,000 prize fund.'

There are audible gasps from around the table as each of us digests the amount. Amazement is replaced by a gritty determination to kill rather than be killed. *£50,000*! That's life changing. I knew it would be a lot, but *£50,000*! Thea is having the same thought process – it's written all over her face. That's enough to buy our way out of Boredomville and to actually have a future.

'Oh my,' Skye says. Beautiful Tayo looks like he has swallowed something sour. Sailor boy Xander almost chokes.

'We have a one in ten chance of winning £50,000.' Thea's eyes are gleaming.

'Who's up for sharing?' Amara says.

Xander throws his hand in the air, grinning from ear to ear. 'I'm in.'

Only Noah's uneasy. He looks really overwhelmed. I try to catch his eye across the table, but he's staring at his hands. Once this table thing is over, I must say 'hi' properly.

Cohin speaks. 'But there is a twist. We are taking the game to another level.' Noah forgotten, my attention's firmly rooted on the shutters rising under the digital clocks, revealing a glass window. Behind the glass is a black bowling ball with a white string sticking out the top and BOMB written on the front. It's cartoony and ridiculous and it's sitting on a whole heap of bank notes, red and green wires snake around the pile of money like a tangle of multi-coloured spaghetti.

'So that's what fifty grand looks like,' whistles Amara.

Cohin speaks. 'Contestants, here is your prize money. But beware. To get the money you must first deactivate the bomb. And there is only one way to stop it.'

'Shut. Up,' shouts Xander, eyes gleaming.

'Each Agent has a code. This code will only be revealed once the Agent has been identified. The combination of both Agents' codes will stop the bomb and release the cash prize. Should the Players or the Agents fail to use the codes within the designated time, the bomb will detonate, and the money will be reduced to ash. Welcome to the Ticking Time Bomb.'

The lights change colour, strobing around the room with a dramatic flashing and the low drumroll growls in our ears. A ticking sound punctuates the effect – louder, louder until BANG.

The explosion makes me jump. My palms are clammy against the glass table, and I brush them against my jeans.

The room falls into an electric silence.

'Will Tayo go to the Confessional. Remaining contestants must wait at the table until further notice.'

Beautiful Tayo stands, salutes us and with a to-die-for smile walks over to the two bright yellow doors and disappears into the one labelled CONFESSIONAL.

The rest of us stay seated.

Cohin disappears, replaced by a cascading waterfall of light.

'I am liking the twist,' Xander says. 'And I am liking the money.'

'Awesome,' Amara says.

'It's not real,' Max says. 'They'll have used prop-money for sure.'

Tattoo boy snorts back a laugh. 'Yeah, 'cause the bomb's real. Contestants get turned into pink mist live on TV.'

Skye pulls a sweet *ewww* face.

Max shuffles on his chair. 'Just saying.'

The waterfall of light morphs back into an image. It's Tayo's master interview, and while he's away we get to watch it.

The image shows him sitting on the stool, one foot resting on the bar, the other stretched out in front of him, arms resting on his thighs. He's so chilled. He looks like he's chatting to an old friend.

'My name is Tayo Asaju. I'm eighteen and I'm from Kentish Town. I've just finished college and am going to university in September to read maths and economics. I love writing poetry,' he holds his hands up. 'Sounds naff, but it's dope, gives me a real sense of place, you know?' He talks to someone off camera. 'Does that sound tragic?' He chuckles. 'And rugby, I play rugby.' He shrugs. 'I also do a bit of modelling which helps pay for college, so all good. I can't wait to get stuck into the game and win the cash. Man, I am competitive, and I love to win.' He points into the camera. 'You can't fool me; I'll see right through you. Watch out, Tayo's coming for you.' Tayo holds his position for a second before breaking and laughing. 'So sad.' His palm rubs his forehead.

I like him more for his bits off the camera than on. Of course, he's a frigging genius, jeez, intimidated much? I wonder what everyone else's secret weapon is.

'Anyone else totally out of their comfort zone?' Noah says.

It's enough to break the silence and we all start talking at once.

Tayo reappears through the yellow door and the hologram disappears from the centre of the table. The conversation stops as he sits.

'S'up?' he says with a confidence that comes from being *that* good-looking. He leans back in his chair, beaming. 'I'm innocent, baby.'

Cohin reappears. 'Will Thea go to the Confessional.'

'Here we go.' Thea pushes her chair back. 'May the best woman win.' As she strides away, I make a mental note to channel some Thea swagger.

We sit at the table for ages, going into the Confessional one by one. There are no clocks in the house. The fierce artificial light gives us no clues, but the August sun is setting behind the high garden wall. I guess they're playing out all our video packages, despite only showing us Tayo's.

It's weird knowing you are being watched. But the longer we sit, the easier it is to fall back into normal habits. I'm not the only one, it's obvious when someone relaxes a little too much then jerks upright and fake smiles once they remember they're live on camera. As everyone comes back from the Confessional there's a subtle change in their body language, as though whatever happened in there altered them – made them more mistrusting.

'Will Rhodri come to the Confessional.'

Rhodri? Tattoo boy stretches casually like he's got all the time in the world.

And I'm last. Why am I surprised? I struggle to hide my thoughts behind my *I am on TV and I'm lovely* face.

Tattoo boy Rhodri gets up, pushing his chair back with his legs, his arms brushing down his jeans. He doesn't bother to look at any of us as he swaggers off to the Confessional.

'What's his problem?' Skye whispers.

'I know, right?' I whisper back.

'He's hot though,' she lowers her voice more, which is stupid as the LAV mic hanging round her neck is gonna pick up even the smallest whisper. 'Those tats.' Who knew that Skye the Great, super-sexy criminal mastermind would be into bad boys?

Cohin morphs into Rhodri.

'Alri? I'm Rhodri, I'm eighteen. I'm an apprentice high voltage sparky from Porthcawl, South Wales.' Rhodri's trademark don't-give-a-damn air oozes through the camera.

He looks even better on camera as the lens picks up the sleeve and the tatts and the smoky green of his albeit unfriendly eyes. 'My dad died when I was thirteen, so I left school and started my apprenticeship to look after my mam and sister. It's cool. I love being a sparky, I do. I love music. I play the piano, drums and the guitar.' He smiles and his eyes sparkle. 'I write songs. If I won the cash, I'd have the money to go further, you know? Maybe do it professionally, give my mam the life she deserves. So yeah, I'm gonna win.' He stares down the lens. 'I got nothing to lose.'

We all stare at the space in the middle of the table processing Rhodri's words long after the image has disappeared.

'Wow,' breathes Skye. 'He's even hotter now.'

'Like Elvis.' Xander checks himself in the mirror wall. We all look at him in confusion. 'He loves his mamma. So hot.'

Max snorts. 'Pah. The I've Had a Hard Life, but I'm Not a Bad Boy trope – so obvious.' He holds his hands up. 'What? It's the oldest trick in the reality book, get the public on your side and you're halfway to the win.'

'The public don't get a say in who wins,' Amara says.

'Really?' Max says. 'How many of you changed your opinion of him when you heard his story?' Half of us look at our hands, not wanting to admit that Max may be right.

'It's a game. Wake up. We're all clichés.' He points to Skye. 'The Softie.' Then at Xander. 'LGBTQ+.' Amara.

'Gay Asian.' Cali. 'E-girl. It's what they do.' He points at Thea. 'Mean Girl.'

Thea says nothing, but I bet she's way more offended than she's letting on.

Noah frowns at him.

'You're the Hot Jock who's full of modesty and doesn't want to be here.' He points his finger excitedly. 'Ooh, bet your mates applied for you.' Max pulls an *I'm not wrong* face.

Amara shuffles in her seat. 'Gay Asian? Ehh he-llo? Mixed race. My Pakistani dad shagged a white woman from Leicester and here I am.'

'Hey, no shame here.' Max holds his hands up. 'Mum's from Cyprus and Dad's British Indian. I'm as mixed as they come.'

Amara leans back in her chair. 'Also, I like boys, so big-time fail.'

Cali folds her arms over her chest and scowls at him through her sharp, straight fringe. 'What's anyone's sexuality got to do with playing a game?'

'You tell him, girl,' Xander pipes up.

Way to make friends, Max. Amara leans towards him. 'So, what are you? Some kind of Mafia fan?' She laughs. 'Like a mad gamer?'

'Hell yeah. Total super fan, gamer AND complete reality-show nerd.' Max chuckles. 'I'm the total cliché, doesn't get more trope than me.'

'You don't say,' Xander says.

Rhodri returns, pulling his seat back and sitting in one fluid movement.

'What did I miss?' His voice is deep, soft and recognisably Welsh.

Thea shifts in her seat. 'Max was sharing his theory that we are all stereotypes and clichés.'

Rhodri doesn't look surprised. 'Ahh, the reality tropes. Got it.' He holds out his arm to show us his sleeve. 'Bad Boy.'

Tayo chuckles from his seat, a wonderfully melodious sound that hugs the table. 'Don't worry guys, the black dude always gets it first.'

'Or the gay Asian,' says Amara.

'E-girl,' Cali almost growls.

'Hey, nerdy gamer here.' Max mimes slitting his throat.

We giggle nervously even though it's not at all funny. Silence.

As I wait for my name to be called, the nerves return.

'Come. On. I am gasping for a drink.' Amara drops her head to her hands.

Cohin morphs into me. 'Will Kass come to the Confessional.'

Amara lifts her head. 'You're up, Girl Next Door.' I do a little curtsey to show I'm all good with the trope thing.

As I leave, Amara starts recounting our earlier conversation in make-up. She's really going into it, almost verbatim. I make a mental note to be careful what I say to her from now on.

97

I stand in front of the bright yellow door. Time to discover my fate. Will I finally get to be the bad guy? At home the Mafia nearly always win, but here with this elite crowd of super fans and A* students, who knows?

I enter the Confessional. Maybe my fate's about to change.

12

The room's not as I expected.

It's small and sparse and prison grey. A tiny table and one chair face a wall with a camera sticking out. Up in the corners are two more cameras, red lights blinking. Next to the table is an easel covered with a black cloth.

I sit. On the table is a large white envelope, with my name written in black. I don't touch it, keeping my hands clutched together under the table, like a silent prayer.

'Kass,' a female voice booms into the room. It's too soft for Pippa, but it doesn't sound like Isla either. 'Please open the envelope and read out the contents.'

Here goes. I try to stop the envelope shaking as I tear off the end. Pulling out the card I read the word out loud.

PLAYER

It's amazing how you can feel so many emotions from one little word. My initial reaction is disappointment, the same disappointment I have every time I play back home and that Mafia card never comes my way. It's like I'm doomed, like my Ancient Greek namesake, to a life of trying to prove my innocence and never being believed.

'How are you feeling, Kass?' Is there a hint of amusement? Is my face that transparent? I look right into the camera and smile a lie.

'Great. Relieved. Being innocent is much easier than being the killer, especially in this fantastic group of super players.'

'You sound very confident.'

The lie's working. 'I am.'

It's probably for the best. At least now I won't have to lie to Thea about being an Agent. I can totally have her back.

'What do you think of your fellow contestants?'

'Um, nice?' My hand moves to my mouth but I can't talk and bite my nails at the same time.

'Is there anyone you suspect?'

I laugh, we've been in the game for about a minute.

'Have you made any special connections?'

'Noah's nice. I think we could be friends. But he could be faking.' I stop. There's a camera lens right in front of me. I mustn't forget I'm talking to the world. 'I like Skye and Max.'

I smile into the camera.

'Kass. We have a task for you. Behind you is a hatch. Open it and put the contents on the table.'

I push my chair back, intrigued. Inside the hatch is a box. Putting it on the table, I sit back down.

'Kass, please open the box and remove the contents.'

I peel back the lid. The inside is filled with packets of biscuits which I place on the table in front of me. Underneath the biscuits is a pile of laminated biscuit pictures, each with Velcro on the back.

'When you applied for the show, we asked you the question: If you were a biscuit, what biscuit would you be?'

I groan silently. I have an idea where this is going.

'Kass, please take the cover from the easel.'

I pull off the black cloth. On the easel are headshots of all the contestants, including me.

'Kass. We would like you to match the biscuits to the contestants.'

I shuffle the biscuit pictures to give me something to do with my hands.

'If completed successfully, you will be rewarded with a key.' The voice continues. 'The keys open various doors in the house including a storeroom, the bedrooms, the garden and the fuse box, which provides access to electricity and hot water. Failure to match the correct biscuits to the contestant will incur a fail. Do you understand?'

I'm trying to listen and figure out the biscuits, while smiling and looking casual for the camera. It's hard.

I have an advantage. I know my biscuit, of course, but I also know Thea's and Noah's. I try to picture the contestants. Picking up the Party Ring and the Pink Wafer, I stick them to Xander and Skye. To be fair, it could be either, but I stick the Pink Wafer on Skye, as I imagine Xander to be the partying kind and a rainbow biscuit seems the right choice for him.

Next, I pick up the Oreo.

'Oreo.' I voice my working out. 'Oreo is the classic

chocolate biscuit filled with just the right amount of filling. It's classy, comforting and a little dark.'

I'm talking rubbish, but I go with it, pretending I'm talking to Thea and Lewis. Looking around the board my eyes fall on Tayo. Too obvious. Cali is next to him with her slightly emo vibe.

'Cali's got a little dark vibe going for her, she would totally go for the Oreo. She's also really cute like the little girl in the advert.' I stick the Oreo on Cali's face.

I press the boring Bourbon into my face. 'I reckon Max is a Hobnob sort.'

For the Jaffa Cake I pretend to waver. 'Jaffa Cake? Should that even be here? It raises many questions: cake or biscuit? Is this person trying to tell us something?'

I put the Jaffa Cake down. 'I've never heard of this one. Don't even know how to say it. Aber… frow, frau? It sounds Welsh to me, so I'm giving that one to Rhodri.' I push it right into his annoying face. 'Chocolate Digestive is easy. It's the king of the biscuits, classy and delicious.' Placing the picture on Tayo I pray I'm not blushing.

'Ginger Nut is fierce, spicy, but very down to earth.' I look at the remaining faces and take a wild guess. 'Amara looks fierce. I reckon she's a fiery Ginger Nut.'

Without realising, I only have the Jammie Dodger and the Jaffa Cake left and I know who both belong to. I mustn't give it away.

'So, a Jammie Dodger's always popular. It's the favourite in my house.' I think of Thea. 'It's cute but not chintzy, there are many layers, biscuit cream and jam and right in the middle is a huge heart.' I stare intently at the pictures. 'I think Thea has a big heart.' I push it onto Thea. 'Sorry, Noah, I'm sure your heart is overflowing too, but Jaffa Cake is the only one left.'

I face front and pat the table. 'Done.'

'Are you happy with your answers Kass?'

'Yeees?' I say. 'It's hard, I've known these people for like two minutes. It's all guess work and gut instinct.'

'You now have a decision to make.'

Oh crap.

'Kass, you have completed the biscuit challenge successfully and may collect a reward. In front of you are ten packets of biscuits, one packet of each representative biscuit. You can choose to take the biscuits for yourself or receive a key. If you choose to take the biscuits, the key will remain here and one door in the house will remain locked.'

'Easy. Biscuits or unlocking the storeroom and food for everybody?' I shrug. 'No brainer.'

'But that's not all.'

My heart sinks.

'If you choose to take the reward for yourself, you will also be awarded a significant game advantage. You have ten seconds to decide.'

'I… What…? I…' My mind is whirring, fast forwarding through sentences like a rehearsal. 'I… To… I… To have a game advantage would be, well an advantage, and let's be fair I could do with one against this lot. But if they find out, they'll think I'm sabotaging and call me out as an Agent. Urghh.' I bury my head in my hands.

'Kass, your time is up.'

'I don't know what to do.'

'I need your answer. Will you take the advantage or take a key?' The voice remains stubbornly neutral.

'Take the key,' I say.

'Is that your final answer?'

I thump my palms on the table. 'Yes. Advantages will come later. Right now it's about building trust.'

The room falls silent.

'Kass, please open the hatch and take out the key.'

I do as I'm told, placing a large key on a blue ribbon on the table.

The voice continues. 'This key will unlock one of five locks within the house.' I beam into the camera. 'One more thing.' Beam extinguished in a skipping heartbeat. 'Kass, you have shown yourself to be a team player, one more likely to play a hero's game than a villain's.'

I pull a modest face while trying to calm the nerves. I'm surprised my mic hasn't picked up on my hammering pulse. Maybe it has, maybe the soundman is cursing me on the other side of the wall.

'Kass, you have been picked for a status upgrade, one that comes with huge responsibility.'

Urghh.

'Please take the envelope from the hatch behind you.'

I'm crap at responsibility. Mum moans daily at me for forgetting to feed the dog, and Dad says I live in LaLa Land ninety per cent of the time. Neither quality is good for big responsibility stakes.

My fingers tap on the glossy black envelope, desperate to open the flap. An advantage would be good, anything that will help me and Thea win.

'Open it, Kass.'

I pull out the card with shaking fingers.

NECROMANCER

Ewww, what even is that? Isn't that some weird wizard type who goes around bringing people back to life?

'Kass, you have been given a very special power.'

'Um, thanks?'

'Kass, The Necromancer has the power to reverse a guilty charge and bring one Player back from execution.' I don't get it. 'If the Jury decides that one Player is guilty and send them to their death, you have the power to overturn their decision and bring that Player back into the game.'

Oh! My face must have gone from blank to beaming in a lifesaving second. 'That's huge!' Those two words don't sound big enough for such an epic ability. I try to expand. 'This is like a superpower. For real. I can actually save someone?' If the time comes when Thea's in trouble, I can bring her back.

'Kass, this ability can only be used once and cannot be used to save yourself, so you must use it wisely.'

I'm nodding faster than Churchill the dog. This is my insurance. Mine and Thea's. What better way to prove I have her back? We can totally rock this game now. A sense of power surges through me.

'Thank you, Kass. You may leave the Confessional.'

I grab the key. I'm tempted to nick a packet of biscuits but realise what a stupid move that would be in a room full of cameras. I leave them on the table, next to the card with one word that has completely changed my game.

13

I walk back into a respectful round of applause. It takes a minute for me to understand.

They were watching me.

Before anyone can speak, the *Lie or Die* theme tune blasts into the house. I freeze.

'We are out of live streaming,' Cohin says. 'All contestants to remain seated at the table.' He disappears. All that's left is the glass-domed Cohin projector.

There's a collective sigh as everyone relaxes. Forgetting we're still recording, even though we're not live streaming, Max opens his mouth wide and does some weird kind of stretching exercises. It's not a good look at any time.

'So, I'm the king of the biscuits?' Tayo adjusts his position, leaning his elbows on the table.

'Felt right.' I sit, praying my face isn't burning. This is so unfair, why me? It's not like they showed anyone else.

Tayo's chuckle is low and mellow. 'Hell yeah.' He points to Noah. 'But no way this dude's a Jaffa Cake.'

Noah grins at Tayo. 'Mate, no one at this table is who they seem.'

'It fits. There's definitely more to him,' I say.

'There's more to all of us, we're all hiding our truths,' Noah says. 'That's the game.'

'There is only one rule,' Max intones loudly. 'Trust no one.'

Thea catches my eye. I don't smile, it's too risky, but I do hold her gaze for a few seconds. She looks away. There's no signs of anyone knowing about my secret status. They could be lying, but I'm not getting that vibe.

'So embarrassing,' I mumble. Skye squeezes my arm.

'You rocked it. You're so natural on camera,' she says.

'I was so nervous.' I start fishing. 'I can't believe you all watched. Why would they do that? It's so random.'

Skye shakes her head, her hair flying prettily around her shoulders. 'We only saw the challenge, from when you got the biscuit box to your decision not to bail on us.' She misreads my look of relief. 'We didn't see your status; they wouldn't show us that.'

I mime a *phew*.

'Or maybe we did.' A Welsh lilt floats across the table. 'Maybe we know *exactly* who you are.' Rhodri's pushing his chair back so the front legs are off the ground in a move that always gets me told off at home.

I struggle to keep my face calm.

'Why would you say that?' Noah says.

Rhodri holds up his hands. 'Because that's the game? No spectators here. Players only.'

'Contestants,' Cohin appears. 'You were given the task of identifying each other from the biscuits you chose to identify as.' Cohin's face spins, virtually looking at each one of us, owl-like and just as wise. 'Three of you matched the correct biscuits to the contestant and therefore were successful in your task. All three of you were given the same option – take the reward for yourself or share with the group. Two of you chose to share. Therefore, two of you are in possession of keys. Rooms without keys will stay locked until further notice.'

Cohin disappears.

'Well, we're all crap,' Thea says with a sad grin.

Cali scowls. 'And someone took the win and the biscuits for themselves.'

'An Agent sabotaging?' Skye says with a cute little shiver.

'Or a hungry person,' says Max. We all look at him. 'Not me … I got it wrong.' He looks at Noah. 'Didn't take you for a Jaffa Cake.' He turns to Cali. 'Didn't get the Oreo vibe with you either.'

Cali raises an eyebrow. 'Oh? And what should I be? A Fortune cookie?'

Max is flustered. 'Um no, obviously. I was thinking you're way more classic, like a Custard Cream?' It's like watching roadkill. 'Or a … Nice?'

I silently will him to stop talking.

Cali stares at him through screwed-up dark eyes. I hold my breath waiting for some almighty take-down. It doesn't come.

'I like Oreos.' Her face relaxes. 'Very dunkable.'

Max nods enthusiastically.

'An Agent could have taken the win for the group to make themselves look innocent.' Tayo's looking at me. My cheeks burn guiltily under his scrutiny.

'Who else got it right?' Skye says.

Amara holds up a key. 'I was like her. No brainer.'

'Anyone want to own up to taking the biscuits?' Skye says.

Cali snorts a no. 'I didn't get any of them.' She points at Thea. 'Except yours. Jammie Dodgers. Excellent choice.'

'Thanks.' Thea beams. Cali seems genuine. Could she be a possible ally?

Max rubs his hands together. 'So, the lying and deception begins. Clever. We must follow the trail of breadcrumbs to the Agents.'

'More like biscuit crumbs,' Xander chuckles.

Rhodri's staring at me. 'How do we know she wasn't playing up to the camera? Could have been a set-up. She could have known we were watching.'

'Not true,' I say, genuinely gobsmacked that he would mistrust me so quickly. 'I had no idea.'

'Then why did they only show us her?' Rhodri says. 'She could be an Agent trying to worm her way into our trust.'

'As could you,' Noah says.

'Nah,' Cali says. 'We all saw her in the task, she was way too obvious to be bluffing.'

'Uh, thanks?' I say.

She grins. 'No prob.'

'Don't overthink it, guys,' Max says. 'It's way too early to play a double bluff.' Despite his words he's staring at me through suspicious eyes.

Why are they all on me? Amara got a key too, don't see anyone grilling her.

The lights snap off and single spots glare down on us, imprisoning us in an individual cage of light. We shut up and sit up.

I'm literally holding my breath.

Cohin reappears in the centre of the table.

'Contestants. Your statuses are set.' He remains hooded, head down. 'The two Agents have been made aware of each other's identity.' Not gonna lie, he's starting to give me the willies.

'There are two factions within you. Players: innocent contestants whose only crime is to want to stay alive. And Agents, whose job is simple: kill or be killed. Should you survive, you will be rewarded with great riches. Who survives? You decide. Who dies? It's up to you.'

Blackout.

Skye leans closer to me.

The room bleeds. Our faces glow eerily as the lights paint us in a blood-red wash. Ten pairs of eyes flit around the table, a circle of terrified expectation hovering in crimson. Xander's clutching Amara's hand. Tayo fades into the shadows. Next to him Noah's bleached white hair turns a subtle shade of candyfloss pink. Rhodri's grinning across the table like nothing ever fazes him.

A siren pierces through the darkness.

The clock on the wall starts to tick…

The noise is loud enough to hear over the screeching siren.

Tick … tick: a lazy beat as the numbers count down. 05:59 and counting.

Tayo booms across the table. 'Six hours?'

'Night's fallen,' Max shouts beside me, his palms pressed to his ears. 'The game's started. This is the Kill Window. Night One.'

'The what?' Cali shouts. 'Spell it out, Fanboy, for those of us who actually have a life.'

'The Kill Window.' Max struggles to be heard. 'The time the Agents have to choose a victim. They have six hours to target and kill one of us.' He shifts in his chair, his elbow knocking mine. 'The Detective has this time to identify an Agent.'

'All contestants may leave the table,' Cohin bellows. 'But beware. Night has fallen. No Player is safe until the Kill Clock stops.'

The siren finishes in a perfectly timed beat. Cohin disappears.

Silence.

All that's left is the ticking of the Kill Clock.

The lights return to the now normal bright.

Relief pinches our faces.

Xander grabs Amara's key and runs for the bedroom door. 'Shotgun first bed.'

Amara chases after him.

Tayo slowly stands, as graceful as a *Strictly* dancer.

112

'How about we open up that storeroom,' he says to me. His voice totally lacks the arrogance I'd expected.

Huh. It's an act, part of his gameplay. He wants me to fall for him so he can get me on my own and stick me with an Agent card. Do not engage.

I smile sweetly and take the key from my pocket.

The key doesn't fit in the storeroom door. Max is more than a little disappointed.

Xander and Amara are trying her key in the bedroom door behind the kitchen, but it's not working.

Xander stamps his foot.

'Try the other door,' Amara says. They run to the other bedroom, the one with the glass window. I head for the first bedroom, but Rhodri blocks my way.

'Try in there.' He opens a kitchen cupboard. Inside is a large, locked box.

'Fuse board,' he says. 'Power.'

Irritated by his assumption I'll just do as I'm told, I open my mouth to argue that he can bloody well jog on. There's a small tug at my elbow. Thea's by my side.

'Power sounds good.' She squeezes my arm. It's weird pretending not to know her. And she's right. I need to wind my neck in and not make enemies.

I try the key in the lock. The fuse box opens.

'Yes!' Rhodri pushes me out of the way and presses the large 'On' button.

'A sparky excited about electricity,' Thea says. 'Cute.'

Looping her arm through mine she leads me towards the excitement.

Xander and Amara have opened the door to Bedroom 2 and are whooping and cheering as if they've won the lottery. They disappear inside the dark room, and we all rush to follow. Amara finds the light switch, illuminating the bedroom as brightly as the living area.

'Power, hot water and beds, not half bad,' Max says. 'Could do with some food though.'

Rhodri pats him on the shoulder. 'Right there with you, buddy.'

The bedroom is long, running about half the length of the living area. Five single beds are made up in a line, each with a grey duvet, pillow and a blanket folded at the bottom. The room is decorated in light pastel greens – neutral and basic. It has that new paint smell. The painted walls are graffitied with the same tags as the living room, the now familiar: Trust no one. The left side wall is a complete bank of floor to ceiling windows. To where? Can't tell. The bright light inside has created an impenetrable black wall. My feet sink into the soft piled carpet, at least that's comfortable.

Amara and Xander are running around. Amara ducks though a door on the far right.

'Shower and bog,' she says.

I shudder at the thought of sleeping in here. The huge glass wall to the living area and the wall of glass out to who knows where makes for one human-sized goldfish bowl. It's not for the self-conscious.

'I guess the other bedroom's staying locked,' Cali says.

Five beds? With the other door locked, does that mean we're sharing?

'I'm thinking we give this room to the girls and sleep in the lounge tonight.' Noah walks in with Tayo and Skye.

'There won't be much sleeping with the Agents about,' Max says.

'We could share?' Amara looks at Xander.

'Bed buddy,' Xander shrieks. They jump on the far bed, next to the window.

'It's well uncomfortable,' Amara moans.

'Of course.' Max plonks himself down on the middle bed. 'Sleep deprivation is a classic form of torture.'

'They're hardly going to torture us.' Thea's voice drips with impatience.

'No,' Max says. 'But the contestants who don't sleep are always the most paranoid. It's just good telly.'

'Do you spend your entire day glued to reality shows?' Amara asks.

Max grins. 'Sometimes I play CoD.'

'Tragic,' Thea says.

Climbing off the end of his bed, Xander whoops. 'I've found a switch.'

'Best switch it then,' says Cali, sounding anything but interested.

Floodlights snap on, illuminating the black outside. It's the garden. Walls a house high, topped with rolls of barbed wire, encircle a square of artificial grass. There's an old tree on the lawn, not sure if it's real or fake. But I'm not focused on the tree.

I'm focused on the body hanging from it.

14

'Oh my god!' Skye cries.

There's crazy movement as ten bodies all cram against the glass and stare into the garden.

'Shiiiit,' breathes Xander.

'Relax, guys,' Tayo's soft voice carries strong over our gasps. 'It's not real. Look.'

'It looks real,' Xander says, flicking his curls.

'Creepy.' Amara shudders.

'There's something in his hand.' Max strains to see. 'It's one of those Agent cards.'

Cali looks away with a non-committal shrug. 'Sad.' She twiddles her earring, a tale-tale move whenever she's uncomfortable.

'Can we go see it?' Xander runs into the living room and rattles the garden door handle.

'It's locked,' Noah says.

'Damn.' Xander comes back into the bedroom.

Tayo's nose is pressed against the glass. 'And so it begins.'

On second look, the body's obviously a dummy. Its head is bowed, a mop of white hair falling over the face. Around its neck is a sign.

'Douglas Broads. Studio Technician,' I read.

'I guess we know the name of the first victim,' Skye says. 'Poor Dougie.'

'Uhhh, hello? Not real,' Max says.

'Suspend your disbelief, Fanboy,' Rhodri says. 'Anyone think it looks a bit like Noah?'

Everyone laughs.

'Didn't that director say something about props and clues,' Cali says. 'Maybe it's one big clue.'

'And it's pointing straight at Noah,' Thea says, waving her hand over her head. 'Bleached hair?'

'Isn't your hair bleached too?' Tayo says softly. 'Could be you.'

'Haha.' Thea faux laughs then stops abruptly. 'My hair's not bleached, its ombré'd.'

'My bad,' Tayo says, turning away from the window.

Amara and Xander saunter over to Noah, reminding me of a pair of hyenas on the prowl. 'Welsh boy's right, it does look like you.' Amara says as they circle him.

'Got something to confess?' Xander says.

Everyone's attention is focused on their banter. The mood is light and fun as they tease Noah. He holds his hands up with the faintest smile on his lips. Ignoring them, I turn back to the dummy. There's something about it that's giving me the willies.

It's weird: my mind is telling me it's a prop, I know it's the dummy from the crawl space, but I can't help the cold chill that's sprinting down my back. It's totally unnerving to see it hanging from the tree like that.

I force my eyes down its arm, from the Agent card clasped in one hand and across the dangling body. I stop.

There's something sticking out of its leg. Pressing against the glass I take a closer look. It's partly hidden by the angle of the body. I twist uncomfortably to get a better look. It looks like a pen sticking out of his leg. A long yellow pen. And I've seen it before.

The EpiPen?

Amara says something I don't catch which is followed by a howling laugh from Xander. I squint at the body, trying to see properly from this angle. It's an EpiPen, I'm sure of it. Just like the one Pippa had. The one that Allergy girl couldn't find.

Why would that be sticking out of Dougie's leg?

Rhodri is teasing Thea about something; her flirty giggle rises over the noise of their banter. Why would the EpiPen be a clue? I don't get it. No one here apart from me and Thea know about Bryony. It doesn't make sense.

'Hey Kass,' Max shouts over the others. 'You're very quiet over there. You know that the quiet ones are usually the first to get targeted?'

'Back off, Max,' Thea says. 'Not all of us are sad little super-geek fanboys.' The protective edge to her tone fills me with warm fuzzy feelings. I've missed her having my back.

Rhodri whoops. 'Touché. That told you, Fanboy.'

Not trusting myself, I check the pen again. Yep, definitely there. I just don't get why or what it's supposed to mean. I briefly consider telling the group but Pippa was very clear about keeping Bryony's accident a secret. I glance up to the cameras. One beady little body is pointing right at me, red light blinking. My stomach rolls like I've been caught doing something I shouldn't. Moving away from the window, I turn to ask Noah how he knew the door was locked but he's gone, the Confessional door is closing slowly.

Max claps his hands. 'I was wondering how they were gonna do the death.' My attention's diverted back to Max and his Fanboy theories.

'In traditional Mafia, the one accredited to Dimitry Davidoff in the 1980s at Moscow State University…'

'Move it on, Fanboy, we are literally on the clock.' Rhodri yawns, throwing himself on a bed.

Ignoring him, Max carries on. 'In traditional Mafia, the game starts with a murder, but never one of the Players. It's always outside the game, a random victim.'

'Doesn't make him any less dead,' says Thea. Max and his big mouth have a Thea-sized target on their back. It's a shame. For all his constant *faux pas*, I like his quirkiness. Plus, he's a total nerd on everything to do with this game which is useful – unless he's an Agent.

'True,' he says. 'But it gives the Agents a free pass for tonight. They now have the advantage of communicating without the stress of having to commit murder.'

''Cause they're the ones stressed about the killing.' Cali snorts.

Max continues. 'As Players, we know we are safe for the next few hours at least.' I notice he keeps saying 'we'

120

when referring to the Players. My gut tells me he's one of us but best keep an eye on him until I can decide who to trust.

'While they plot which one of us is next,' Thea says.

Rhodri stretches his arms lazily above his head.

'As long as it's not me,' he says. 'I am fine with them plotting all night.'

'And the Detective?' Max says. 'They're gonna be trying to get to the Confessional. Tricky, they could easily bump into the Agents and…' He makes his finger into a gun and mimes shooting himself.

'Fanboy. Do you *ever* shut up?' Rhodri says.

'Well, if I *was* the Detective, yours would be the first name I'd put forward,' Max says.

Rhodri rests his hands under his head. 'Sweet. Then you would know I'm innocent. I'm a lover not a fighter.'

We ignore him.

'We should get some rest. We'll not get much opportunity for the next four nights.' Max sits on the bed next to Rhodri. 'They won't let us rest during the day: way too boring.'

'He's right.' Tayo walks into the bedroom, followed by Noah. I hadn't even noticed Tayo leaving, I need to get my head in the game. 'We should all try to rest.' He speaks with a calm confidence that immediately gets all our attention. 'How about you showing some class and letting the girls have the beds?'

Rhodri pats the mattress. 'Anyone is welcome to join

me.' His Welsh accent lilts seductively, making it almost an attractive proposition. Almost.

'Don't you think we should all stay together?' Skye says. 'So we can keep an eye on everyone's movements?'

'I'd love to know who has the biscuits.' Xander rubs his tummy. 'Starving.'

Noah crosses his arms. 'There are sofas next door, or the beds in here. To be honest, I'm way too wired to sleep. I guess it's wherever you're comfortable.' He looks at Tayo. 'Tayo and I are on the sofas.' Tayo nods his confirmation, and they walk out shoulder to shoulder like a couple of old friends.

Max bolts up off the bed.

'Stand down, Fanboy.' Rhodri swings his legs over the bed. 'I'll take one for the team. Besides someone's got to keep an eye on Jaffa and the King.' He lollops out of the room. 'Sweet dreams, losers, don't let the Agents bite.'

Max falls back onto his bed with a thump.

'Wanna share?' Skye grins at me.

'Sure.' I grin back.

Amara and Xander's bed is nearest the garden window. Cali takes the bed next to them, Max in the middle, then Thea. Skye and I take the bed on the end, nearest the bathroom. I make sure I'm on the side next to Thea. Skye disappears into the bathroom, glancing at the cameras as she goes. They don't follow her.

I'm getting a bit more used to the blinking lights of the cameras huddled in the corners of the rooms, but the whirring sound they make when they turn towards the action still weirds me out. I have to consciously stop myself from freezing whenever I hear it.

Behind the beds is a bank of mirrors. Xander and Amara are pissing around in front of them, peering right into the glass. Their loud banter's giving me a headache, so I leave rather than let them wind me up. Wandering into the living area, I'm drawn to the £50,000 money mountain behind the glass.

'Hey.' Noah's at my shoulder, holding out a bottle. 'Water rations. Hopefully they'll open the storeroom in the morning.'

'Thanks.' I take the water but don't open it. No way am I drinking fluids yet; I am so not ready for the whole bathroom thing. I notice he hasn't opened his either. We stand in awkward silence staring at the money. 'How cool is that?' I ask. 'The money, not the bomb.'

'Very cool.' He doesn't exactly sound excited.

'Dougie was a shock, totally didn't see that coming,' I say, trying to make conversation.

Noah stares out to the garden, his brows furrowed in confusion. 'Yeah, big surprise.'

The Noah I met in the cafe is very different from Noah in the house. 'You okay?'

'Bit overwhelmed.' He tears his eyes away from the garden, gesturing to the cameras. 'Guess I'm camera shy. Who knew?'

A camera turns towards us with the familiar whirl. My heart jumps a beat as the red recording light snaps on.

123

'Me too,' I whisper. Now I know it's there, it's taking all my willpower not to look at it. Noah points to my microphone.

'They can hear you even when you whisper.'

Amara storms past us with Xander close on her heels and heads through the yellow door of the Confessional.

'Something's got them worked up,' Noah says. As I walk away, he catches my arm.

'I've got your back.' He half grins, half grimaces. 'Just wanted to tell you.'

'Me too,' I say, conscious of the whirring in my ear. We are being watched right now. I look up at the camera slowly so his eyes follow. He nods.

'Total shit show.' Amara and Xander storm past again. 'They're not releasing the suitcases,' Amara says to anyone listening. 'Won't tell us when we are gonna get them.' She grabs some bottles of water from the kitchen, throwing one to Xander.

'So unfair,' Xander bleats. 'I need my eye mask.'

'First World problems,' Noah mutters.

'And they want you.' Xander points to the Confessional. 'In there, something about your microphone.' Spinning on his heel, he disappears into the bedroom behind Amara.

'They've bonded quickly,' Noah says. He hurries towards the Confessional leaving me alone in the huge living space.

I half expect Cohin to be watching me from the table, but no one's there, hologram or human. Tayo's lounging on the sofa. I hesitate, I should go speak to him, but he's just too intimidating. I head back into the bedroom. Thea's in bed, fully dressed under her duvet, her shoes placed neatly beside the bed. Max is lying on the bed next to her.

'You'd better not snore,' Thea's saying to him. 'Or fart.' Banging her pillow with her fist, she turns her back on him.

Skye comes back from the bathroom. Her hair's pulled back into a night braid. Even without make-up she looks perfect. I try to ignore the pang of envy.

'It's alright in there,' she says. 'One camera, no red light, none in the loos. I think they'll only record if there's drama. I covered my mic with some loo paper when I … you know.' I nod, too much info. I'm gonna wait, even if I am bursting. It's too embarrassing.

Amara and Xander have tucked down in the end bed. We may have to kill them for being too annoying. Noah's right, they've formed a strong bond, but you could say the same about him and Tayo, me and Skye. Just because you're friendly with someone doesn't make you both automatically Agents. It's easy to get paranoid in here. Must keep a level head.

Climbing into bed beside Skye, in a room of strangers is weird. I turn to Thea. Her face says exactly the same. I wonder if Lewis is back. There's a camera right above me – could he be watching? I dare a quick smile into it, saying a mental goodnight.

Skye sits up, peering over me to Thea.

'Should we take it in turns to stay awake?' she whispers. 'To watch?'

Cali's sparko, which is amazing as she's next to Amara and Xander who are being really loud. Max's breathing is steady, each out breath whistling loudly through his teeth.

'I'll watch,' I say. There's no way I'm gonna fall asleep in this goldfish bowl of sharks. Relief floods Skye's face.

'Great.' She settles down beside me.

As her head hits the pillow the bedroom light flips off, plunging the room into dark. Night lights snap on, little rows of beady lights running along the floor, like a mini motorway, signposting the exits.

I stare at the ceiling, trying to avoid the flashing red from the cameras as they sweep their relentless gaze across the room and back again, never blinking, never sleeping, never losing sight of us.

Either the bed is surprisingly comfy, or my adrenaline high is wearing off rapidly. With Amara and Xander finally settled, the rhythmic breathing of bodies is like waves lapping on the beach. Soon I'm fighting my eyes as they stubbornly close, the epic events of the day catching up with me. I struggle to keep my watch but everyone's asleep and right now, exhaustion is a stronger force than paranoia. I allow myself to drift off.

It won't matter, just for a minute or two.

15

Someone's poking me.

I jolt awake. Thea's face is in mine, her finger firmly planted over her mouth in a silent *Shhh*, her wide eyes instructing me to keep quiet.

I'm sleep groggy. I rub my eyes, unsure whether I'm still dreaming. The pinch confirms I'm very much awake. I scream a silent *Owww* at her as my reality comes flooding back.

Grumpy and awake, I crawl carefully out of bed without waking Skye. A string of red lights outlines the ceiling as the cameras whirr awake. I pad softly after Thea. Max is snoring. The combined rising and falling of breaths is surprisingly loud in the total quiet of the house. Through the glass, the two large mounds on the sofas must be Tayo and Rhodri. Noah's curled up in the chair. I close the bathroom door softly behind me.

Thea's jumping up and down with excitement. 'Can you believe this?'

My eyes take in the modern bathroom, shower, sinks, gleaming white tiles. There are cameras in here but no red light. There are two cubicle doors in the corner. I dive into one. Having seen the absence of recording lights and having Thea on guard makes me finally able to 'go' and I am busting.

'We really have to stop meeting in toilets,' I say,

washing my hands in the shiny sink, loving the posh soap so much I do them twice. Grabbing a towel, I turn to her. 'So, what's the plan?'

'I'm innocent,' she says. 'You?'

'Same.'

'Hand on heart?' Thea stares at me.

'Yes,' I say.

'Swear on your life.'

'On my life,' I say, a bit pissed off that she would doubt my word.

'Okay,' she says. 'We should stay quiet for the first round, keep under the radar. But watch *everyone*.'

I get it. Those who are in your face in the first round usually end up getting accused themselves.

'That dummy in the garden freaks me out,' Thea says, washing her hands.

I frown, glancing up, but there's no red light on the camera in the corner: we are not being watched. 'Did you see the EpiPen sticking out of its leg?' I whisper.

'What's an EpiPen? Isn't that something to do with anaphylactic shock, like allergies?' Her expression changes as the penny drops. 'Allergy girl?' I gesture for her to whisper.

'I swear I saw one sticking out of its leg,' I whisper, my eyes glued to the sleeping camera.

She pulls a face and shakes her head. 'Why would they do that? That's just wrong on so many levels. No,' she says with a finality you can't argue with. 'Doesn't make sense. You saw wrong. It's easy to get paranoid in here.

And we are not supposed to know about,' she mouths '*Bryony*'. 'So…' she gestures locking her lips. 'Lewis could get into a whole heap of trouble for telling me.'

I nod. She's probably right, but I can't help the niggling voice in my head reminding me what I saw.

'I get it though,' she talks normally. 'He is creepy as, totally weirding me out.'

I smile as she faux shudders into the mirror. I'm loving this, it's almost like old times with her. 'I've seen him naked, he's totally harmless.'

'What?' Thea's face is a picture.

'He was in the space under the set,' I explain, grinning. 'Found him when I fell through, in nothing but his birthday suit. He looked like…' I stop. Not entirely sure I should be talking about this when I'm trying to prove to Thea that I don't think about boys all the time. I change the subject quickly. 'I wonder who's the Detective?'

'Keep your eyes open,' she says. 'I proper don't trust Amara or Xander or Max. I'm going to watch all of them for both of us.'

'Max's okay,' I say. 'Just a nerd.'

'And what's with the blonde one, he's totally jumpy.'

'Noah? He's fine, just nervous,' I say. 'I like him.'

'Just stay alert, okay.' Thea screws up her nose. 'I like Rhodri.'

'Like? Or *like*?' I giggle.

'In the game, stupid.' The pink blush appearing on her cheeks says otherwise. 'He could be the Detective?'

'Based on the fact that you think he's sexy as hell?' I laugh. Let's face it there's nothing else to go on.

'Stop it,' she grins. 'I do love a Welsh accent. I'll keep a special eye on him.'

'You do that,' I say. 'Remember the plan: lie, lie, lie, stick together and pick them off one by one.'

'Shhh,' Thea says. 'You can't say that in here. My god, Kass, this is exactly what I mean, you don't think.'

'No one is listening,' I say quickly, trying to pull it back.

Thea nods to the camera in the corner, the recording light is blazing red.

'It's fine,' I say again, with a dismissive shake of my hand. 'What I meant is, don't let the fact you like him cloud your judgement, he could be an Agent.'

'Course,' she says. 'I would never let a boy cloud...'

Awkward. Will I ever get this JB thing off my back?

There's not much else to say and we are totally paranoid about getting caught. Thea hugs me and leaves.

I hang back, giving her a minute to get back into bed.

As I leave, Isla's directorial voice plays in my head. *If the words come from your mouth, then you only have yourself to blame.*

Thea's snuggled back down in bed. Creeping back into the quiet room makes my nerves run wild. If anyone sees me, I could be accused of doing something suspicious and Agent-like. My mouth is cardboard dry. Sitting on my bed, I reach for my bottle of water, but it's gone. Someone's nicked it. Cali's buried under her duvet, her arm poking out from under her pillow. Amara and Xander are quiet in the end bed – I bet it was them. Damn. I'm thirsty and the NOT FOR DRINKING sign above the bathroom sink has put me off the tap water. There're more bottles in the kitchen.

I move quickly out of the bedroom and through the living area, bypassing the boys on the sofa. Once in the kitchen, I exhale slowly and quietly, convinced I'll wake the entire house.

The whirring of a camera above makes me shiver.

There's no water. The fridge is empty and I daren't open up all the cupboards, so I have no choice but to drink the tap water. Never has the sound of running water hitting glass sounded so loud. I drink greedily, gulping it down, forgetting where I am for the smallest second, safely hidden in the darkness.

A shadow to my left makes me jump. Someone's moving around. Agent? It disappears around the corner. I mentally draw a map of the room, there's nothing in that corner. I hold my breath until my lungs burn, waiting for them to reappear.

Nothing.

The house is sleep quiet. I can't risk moving in case I'm seen, or worse come face to face with an Agent – way to get targeted. It's all very well for Max to say the Agents won't kill tonight, but what if he's wrong? Or worse, what if he's an Agent and he's waiting for some idiot to wander around the house in the middle of the night. I stand petrified in the kitchen, until my legs stiffen and my calves scream. I can't get carded now, not when Thea is just starting to be normal with me again. The Kill Clock's counting down in the living room, reminding me that I'm completely vulnerable. Why didn't I think? Risking my whole game on a stupid drink of water.

Slowly I flex my muscles and plan my path back to bed. Adrenaline accelerates me so fast I'm standing back in the bedroom doorway before I can say *Carded*.

I check the far corner. It's empty. As my eyes run over the boys sleeping on the sofas, I freeze.

Tayo's awake.

He's staring right at me. I dive into bed, pulling the sheet over my head. My heart's banging so loud it's gonna wake Skye. My brain's whirling. It makes no sense. There was nowhere to go, and yet that shadow disappeared as mysteriously as Amelia Earhart.

I turn the problem over in my head, my conviction waning the more I fail to solve it. By the time I fall asleep I have done a pretty good job of convincing myself it was all a figment of my very paranoid imagination.

16

'Make it stop,' wails Xander.

The siren rips through the bedroom like a stampeding army, attacking our ears with its ear-splitting war cry. I don't so much wake up as get yanked out of sleep backwards, upside down and by my ankles. I sit up next to a bewildered Skye, head thumping from the relentless noise and way too little sleep.

Thea's sitting on the side of her bed. Xander's up, his hands clamped over his ears, screaming dramatically. Max pulls the duvet back over his head with an unimpressed groan. Only Amara doesn't react, huddled beneath the sheets.

Thea throws her pillow at Max. 'Wake up.' She wanders to the table with Skye.

Xander shakes Max. 'It might stop if we all get up.' He's immediately distracted by his reflection, messing around with his lazy curls in the mirrors.

Max blunders out of bed and into the living room. Stretching, I follow him.

Tayo's on the sofa, readjusting his locs. He looks sexy as, with a half-awake, sleep-tussled look on his face.

'I'll be there now,' Rhodri shouts from the kitchen. He's barefoot and topless and it's hard to miss the muscled six pack as he shamelessly wanders around. From the flush appearing on Thea's cheeks, she's definitely noticed too.

Noah's at the table, gesturing for us to sit, looking like he hasn't slept a wink. 'Someone needs to wake Amara.'

'Am-ara,' Xander shouts as he sits at the table, turning to stare into the mirror. 'My head is banging,' he moans. 'And my mouth.' He stretches his mouth open and sticks his tongue. 'Need water.'

Still the siren screams.

Rhodri's still messing about in the kitchen. If he's trying to piss us off, it's working.

'I need coffee.' Thea covers her ears with her hands. Gesturing to me, she shouts. 'Microphone.'

Damn. It's by the side of the bed. I run back into the bedroom.

'Where's Cali?' Skye shouts from the table. I shrug a *don't know* through the glass window.

'Urgh.' Xander stands and shouts. 'Amara.' He runs back into the bedroom. 'I mean, wow. That girl could sleep through a war.'

He throws the duvet back, revealing Amara. Still no movement. 'Babes, wake up.' Glancing up at the cameras, he waits for them to turn in his direction before comedy jumping back, hands to face, a shrieking scream leaving his lips. 'I don't believe it, she's dead.'

He screams to the others through the glass window. 'She's dead.' Hands on head, eyes popping, full-on playing up to the cameras. 'She's been mur-dered.'

'Dude, what are you doing?' Rhodri wanders towards the bedroom doorway.

Xander stops his over-the-top reaction and frowns at Rhodri, hands on hips. 'What Isla the Director said. It's a clue, I'm leaning in.'

'All contestants to sit at the table, immediately.' Cohin's voice booms over the siren. Everyone obediently heads for the table, leaving me and Xander in the bedroom.

Looping the mic cable over my head I look over at Amara. My first reaction is to scream before I remember I'm on a murder-mystery show and Isla's words about props: *All are designed to get your investigative juices working … the more you do, the more entertaining you will be.* I quickly stop myself, don't want to be *that* contestant, the one labelled the drama queen or the screamer, that's not the kind of entertaining I want to be. Checking myself, I prepare to play the game, however gross it may be. Amara's lying in bed, curled up. A line of white dribble snakes from mouth to pillow. She must have had this done properly, like from the make-up lady, it's too good to be a do-it-yourself. The blue tinge to her lips is so professionally done. One arm outstretched. Clutched in her hand is a biscuit.

'Poison.' Xander gestures to her lips and the drool. 'I bet it's poison. She ate the biscuit and…' He swipes his hand across his throat, making sure he's angled properly for the camera. 'Oh my god, so cool. I had no clue. I was next to her all night.'

There's something on the floor next to the bed.

'Nooo way.' Xander splutters as he runs to pick up the Agent card and then comes back to me. 'How? When? I was sleeping right there.' Xander is massively distracted by the cameras and giving a truly Oscar-winning performance, he's leaning so far into this he's defying gravity.

'I thought we were supposed to go to the Confessional when we got killed?' I whisper to him, remembering Isla's instructions. 'Why is she still here, pretending to be dead?'

Xander's head bobs up and down excitedly. 'She's a drama student, this is her big chance, no way was she gonna go quietly. Good on her.' He whispers, 'You are rocking it, girl.'

'All contestants to return to the table.' Cohin's voice is stern. The siren screams even louder. Xander backs out towards the table, pulling me with him.

'Sorry,' he mouths to the cameras. Looking at me he pulls an *Eek*. 'Guess they don't want us to blow her cover,' he whispers. 'She's awesome. I would be pissing myself.'

It's true, Amara is brilliant at playing dead. She's not making one movement. I hover in the doorway, uncertain. It really does look real – I can't even see her breathing.

'Are you sure she's alright? Shouldn't we check?'

'Girl, she will love you forever. Hollywood, remember, she's going all the way.' He pulls me out of the bedroom. 'They have stuff to make her look like that, it's all good,' he whispers in my ear. 'That's why they want us at the table, if we get too close, we'll make her laugh.'

Xander flaps his arms excitedly as he flops into a chair, throwing the card on the table. 'So cool.' It skids to a stop in the middle, the large red 'A' staring up at us.

'Poor Amara,' Skye says.

'Uh hello? Murder-mystery game?' Xander's face is one big *doh*. 'If we're gonna die, best do it in style.'

'I'm planning on winning.' Rhodri points to the money behind the glass. 'That money's mine.'

I must admit that there is something endearing about Rhodri's determination to win for his family. I quickly squash that thought: Thea likes him and anyway, he's a proper dick.

Max is shaking his head. 'Not cool. One kill per night. That's the rules. Dougie was the kill.'

'Well, she's definitely been carded.' I sit at the table. 'Right in the middle of us.'

'One per night. That's how I've always played it. One per night.' Max keeps muttering.

'Calm down, Fanboy,' Rhodri says. 'Maybe they changed the rules. Did anyone bother to read them?'

'Will all contestants come to the table.' Cohin appears again, his voice stern.

'Where *is* Cali?' Skye shouts.

We all look around. She's nowhere to be seen.

'CALI,' Tayo shouts over the noise.

Xander joins in, 'CALI.'

Still no sign of her.

'You don't think the Agents got her too?' Skye shouts, her eyes as big as saucers. 'You don't think *she's* an Agent?'

'No way.' Max gestures to the dummy still hanging on the tree. 'One kill per night. It should only be Dougie.

And we're supposed to go to the Confessional when we get carded. That's the rules.'

Tayo raises his voice to be heard. '*The lady doth protest too much, methinks.* Poison a biscuit, did you?' We all look at him. 'What?' he chuckles. 'He's the only one who gets to lean in?'

Max shrugs. 'Why bother telling us the rules if they're just going to change them?'

'That's the game, brother.' Rhodri thumps him on the back. 'We are in for one hell of a ride.'

Cali appears from the bathroom. Her jet-black hair has been swept up in a high pony and her face looks much less harsh without the heavy black eyeliner.

'Hurry up,' Xander shouts.

She sits and the siren stops.

'Thank god,' Skye says.

'My ears are still ringing,' Max moans.

'You couldn't hear it?' Tayo asks her.

'We've all gone deaf because of you,' Xander wails.

Cali shrugs and points to the bedroom. 'Is that?'

Thea nods. 'Amara.'

'Dead?'

'Yep.'

'Agent?'

'Carded in her sleep.'

'Wow.' Cali flops back in her chair.

'Kass thought it was real,' Xander says snidely, and everyone laughs.

My cheeks start to burn. 'No, I didn't exactly say that. I just wanted to check she was alright.'

'I repeat. Murder-mystery show? Clue's in the "murder"?' Xander says. 'Hundreds of cameras watching our every breath – think they would know if it was her last.'

More laughter.

'Bless, Girl Next Door really is too innocent for this game,' Thea says. I glare at her.

'Or maybe she isn't,' Tayo says thoughtfully.

A high-pitched mechanical groaning punctures the air as a wall of white shutters lowers across the bedroom glass.

Cali jumps up. 'Shit, my microphone.'

She runs to the bedroom door and tugs. It doesn't open. She sits back down.

'Electric locks on all the doors,' Rhodri says, knowingly. 'Operated by the powers that be.'

Thea shudders. 'Gives me the creeps. Knowing they can lock the doors at any time. We could get trapped in here.'

'They'll have an emergency override.' Rhodri nods his head like he knows. 'They have to.' I knew that. Just because he's an apprentice electric-whatever doesn't mean we need his mansplaining. Knob.

The shutters descend, shutting out the bedroom.

Crowd noises start playing through the speakers, so loud we have to shout again.

'It's so we don't hear them in there,' Tayo shouts. 'With Amara.'

'I'm getting a headache,' Skye says, pulling a face.

We wait at the table, still half asleep. The noise doesn't last long, stopping abruptly as the shutters rise and the bedroom becomes visible. Amara's gone. There must be a secret door in the bedroom too. Knowing someone can come in and out while we sleep wigs me out far more than the doors locking without our control. But I guess that's what we signed up for.

'Day One breaks.' Cohin appears again. 'Contestants, while you were sleeping the Agents struck again. Amara was murdered in her bed.'

Rhodri swallows a giggle, his face buried behind his hand. Skye scowls at him. He pulls a face. 'Death by Hobnob?'

A nervous giggle erupts around the table.

Cohin morphs into the head and shoulders of Amara.

'Oh My GOD, guys, I got murdered. That sucks.' Her face turns fierce as she spins around. 'Didn't see it coming. I demand justice. Players wake up and get those Agents.'

She morphs back to Cohin. 'One of you is dead. Who will be next?'

Cohin disappears.

'Doesn't she tell us what she was?' Cali asks.

Max shakes his head. 'Only the executed reveal who they are. The murdered don't get to have a voice.'

'Well, that's sad,' Skye says. 'And a little annoying, how are we supposed to know if she was a Player?'

Xander jumps up. 'We look at the clues,' he says gesturing to the bedroom. 'She had a biscuit in her hand and her mouth was all gross, so I say that's a clue.'

'Calm down, Sherlock.' Rhodri chuckles.

Xander flops back into his chair.

'So, we know someone won the challenge and chose to take an advantage,' Tayo says. 'That advantage could have been to take out an extra Player.'

We all nod our agreement. 'Was it you?' He is staring right at Xander.

A pink flush creeps up Xander's cheeks. 'Uh, no? Amara was my friend.'

'Doesn't mean you didn't kill her,' Skye says.

'Well, I didn't,' he says, with a non-committal shrug.

'You had that whole poisoned theory going.' Tayo stares at Xander who shuffles uncomfortably under his scrutiny.

'*He* lied to us.' Xander points at Max.

'Sorry?' Max splutters into his drink.

'You said we were safe. You said they wouldn't kill again so we all relaxed, and she got caught off guard. We trusted you.'

'Excuse me?' Max says. 'I was simply stating the game rules.' He gestures to the walls and the huge *Trust no one* graffiti. 'Can't you read?'

Everyone laughs. Xander's eyes turn angry as his gaze sweeps the table. Finding another target, he attacks.

'Where were you?' Xander pounces on Cali.

Cali stops laughing. 'What's it to you?'

'Washing the poison off your hands?' He stares at Cali intensely.

Cali stares back, not at all intimidated. 'There's leaning in and then there's drowning in it.'

Xander holds his hands up, pulling a shock face. 'You do you and I'll do me.'

Cali's face is one big grumpy scowl.

Thea turns to Cali. 'Didn't you see anything? You were right next to her.'

Cali points to Xander. 'HE was in the same bed.'

Xander shrugs. 'Heavy sleeper. But I did wake up in the night and your bed was empty.'

Rhodri rests his head on his arms.

'Interesting.' Cali scowls.

'This isn't a need-to-know kinda show,' Rhodri says to her. 'Better be talking or you'll be walking.' I struggle not to smile, don't want to give him the satisfaction of knowing I find him funny. He leans back in his chair pretending to study the ceiling. 'I would die for coffee.'

'Probably not the best choice of words.' Tayo chuckles. 'But I'm with you, coffee would be good right now. And food.'

'Any idea what the time is?' I ask. The Kill Clock has stopped and reset to 00:00. It's early. The sun has only just emerged over the garden wall, its newborn light tiptoeing across the grass.

'Feel like I've had no sleep at all.' Thea yawns.

'I slept lush,' says Rhodri. 'Ready to face the day.'

'Can't you put a shirt on?' Cali says.

'Not bothered,' Rhodri says. 'These abs could get me a modelling contract.'

Max snorts.

'Seriously,' Thea's saying to Cali. 'You can't have secrets in here. We're all way too paranoid, what with Amara being murdered right under our noses.'

'I was in the shower,' Cali says. 'Fanboy was snoring all night and I couldn't sleep. Thought a shower might clear my head.'

Looking a little more closely, Cali's hair is damp.

'It's the paranoia that will get you out in the first rounds.' Max wags his finger.

'I don't trust anything you say,' Xander says.

'Finally, we're playing the game.' Tayo grins.

'Do you think they're filming?' Skye whispers.

Thea giggles. 'Yeah? What part of reality show you not getting?'

'We're not streaming, so I thought...' Skye says.

Xander rocks in his chair, copying Rhodri. 'Everything is recorded, then the interesting bits are cut into stories to make up the hour programme.'

'So, if you're boring, you won't get airtime,' Rhodri says. 'And let that be a warning, my friends. Make no mistake...' Rhodri's interrupted by a flickering light in the middle of the table.

Cohin appears, head bowed and hooded.

'I demand coffee.' Rhodri slams his palm on the table.

'Don't piss off the holographic oojamaflip,' Thea says.

'Oojamaflip?' Rhodri gives Thea a look that makes her blush and tilt her head. I recognise the play. She fancies him, hundred per cent.

Cohin begins. 'Please note the second countdown clock.'

We all turn to the clock wall. Below the Kill Clock is another set of digital numbers, also set at 00:00.

'Contestants, this is your Accusation Window. Once the clock starts, you have a small window of time to accuse someone of Amara's murder. Once a contestant is accused and seconded, they will be taken to the Courtroom to be tried.' Cohin morphs from one of us to the next. 'Find the Agents, deactivate the bomb, win the money. You have the fate of each other in your hands. It's time to *Lie or Die.*'

'Da, da, daaaaah,' Rhodri sings. 'Bit OTT.'

'I like it,' Max says. 'Ramping up the tension. Talk about pressure.'

Tayo looks at him.

'If we get it wrong, a Player dies,' Max says. 'That means they're out, finished, no more game.'

'No more fame.' Xander sits back in his chair.

'Deady, dead, dead,' Max half sings. 'Dead.'

We all fall silent.

'Metaphorically,' says Max.

'Well, your reputation's dead, and your chance to

become someone and actually do something with your life,' Xander says. 'You'll just end up in the loser graveyard with all the other reality contestants no one remembers.'

'Thanks for clearing that up,' Tayo chuckles.

'So, is he gonna tell us when this Accusation Window opens or what?' Cali says.

All our gazes lift to the clock, still set stubbornly at 00:00.

'I guess we have to watch,' Thea says.

'Be alert people.' Rhodri bangs his fist on the table, making us jump.

'Be cool, bro,' Tayo says quietly.

'I can't believe Amara's gone,' Xander wails.

'Are they gonna make us all do that if we get carded?' Skye says. 'I was crap at drama.'

'There's an easy solution,' Thea says. 'Don't die.'

'Love it,' Rhodri rubs his hands together. 'Let's get killing.'

Cohin has returned to his bowed head, neutral position. 'The remaining rooms are now open.'

Bodies explode from the table. I can't find Noah; he's disappeared in the confusion. He was sat at the table, wasn't he? Thea and Xander are the first to reach the storeroom, flinging open the door. I follow, waiting to see if Noah appears from our bedroom or the bathroom.

'Suitcases,' Xander screams, Amara forgotten.

Rhodri and Max push past Xander. 'Coffee,' they sing, jumping up and down.

Xander is literally kissing his suitcase. He carries it to the bedroom with Thea pulling hers behind her.

'Priorities,' Tayo says.

Rhodri waves a bag of coffee in the air. Max carries a platter of pastries and fresh bread.

The storeroom is small, made smaller by Tayo's huge frame dangling over the door. I hang back. Wandering to the window I look into the garden. Dougie's still there, hanging lifelessly from the tree but when I look at his leg, the EpiPen is nowhere to be seen. I check the floor in case it fell off; there's nothing.

Weird? I shake my head. Maybe Thea's right and this place is getting to me.

Noah appears from the direction of the Confessional.

'All we need now is some biscuits.' He stands at my shoulder. 'Bourbon?' He raises his eyebrows at me. What's he trying to say? Is he trying to say anything? Tayo's watching us with a curious expression. Thea's right, we are all totally paranoid and Amara's murder has made it a million times worse. I still can't get her lifeless body out of my head.

'Where d'you go?' I ask.

'Confessional.' He's even paler than yesterday. He looks like he's about to say something but changes his mind. He groans. 'Glad they've opened the other bedroom, at least we all have a bed tonight.'

'I guess the chair wasn't very comfortable?' I ask.

'Understatement,' he says. I wait for more, but he

stares out the window at Dougie. I don't get it: where's the chatty, cheeky boy I met in the cafe? Distracted by the smell of coffee, I park the thought.

Noah nudges my arm. 'Kass, I want you to know…'

Thea appears by my side. 'You two having a private chat, or can anyone join in?'

'Be right back.' Noah disappears into the boys' bedroom.

'What's his deal?' says Thea.

'Nothing,' I say. 'He had no sleep on that crappy chair.'

'Did he talk about us?' Thea says.

'What?'

'He knows we're friends,' Thea whispers.

'You're being paranoid.'

'Am not,' she says. The quick flick of her hair says otherwise. She nods to Dougie. 'Where's this pen then?'

Now I'm the one on the back foot. 'You were right,' I say reluctantly.

'A-ha!' she shouts a little too loudly, her face covered with a gleeful *I told you so*. 'Who's paranoid now?'

Breakfast never tasted so good, I scoff three pastries, and I was the polite one. Skye had three and a croissant. Max is still going, I stopped counting at six. Tayo ate loads. But Noah took only one piece, which he's barely touched.

It didn't go unnoticed.

'Not eating?' Xander says, his mouth full. 'Full up with biscuits, or were you too busy poisoning them?'

Noah ignores him. 'We need to keep an eye on that clock. If we miss the Accusation Window, we miss our chance to nominate.'

'On it,' Tayo says.

After we've stuffed ourselves, everyone disappears into the bedrooms, leaving Cali, me and Rhodri to clear up.

'I didn't kill Amara. I was in the shower.' Cali passes me the cups to wash. 'I came on. Went to the Confessional. Had to go all Bumblebee to open my suitcase. Needed to shower. You get it, right?'

'Sure.' I'm not a hundred per cent sure I believe her. It's difficult to believe anyone when the walls are plastered with *Trust no one*. With the Accusation Window opening soon, her confession is perfectly timed. Has Cali singled me out as the soft touch? Rhodri's clearing the table, he can't hear us.

'I did hear someone moving around in the night,' Cali says.

I try to hide the look of guilt.

She leans in. 'By the table, and when I went to the Confessional, I saw someone.'

My heart skips a beat. Did she see me and Thea?

'I got up for the loo in the night.' I stumble over the words. 'And for water. I was in the kitchen.'

'No, it was in here,' she says.

'Tayo?' I mouth.

148

'Smaller.' We look at Rhodri.

'What?' he says.

'Anything else to wash up?' I say, smiling at Skye as she heads towards the Confessional.

'Nope,' he says. 'But you two look guilty as hell.'

Cali flushes.

'Cali heard someone last night,' I say.

'In here,' Cali says.

'Ahhh, and you think it was me?' Rhodri says. 'I'm a Player. Sleeping like a baby, I was. You?'

'Player.' I believe him, when I was in the kitchen, he was asleep on the sofa.

'Jeez, man.' Noah and Tayo burst out of the bedroom holding their noses, Max following. 'That's a weapon of mass destruction.'

Max throws himself on the sofa, chuckling cheekily. 'Must have been the coffee.'

Noah gestures to Rhodri. 'Needed to evacuate the bedroom. Toxic waste.'

'What was the safe word? Bumblebee?' Tayo asks.

Rhodri laughs.

I grab my suitcase from the storeroom, thinking about Cali's words and wondering why she didn't say that she was a Player too.

17

We've been called to the living area. Wooden podiums are lined up in front of the garden window, numbered 1–9.

'Contestants,' Cohin says. 'The public have been getting to know you. Since yesterday, they have been voting for their favourite contestants.'

'This is gonna be carnage,' Skye says, giving me a look I can't read.

'I will ask a question,' Cohin says. 'You must stand behind the number you think corresponds to you. Nine being the most popular and one being the least. Contestants may confer. If you successfully arrange yourselves in the same order as the public, you will win a group reward.'

'Better than sitting around here all morning,' says Rhodri.

'You have sixty seconds. Will contestants line up in the order of most likable.'

'Let's get this party started.' Rhodri heads for the top position, jumping on podium nine. 'Sixty seconds, guys.' Everyone rushes to a podium.

'I'll take the bottom.' Max stands on one.

'Let's not be modest, people,' Rhodri shouts. 'I want the reward.'

Noah jumps on eight.

Skye hovers indecisively.

'Go with your gut.' Tayo smiles encouragement as Skye steps on seven. Tayo takes six.

Thea jumps on five and with Cali on four, Xander moves down to three. I jump on two as the siren blasts.

We look around at each other.

'Contestants. You have failed to guess the correct order.'

'Oh. Come. On,' Rhodri shouts.

Cohin continues. 'When I call your name, move to the correct podium.'

Butterflies gather in my stomach as I hope for the shortest second that I may be further up the line.

'The public voted Tayo as the most likable.'

Tayo moves calmly to nine. Rhodri pulls a *not-bothered* face as he jumps off.

'Eight is Rhodri,' Cohin says. Rhodri jumps onto eight, smugness tattooed all over his face.

I don't get it. How is he likeable?

We shuffle into our new places.

Seven – Skye

Six – Noah

Five – Xander

Four – Me. I'm quite happy with that, it doesn't suck.

Three – Max

Two – Thea.

'The least likeable contestant is Cali.'

'Let's remember this isn't real, these people don't know us,' says Max.

'Thanks, Fanboy,' Cali says. 'Feeling so much better now.'

'How's the view from down there?' Rhodri taunts.

'Get lost, Rhodri,' Max snaps.

Rhodri feigns horror. 'Ooh, Fanboy's sad.'

Cohin speaks. 'Will contestants now rearrange into the most entertaining.'

'Let's just get it done, guys.' Noah stands on one.

'I'm staying put.' Max remains on three.

'Skye, you need to be up here,' Rhodri shouts, back on nine.

'I'm okay here.' She jumps on four.

'Welsh boy's right,' Thea says to Skye. 'It's about how the public see you, and they like you.' Skye moves to seven. Thea jumps on four.

Xander stays on five.

Tayo stands in front of Max. 'You are way too entertaining to be at the bottom.'

Max moves up to six. Cali stands on three.

Tayo looks at me. 'Reckon you're high up.' A warm fuzzy glow propels me onto eight as Tayo jumps on two. The siren sounds.

'Contestants have failed. I can reveal that the most entertaining contestant is…' The butterflies are back, begging Cohin to say me. 'Rhodri.'

'Come on.' Rhodri bangs his chest, Tarzan-like.

What? No way is he the most entertaining. What are the public seeing that we're not? If there was a most arrogant, he'd be on podium twelve.

Cohin calls out the order. A quiet awkwardness falls over the room as the numbers get lower, until:

Four –Thea

Three – Cali

Two – Me

One – Max.

'We suck.' Thea flicks her hair back, her tell-tale tic. She's not happy.

I hang my head to hide my face. It's one thing to know you're boring but quite another to have it confirmed by the viewing public. I'm sure Max is at the bottom because of his earlier dodgy trope comments. The public likes to punish. Girl Next Door is exactly that, totally forgettable, and nobody could be bothered to vote otherwise.

'Hey, don't sweat it,' Cali whispers from the next loser podium. 'We'll show them.'

She's right. These people don't know me, so how can they judge me? It's no coincidence the top five podiums are filled, once again, with the shiniest people.

'Contestants move to the following positions:

Nine – Noah

Eight – Thea

Seven – Kass

Six – Cali

Five – Max

Four – Xander

Three – Rhodri

Two – Skye

One – Tayo.'

We stand in our new positions, Noah at the top and Tayo at the bottom. I should feel good. It's the highest I've placed in this stupid game. But beautiful Tayo and bad boy Rhodri, Skye the Great and Xander with his cherub good looks and fashionista style are all at the bottom. My sixth sense tingles a warning.

'Contestants, we asked the public to list you in order of most deceitful. We have placed you in the correct order for your own entertainment. The task is now over.'

Cohin disappears.

'Wow,' says Noah. 'They really don't like me.'

'Or me,' I say. Thea's next to me. Do the public think we're deceitful because we're hiding our friendship?

The Accusation Clock begins its countdown.

'Look.' Cali nods to the clock.

Max rubs his hands together. 'Now we're talking, that game makes total sense now.'

Thea jumps off first, heading straight to the bedroom, Xander follows. Rhodri swaggers around the living area, his head even bigger.

'I guess we didn't win the reward.' Skye perches on a stool.

'No big,' Tayo says. 'Doesn't matter what the public think.'

'Easy for you to say,' Cali says. 'You were on the top for everything.'

'At least you weren't the most deceitful,' says Noah. 'That one stung.'

'Why?' Skye asks.

'Why did it sting?' says Noah.

'Why were you on the top?'

She has a point. Why do the public think Noah is the most deceitful?

She turns to Tayo. 'Do you think the public know who the Agents are and they're sending us a message?'

'Did you kill Amara?' Xander walks up to me, his face dark. 'Is that why?'

'No, I'm not an Agent,' I say trying to sound calm and genuine. I hold Xander's suspicious stare as my cheeks heat up guiltily. It's so annoying, why do I always sound like I'm lying?

'I believe her.' Skye jumps off her stool with a grace I lack and heads into the Confessional before I can thank her.

'The public didn't,' Xander says.

'Sometimes the public aren't shown the real truth,' Tayo says.

'What he said,' says Max. 'We have no control over the story. If production decide you're a villain there's nothing you can do to stop it.'

'Nobody's a victim in here. If you don't like it, change it.' Thea appears from the bedroom. She's changed into a low-cut cropped vest top. Does she think more cleavage is gonna make her more likeable?

'Nice top,' Rhodri says, his eyes firmly planted on her tits. I guess it's working but I'm disappointed she's sold out so quickly.

'It doesn't mean anything,' Cali says. 'It's not like they get to vote us out.'

'Nope we get to do that all by ourselves,' says Rhodri from the sofa. 'But the public have given us much to consider.'

Tayo waves at the clock. 'We have less than an hour, guys.'

Everyone's talking in whispers. Small groups form in huddles as we all desperately unpick the public's reactions for clues.

I have no idea who's an Agent. Do the public really think that Noah is the most deceitful or did they simply not care enough to vote for him? I trust Skye, not picking up on any tics and she's proved she has my back. Can't get a read on beautiful Tayo but I'm leaning towards Player. Xander needs to chill, he's totally over-playing the Amara friendship thing for the cameras.

Rhodri's even more annoying now he knows the public are on his side. Max knows so much about this game; he could be very dangerous. That leaves Cali who's desperately trying to prove she's a Player but took a shower the exact same time we found Amara.

Urghh, it's so hard.

Thea catches my eye. I know exactly what she's thinking – don't make waves, it's too early in the game.

Perching on the stool next to Noah, I lower my voice. 'It was you I saw last night, wasn't it?' I catch the small tattoo on the underside of his wrist again. It's a dove.

His eyes fix on mine, ice blue and begging. 'It's not what you think. You need to trust me.'

'I do,' I say. The last niggles of doubt are washed away by the expression on his face right now. I'm certain he's not lying, my tic detector's not even whimpering.

The Accusation Clock counts down, but we do nothing. Forty minutes pass and still no one comes close to an accusation.

'Okay,' says Rhodri from the comfy chair. 'I'll start. I accuse Max.'

'Why me?' Max humphs.

'Don't we have to give a reason?' Skye asks.

Rhodri holds his arms up in the air and pulls a face. 'Because he ate all the pastries? And he destroyed the bathroom.'

'Fair point.' Max chuckles. 'I did do that. But you can't fry the nerd in the first round. Think of the haters.

'Haters gonna hate,' grins Rhodri. 'Who'll second me against Fanboy nerdy?'

No one will meet his eye.

'Not the best play, my friend,' Max says, grinning back. 'I accuse you right back, Tom Jones.'

'What have you got against the Welsh?'

'Fanboy nerdy?'

'Fair dos,' says Rhodri. 'Now we're rocking.'

'Seriously?' Thea says.

'It's quite customary for the first accusations to be banal,' Max says. 'We haven't had time to thoroughly investigate each other. That makes us all vulnerable.'

'I accuse you for using the word banal,' says Rhodri. Max almost chokes on a crisp.

'We need to take it seriously. What he said.' Xander points to Max.

Rhodri shifts position in the chair. 'Do go on.'

'Did anyone see or hear anything last night?' Xander scowls at Rhodri.

There's a lot of head shaking and puzzled faces as we all play dumb.

'Guys, come on,' Noah says. 'This is hard, but it's part of the game.'

Xander glares at Noah. 'Maybe we should accuse you.'

Noah shrugs. 'We're here to play a game, not make friends.'

'Coming from Mr Most Deceitful, don't forget,' says Xander.

'That was just a stupid game,' Cali says.

Xander pulls a face. 'Also interesting, coming from the least likable.'

Cali's eyes narrow.

'I saw something,' I say, trying to divert the negative

attention away from Noah. 'Someone was moving around in here. Last night.' All eyes turn to me. 'I got up for a drink and I saw someone.'

'Interesting.' Tayo leans in to listen.

'Where?' says Cali.

'Who?' asks Thea.

'You sound a little defensive there,' Rhodri says.

Thea flushes. 'Jog on. Who's to say it wasn't you?'

Rhodri stares into her eyes. 'It wasn't me.'

Thea giggles, she's totally crushing on Welsh boy.

I shake my head. 'Rhodri was on the sofa.'

Xander turns to me. 'You could be working together.'

'If hell froze over,' I mutter, scouring the room for an ally. My eyes rest on Skye.

'Kass was sleeping in the bed with me, and she was only gone for an instant.'

I silently thank her for a second time.

Tayo turns to Thea. 'You're quiet, Thea?'

Thea turns serious. 'I heard movement next to me.'

Xander smiles triumphantly. 'Kass.'

Thea frowns. 'The other side.'

Xander sings, 'Ca-li.'

'Oh, come on,' Cali shouts.

'She did disappear this morning,' Skye says.

'Agreed,' says Rhodri, still fidgeting in the chair. 'She was pretty shady about where she had been.'

'Was not,' Cali argues, but no one's listening.

'I accuse Cali,' Xander shouts.

159

'Seconded,' Rhodri says.

My heart skips. How quick did that happen?

'Brutal.' Tayo whistles.

'This is bullshit,' Cali says. She twiddles her earring.

'Guys?' Rhodri's holding an empty biscuit packet. 'Look what I found down the side of the chair.' He lifts his other hand. 'And this.' He's holding a small black bottle, there's a word written on the front in the same cartoon writing as the bomb.

POISON

'I knew it.' Xander fist pumps the air. 'I said it was poison.'

Max shouts excitedly. 'It's a clue. It's a biscuit clue. Amara was holding one. The biscuit could lead us to the Agent.'

'Chocolate Digestives,' Skye says. 'The ones from the challenge.' Everyone looks at Tayo.

Suddenly in the spotlight, he doesn't panic. 'My biscuits, not my moves.'

'Way too obvious,' says Thea.

'Agreed,' says Skye.

'Maybe it's a double bluff,' says Xander.

'Loving this talking about me like I'm not here,' Tayo says. 'This game changes on a dime.'

'I saw you last night,' I jump in. 'Sorry, but you were awake.'

Tayo raises his hands and smiles. 'Do what you gotta do, but I'm telling you, I'm not your man.'

He's way too chilled to be lying.

Xander launches an attack Rhodri's way. 'How do we know they weren't yours?'

'Don't shoot the messenger, dude.' Rhodri points to his six pack. 'You think I got this by trash eating?'

'Too obvious.' Thea jumps to his defence. 'Who was sleeping there?'

Shit.

'I was,' Noah says.

'It's Jaffa Cake.' Rhodri faux gasps.

'Was it you?' Skye asks Noah. 'Did you take the biscuits and throw the task so we couldn't open the storeroom?'

Noah shuffles uncomfortably, two small pink dots appear on his cheeks like a tell-tale guilty blush.

'Dude,' Rhodri says. 'Did you eat all the biscuits and card Amara because she was on to you? Or was it because she was so bloody annoying?'

'Oh my god, take this seriously,' shouts Skye. Rhodri looks as shocked as the rest of us. Skye takes a noisy breath. 'Sorry.' She half smiles at him. 'Too much pressure.'

Rhodri nods, his face suddenly serious. 'I nominate Noah,' he says, watching her.

'Seconded,' Skye says, not taking her eyes from Rhodri.

I did not see that coming. Noah doesn't react. Why am I more blindsided than him?

'Is Cali free now?' Thea asks.

Max shakes his head. 'Up to two accusations can be made at one time.'

Cohin appears. 'All contestants assemble at the table.'

We obediently move. The cameras spin and whirr above us.

Cohin continues, head bowed. 'Two have been accused and seconded. The trial is set. Accused, you have two hours to build your defence. Whoever is found guilty will be sent to the electric chair.'

I finally catch Noah's eye. 'I'm sorry,' he mouths, leaving me even more confused than before.

Cohin disappears.

'What just happened?' I whisper.

'The game got real.' A huge smile spills over Max's face. 'And it's awesome.'

18

We are back in the Courtroom, only this time it isn't a rehearsal. Someone's about to go home.

The cameras are recording, blinking red lights hovering in the air. Noah and Cali are stood in the docks either side of the Judge's chair. I wonder how it feels to be accused. The thought makes me shudder. The rest of us are on the benches.

We have all the power. We decide who leaves the game, their chance of money and fame gone. The pressure weighs heavily on my shoulders.

I don't want it to be Noah. It's crazy, I've known him for like twenty-four hours, but I have this irrational instinct to protect him. I made a promise to have his back, and he promised to have mine. I plan on seeing it though till the endgame.

Unless I've read him completely wrong and he's taking me for a pathetic loser who he's totally manipulating.

Arghh, I hate this game! Never have I been so sure of something yet doubted myself so much.

The lights are softer on the benches, we can relax a little. Not so for Cali and Noah, who are both bathed in their own bright halos of guilt.

Cohin appears, sat cleverly in the Judge's seat, raised higher than the two defendants. He's facing us, hood down. Callous hands with spindly fingers rest virtually on the desk. He's so real. If I wasn't so intimidated by all of this, I'd be impressed right now.

The accused are facing us. In the left dock, Cali's holding her head high, staring us down, daring us to vote to kill and send her home. Noah's stance is less aggressive. Head down, shoulders drooped, he's already given up.

'Members of the jury, two stand before you accused of the murder of Amara Pells. Will the first accuser step forward and make their case.'

Xander steps behind the central lectern. He faces the Judge, bathed in his own pool of light. He reads from the card prompt on the stand, chin raised, head tilted towards the cameras.

'I accuse Cali Zhu of the murder of my friend, Amara.' Brilliant, he's gonna milk this for airtime. He launches into his attack. 'She's so guilty. Last night, I heard noises in the bedroom and this morning she'd disappeared. When we asked her, she was really defensive and said she was,' his fingers make speech marks, 'taking a shower, but she didn't tell any of us and none of us heard the shower. When I went in the bathroom this morning, the shower hadn't been used. She wasn't even wet, and I know for a fact she didn't use the hairdryer 'cause we would have heard her.'

Well, that was a lie, her hair was wet.

Cohin turns to Cali. 'Defendant Cali Zhu do you have anything to say in your defence?'

Cali scowls. 'I got out of bed to use the bathroom and

I was in the shower,' she says, flushing a deep red. 'And I went to the Confessional.'

'Why would you go there in the middle of the night?' Xander says.

'Uh, that's private?' Cali tugs on her earring.

'You were meeting the other Agent.' Xander's puffed up like a little peacock. 'You decided to murder Amara.'

Cali is flustered. 'No. I…' She looks up at one of the cameras. 'You were with Amara all night. How could I have done it without you knowing?'

Xander goes quiet.

'Oops,' Max whispers to me. 'Plot hole.'

Xander pulls himself up straight and shouts. 'Why did you go to the Confessional?'

I can't look at Cali. We both know she's not willing to tell the world that she came on, and that's totally fair. Like a cornered animal, she lashes out desperately. 'I heard noises too. I saw someone moving around.' *Shit*. I told her I was in the kitchen last night, she's gonna totally throw me under the bus.

Xander sneers. 'Who?'

Cali holds his stare. I hold my breath.

'You.'

Xander's laugh fills the Courtroom. I breathe out.

Cali looks up at the jury. 'It's true. I saw him get out of bed and go to the Confessional.'

'You're only saying that to get back at me for accusing you,' says Xander.

Cali's head moves back and forth as she searches the benches for an ally. Her gaze lands on me. 'I swear.'

I squirm under her desperate watch.

Max nudges me. 'Don't stress about it. It's them or us.'

He's right. But I'm finding it hard to look Cali in the eyes.

'Defendant Cali Zhu, you may sit.' Cohin turns to Noah. 'Defendant Noah Winston, you too have been accused of the murder of Amara Pells.' Cohin looks forward. 'Who accuses this defendant?'

Rhodri's already shuffling along his row. 'That'll be me.' He stands straight, arms resting confidently on the lectern. 'This is a tale of crunchy, chocolatey biscuits … and poison.' He turns to us. 'It starts with a challenge about identity, which was thrown by a couple of gameplayers, or should I say, Agents.' He pauses for dramatic effect, holding the vial of poison high in the air. 'I have actual evidence that this defendant,' he points at Noah, 'is an Agent and therefore should pay the price of tyranny and murder.'

Shit, he's good.

Noah looks straight at Rhodri.

'I'm innocent.' He doesn't sound convincing. 'I've been set up.'

Rhodri waves the small bottle in the air, making sure the word 'Poison' can be seen clearly. 'The clues were all there. This was found down the side of the very chair you were sleeping on.' Reaching into his pocket he pulls out the empty biscuit packet. 'And these. We were all starving at breakfast.' He points to Noah. 'All except you. Why?' He throws his arms in the air. 'Because Noah ate all the biscuits.' He turns back to Noah. 'But you kept one back for your victim. You betrayed us. The public sent us a warning. They may not have liked Cali. They may not have found her entertaining, but they thought you were the most deceitful. Why would they think that unless they saw something we haven't? They knew you were an Agent.' He points dramatically to Noah. 'They saw you brutally murder Dougie Broads and callously hang him on that tree.'

It's totally ridiculous and far-fetched but Rhodri's so entertaining I'm starting to get why the public love him so much.

'Come on, Noah, stick up for yourself,' I whisper under my breath.

'Doesn't look good,' Max says.

'Defendant do you wish to speak?'

Noah says nothing. He stands in the dock, looking, to be fair, very guilty. Is he that freaked out by the cameras that he can't talk? His ocean blue eyes sparkle intensely. 'I'm innocent.'

There's nothing in his body language or his expression that says liar. In that split second, I know he's telling the truth. This game's all about people you trust. If I can get to the end with him and Thea, I know we can win. If I could just talk to him. Cali's smiling, she knows she's safe.

Cohin speaks to us. 'Jury. It's time to vote.'

I take the voting pad from underneath my seat and hold it in my sweaty palm. The first vote is for Cali, the second, Noah. The lights dim on the benches. I catch Skye's eye.

'You have to pick one,' she whispers. 'It's just a game. And it's a no-brainer. This is an easy vote, go for the obvious.'

Knowing we have one guilty vote and one save doesn't make it any easier. I press red for Cali and green for Noah. It's not enough. Skye has just confirmed what everyone is thinking.

Noah will be the first executed.

Cohin speaks. 'The votes have been counted and verified and I can now confirm that with a vote of six votes to one, one defendant has been found guilty.'

Noah's face is bowed, his expression hidden. I can't stand it. I don't want him to go out first.

'Wait,' I shout. All eyes turn to me. 'I am the Necromancer and I want to save Noah.'

Noah's head snaps up, his expression confused. A small cry comes from the other side of the dock as Cali's smile disappears in an instant. The cameras whirr as they move position, focusing on me, Cali and Noah.

Cohin doesn't move. For a second it looks like he's frozen. He turns to face the Jury. 'I can confirm that you are the Necromancer and you have the power to save.'

'What?' Noah raises his voice. 'No.' He's looking at

the cameras as if talking to someone other than us. 'That's not right.'

'Are you sure you want to play your advantage?' Cohin says. I swear the lights over me have got brighter.

'Yes,' I say.

'Can I confirm that you wish to play your advantage to save Noah?'

'Kass, don't do this,' Noah shouts.

'Yes.' I hold my ground. 'I want to save Noah.'

'Kass no,' Noah screams.

The lights snap from me to Noah and Cali, trapping them both in their yellow light. Cohin speaks. 'I can confirm that Noah has been saved and is therefore excluded from this vote. All votes for Noah do not count.'

More rumblings from the benches. I can't tell who looks more shocked, Noah or Cali. 'With one vote against, defendant Cali Zhu has been found guilty.'

'No way,' Max says. 'Talk about a twist.'

'Defendant Noah Winston you are free. Take your place on the benches.'

'No,' Noah cries. 'This isn't right. What the hell is going on?' He's talking directly at Cohin but he's making no sense. Why wouldn't he want me to save him?

Cohin repeats. 'Defendant Noah, take your position on the benches.'

Noah bangs his fist on the dock but does as he's told and climbs down. Passing me, he glares angrily.

I don't have time to react. Cohin places a black cap on his head and turns to Cali.

'Cali Zhu. You have been found guilty of murder. The sentence is death. Do you have any final words?'

'This is bullshit,' Cali spits. 'She's obviously an Agent playing to save her boyfriend. It's fixed.'

Skye squeezes my arm. 'They'll edit that bit out.'

Cohin speaks again, his voice neutral, totally devoid of emotion. 'Cali Zhu the Jury has spoken. You have been found guilty. The sentence is death. May the gods have mercy on your soul.'

Cali reaches for the hood. As she moves from the dock to the electric chair, she casts the evils. 'Don't trust anyone.'

Sitting in the chair, she throws the hood over her head.

'This is not supposed to happen,' Noah cries from the back bench. 'We need to stop it.'

Tayo is holding him back, keeping him firmly on the bench. 'You should be feeling good right about now.'

Noah's fighting to get free but Tayo's holding him tight. 'Dude, relax.'

The lights fade to a single spot over the electric chair. As we watch, silent and wide-eyed, the light turns from yellow to red. The chair vibrates. A buzzing grows louder in our ears, masking Noah's desperate cries. Cali shakes, harder and harder. She makes a choking noise, creepy and guttural, way better than my pathetic attempt. She's so good.

The buzzing builds to a crescendo. Puffs of smoke are filling the dock, smothering her as she writhes in the chair.

'Total respect, she is killing it,' Rhodri says. 'Excuse the pun.'

The red light bleeds stronger and stronger until one last gargled gasping scream from Cali and the room snaps to black.

'Awesome,' mumbles Max.

A weird smell saturates the air. It's making my stomach turn.

When the lights come up, Cali's gone. I'm impressed she didn't scream as she fell through the trapdoor.

Cohin speaks. 'Members of the Jury you have survived the first night. Do not become complacent or you will not last the next.'

'Nice,' Tayo says.

Thea is wafting her hand in front of her nose. 'Smoke machine's a bit much,' she pushes past me. 'Stinks.'

'I thought the effects were pretty special,' says Tayo. He slaps Noah on the back. 'Second chance, mate. Aren't you happy?'

Climbing off the bench, I head back through the yellow door to the main house. Noah's giving me a look so toxic, I don't need my superpower to translate. While every bone in my body is screaming that I did the right thing, the look he is giving me right now is shouting in my face that I have, hundred million per cent, majorly screwed up.

19

The mood is pretty up when we return to the house. The boys disappear into their bedroom for a debrief and the rest of us head into our room. I tried to talk to Noah, but he went straight to the Confessional and hasn't come out yet.

Skye smiles at me. 'Great moves from Girl Next Door. Did not see that coming.'

'Me neither. What Cali said: Trust no one,' Thea says. I wince. She's so mad at me right now. Loyalty and friendship are her two mantras and, in her eyes, I just messed it all up again by saving Noah when I could have kept the card for her. Thea glares at me. 'I guess no one is your friend in here.'

The barb stings with unfairness. Why should I explain myself? This was my decision, my gameplay. And I've made an ally from it which will benefit both of us ... or I thought I had.

'Very cool.' Skye perches on the end of the bed. 'Can you use it again?'

'I don't think so. It was a one-time deal.'

'Shame,' Skye says.

Xander appears and dives on Amara's bed, rolling around like a happy puppy.

'Really?' says Thea.

'What?' Xander rolls onto his elbows. 'Cali messed up. End of. It's gonna happen to most of us, better get used to it.'

'Sucks to be the first voted out though,' Skye says from the end bed.

'That's the game. It's not personal. We all knew what we were signing up for,' Xander says. 'I'm glad I got justice for Amara. Cali was totally guilty.'

'I thought you voted for Noah,' Thea says.

Xander shrugs. 'I'll get him next time, he's definitely an Agent. Did you see him? Boy had no argument. I reckon they were in it together.'

'Talk like that's gonna get you murdered in your sleep,' Thea warns.

'Not bothered,' Xander says.

'Why is he sleeping in here?' I say. 'This is the girls' room.'

'I don't need to conform to gender stereotypes,' Xander says. 'I belong in here. Besides I miss her. She was my soulmate.'

'You knew her for twenty-four hours,' Thea says.

'When you know, you know,' Xander says hugging Amara's pillow. 'Besides, a day in here is like a month on the outside.'

Thea coughs a *Bullshit.*

'Shame you didn't know she was being carded when you were sleeping right next to her,' I say.

Xander pulls a face, then turns away, chewing his lip. Talk about playing up to the cameras. Xander is definitely on my radar.

'Wonder when they're gonna tell us if she was an

Agent or a Player?' Thea makes a point of talking to Skye, not me.

'Probably letting us stew for a while,' Skye says. 'You know, to add to the tension.'

'They don't need to make it any more tense.' I try to make a joke. 'I'm balancing on a knife edge.'

'Mind you don't cut yourself,' Thea says.

Everyone awkward giggles.

Skye gestures to the beds. 'Shall we all move up one now Max has moved next door?'

'I'm not moving.' Thea plonks herself onto the bed next to us. She glares at me. Brilliant, after everything, my one move to save Noah has sent her right back to resting bitch face.

'Fine.' I grab my still unpacked suitcase and move over to Max's bed. I'm in the middle now, moving around is gonna be harder.

Thea heads to the bathroom and I follow. I really should sort my suitcase but right now I need to do some serious damage control. I can unpack and change after I've put things right.

'Well?' she says.

I close the bathroom door behind me. The camera in the corner turns in our direction, and my mic hangs heavy around my neck.

'Hi?' I whisper, turning on the taps, hoping the sound of the fast water hitting the shiny ceramic sink will dull our conversation. 'Can we talk?'

'Oh, *now* you want to talk?' She's forgetting to whisper. I turn the tap more.

'That's not fair,' I say.

'Why did you do that?' she says.

I have no idea. 'It felt like the right thing to do?'

'Using your advantage on some random boy?'

'He's not a random boy; he's my friend.'

Thea humphs impatiently. 'You're supposed to have my back, and instead you go save a boy you've known for two seconds. Why didn't you save it for me?'

'I *do* have your back.' The taps won't go any more, so I angle my mic closer to them.

'We had a plan to look out for each other, or had you forgotten? We could have used that card together, for ourselves,' she says. 'You totally blindsided me.'

'That's not what happened,' I say.

She throws her hand towards the camera. 'It's recorded. Watch it back. You lied. What are *they* gonna think?'

By *they*, I assume she means the public, who, if I'm honest, I didn't think about at all, but Thea is all over public image.

'Maybe they'll see it as a nice gesture?' I say.

'Just when I think I can trust you, you go and mess it all up again.'

'I haven't,' I say. 'I had no idea that saving Noah would be such a big deal.'

'Oh my god, Kass. Listen to yourself.' She flings her hands in the air in despair and storms into the toilet cubicle, locking it noisily, leaving me standing like an utter plonker, crouched over the running sink.

When Thea's mad it's always best to leave her to cool off. Easier said than done in a locked set with nowhere to hide.

Turning off the tap, I hover outside the toilet door.

'Go away,' she says.

There's no point trying to talk, so I head back into the bedroom. Xander gives me a weird look and Skye fires a sympathetic smile my way. Could they hear? Urghh, now I'm paranoid.

I leave the room. I'm desperate to get out of my cute sushi T-shirt, but my need to create distance from my angry best friend overrules.

'I wish they'd take Dougie down.' Skye's by my shoulder. 'I mean, I know he's not real, but it still gives me the creeps.'

I don't say anything, my head's too full of Thea. Have I really messed everything up again?

'You okay? Thea really didn't like you saving Noah,' she asks.

I'm about to launch into a massive moan about classic Thea, before I remember that nobody knows we are friends. 'I know, right?'

'Why did you?' Skye says.

Even when screwed up in concentration, her face is pretty.

'Why did I what?' I try to stall.

'Save him. He obviously didn't want to be.'

My eyes sweep the living area. Tayo's sat on the sofa, Max is in the kitchen. Noah's nowhere to be seen.

'Felt like the right thing to do,' I say.

'Did you think Cali was an Agent?'

'No.'

'But you voted for her. She only had one vote and I'm guessing you didn't vote for Noah.'

Guilt makes my face flush.

'Interesting. I thought you two were friends. I guess none of us are really friends in here, are we?'

She walks ahead of me to the kitchen. *Way to go, Kass.* I'm really screwing this up. I catch Tayo's eye and smile. He smiles back, totally cool with being caught staring.

I hover in the doorway of the boys' bedroom. Rhodri appears from the bathroom, nothing but a towel wrapped around his waist.

'S'up?' he says. The bedroom's the same as ours, minus the window to the garden. Five beds line the long wall with a mirror running behind them.

Rhodri's taken the bed at the far end. I recognise the *Star Wars* T thrown onto the bed next to him – Max's. There's no evidence to suggest which of the last three beds is Noah's or Tayo's, both look like they haven't even been sat on yet. A holdall sits open on one, while the bed nearest the bathroom has a rucksack leaning against it.

'Have you seen Noah?' I try to keep my eyes off Rhodri's sleeve and the tattoo covering half of his back and pretend to be cool with the fact he's half naked.

'Need to talk tactics?' He grins. 'Ballsy move you made in there. Hope it doesn't come back to bite you on the arse.'

Is that a threat?

I wander round the living area. Noah must still be in the Confessional. I flump onto the sofa opposite Tayo.

'You find him?' Tayo says. My face must be talking without the need of my mouth. 'He was pretty shook up, probably needs a minute.'

The Kill Clock's poised to start any moment. I push myself off the sofa to go and unpack my suitcase when Max appears from the direction of the Confessional, carrying a stack of boxes. 'Pizza!'

Noah appears from the Courtroom door. What's he doing in there? Suitcase forgotten, I head straight towards him, but Tayo gets to him first. They're talking, heads close, I feel weird interrupting, so I sit back at the table and wait.

'How are you, after your miraculous save?' Thea coos to Noah as he and Tayo help themselves to pizza. 'I had no idea that you two were so close.'

Noah grimaces. 'We're not.' He won't look at me – what *is* his problem?

Xander grabs the veggie pizza and takes it to his side of the table. 'A move like that could get everyone talking.'

178

'Everyone is talking.' Noah takes a bite of pizza.

'I prefer to stay under the radar,' says Rhodri.

'Not like I had a choice.' Noah's tone stings.

'Oh, don't be a ball-ache.' Rhodri reaches for the pepperoni pizza. 'Girl Next Door obviously saw something in you.'

'Guess Girl Next Door thinks I need saving.'

'I'm right here, guys.' I take a bite of pizza. It tastes like cardboard. 'Next time I try to do something nice, remind me not to.'

'Trust no one.' Xander nudges Max. 'It's written on the walls.'

Everyone laughs. I pretend to go along with it. 'You got that right.'

'Pass the veggie,' says Max.

The room turns red and the sirens batter our ears. The Kill Clock starts to countdown.

'Night Two,' says Max.

'Good luck everyone,' says Thea.

'Okay, you sneaky Agent bastards.' Tayo waves his pizza at us. 'Come and get us.'

20

I can't sleep. I'm terrified an Agent's gonna appear and card me. I stare up at the ceiling thinking of Swift-isms to banter when I see Lewis. Is he watching? *You're Not Sorry* pretty much sums up my actions in the last twenty-four hours.

And I'm not sorry I saved Noah, whatever his problem is. My gut is telling me he's not a double-bluffing Agent but my head's over-thinking everything. I am sorry I've upset Thea. Just as I think I'm making things right I mess it up all over again.

I chuckle as *I Did Something Bad* fills my head. *You're On Your Own Kid*, that's what Lewis would say before accusing me of mad stalking a total stranger.

I roll over, punching the pillow. Nice one, now I'm thinking in Swift-isms. This place is getting to me.

There's shuffling. Skye's snoring gently in her own bed and Thea's sparko. How is that even possible? I envy their ability to sleep through the pressure. I check the other bed. Xander's up, heading towards the bathroom. I shut my eyes as he passes, convinced he'll hear my thumping heart. I count to five before opening them, waiting to see if he is followed.

Nothing.

After barely any time he creeps back, climbing into bed. I wait until I'm certain he's asleep before sitting up.

There's movement in the living area.

Someone moves right past the glass. I duck under the duvet. No one's sleeping in there tonight, the boys are next door. There's no reason for anyone to be wandering around, unless they're Agents or the Detective. Either way, if I can get a good glimpse of them, it will up my game a million per cent and any good news I can give Thea may counteract my Noah mess-up. Peeling off the covers, I tiptoe out of the bedroom.

My eyes sweep the corners of the living room, searching for movement but there's nothing. Reaching the kitchen, my head's spinning with questions.

Did I imagine it? People don't just disappear.

Or do they?

Last night, somebody disappeared from this exact same spot. I creep into the corner where the mystery shadow vanished. It's empty; my eyes search the floor, the walls and past the storeroom door.

The storeroom.

Duh. How did I miss that?

Shelves cover the walls from top to floor, filled with enough supplies to feed an army. I reach for the light switch, then stop myself. I hold my breath, my ears straining for any noise, half expecting Max to be snack-binging. It's empty.

The banging in my chest has been replaced by mad butterflies.

I move to the back of the room. The camera-runs are

behind the wall, there could easily be a secret door. My hands splay across the wall searching until my fingers hit the edges of something. I'm right, there is a door and it's open, just a little.

If I go through, I'm pretty sure I'll be breaking the rules. I check the ceiling for little red lights, nothing. The door swings open in my grip. I'm buzzing. If I can find our mystery nightwalker and identify them as an Agent, I've a pretty good chance of getting to the end with Thea. I push myself through the door and into the camera-run.

It's cold and midnight black. Edging forward, my foot hits the camera track. Left, or right? No clue what to do now I'm here and wishing I had a torch, I turn left, walking slowly, feeling the metal track cold beneath my toes as my eyes adjust to the dark. The inside wall turns to glass. I can see into the boys' bedroom.

I count the sleeping bodies. There's an empty bed.

Noah's missing.

A loud crash is followed by a muffled cry making me jump. The noise was in the camera-run.

'Noah?' I whisper.

Nothing.

I walk back towards the noise. What is Noah doing?

The tunnel gets darker. Passing the storeroom door, I resist the urge to dive back inside and hide under my duvet.

More shuffling. Nearer this time.

The yellow hazard tape runs along the camera-run

floor. A small section forks off and runs under the wall. That's where the sound came from, for sure. Crouching, I recognise the Courtroom crawl space.

The exit light that lit the space is broken. The darkness under the set is like a wall, thick and impenetrable, even the hazard tape's bright yellow is impossible to see.

I feel my way forward on my hands and knees cursing my Scooby-Doo nosiness, while rehearsing all the things I'm gonna say to Noah when I find him. The residual smell of the smoke machine lingers in this claustrophobic space, mingling with something else, a strong smell I can't place. The cloying scent sticks in my nose. It's gross.

My fingers hit something hard and smooth. I tug, it's heavy. It doesn't move. It's another freaking dummy, it must have fallen and is blocking the way. At least they've dressed it, black tights cover the legs sticking out in front of me. My hands are clutching cold leather. My fingers move down across hard metal buckles and find thick rubber treads. I'm clutching a boot. A platform combat boot.

Cali had the exact same pair. Why would they dress the dummy up like Cali?

A movement beside me makes me scream.

A hand clamps itself firmly over my mouth.

'Shhhh,' a voice whispers in my ear. I buck my body backwards to escape, more instinct than gameplan. It doesn't work. An arm coils round my waist, the hand stays firmly over my mouth. 'Kass, please.'

It's Noah.

'I'm gonna take my hand away and I need you to not freak out,' he whispers. 'I'm not an Agent and I'm not going to card you.'

Holy crap! I need to calm down.

'I need you to take off your battery pack and give it to me before you say anything,' he whispers. Unclasping the battery pack, I hand it to him, as my eyes adjust to the dark. He grabs the microphone cable around my neck and unplugs the end from the pack.

'Okay.' He slowly removes his hand from my mouth.

'You scared the shit out of me,' I whisper in one long breath. 'We're not supposed to take those off.'

'I don't want to be heard,' he says. 'Or caught.'

'It's Cali, right?' I correct myself. 'I mean not Cali, Cali. The dummy's been dressed as her, which is really dark, not gonna lie.'

'Kass… This isn't the dummy. This *is* Cali.'

'Yeah, right.'

Noah surprises me by grabbing my arms.

'What?' I say. 'I know it's a dummy, I saw one in the dry run. Stop trying to wind me up.'

'Kass, please listen. The dummy is on the tree. There are no other dummies.' He stops for me to register his words. He's right. Dougie is still hanging on the tree with the same bleached hair as the dummy I found down here.

'But, if the dummy's in the garden, then who?' I squint in the gloom and look at the body. They do look exactly like Cali's combats.

'This is Cali. And she's dead. For real.' He sounds scared.

'Okay?' I play along. I can feel his eyes boring into me, his super-pale face popping against the darkness. I force myself to look at the body, like *really* look. It's crumpled like a ragdoll, like it's fallen through the trapdoor, arms and legs splayed out in weird positions. It's one big silhouette, facing up towards the ceiling. I can't see the face; it's covered by the *Lie or Die* hood.

Could this really be Cali?

My hand hovers over the body, should I check for a pulse? I stop myself, annoyed that I almost fell for it. This is a wind up, it's a dummy, it has to be. The weird smell down here is making me gag. Pushing past him, I crawl back through the hole in the wall. 'Not funny. Is this payback for saving you? 'Cause that's just twisted.' I make my way back up the camera-run to the storeroom, feeling my way in the dark, anger driving me forward.

'Kass, please.' He follows behind me. 'I'm serious. This isn't part of the game.'

'Nice one.' I refuse to stop, shuffling forward towards the storeroom. 'Okay, I'll play. Say she's had some terrible accident and is lying dead under the set. How would you possibly know that? And why would they just leave her here?' He doesn't answer. 'Thought so, stop jerking me around.'

'What are you doing here? You shouldn't even be here.'

185

His change of subject puts me on the back foot.

'I … I was following a hunch,' I stop.

'You were following me more like. Damn it, Kass, what is wrong with you?'

His accusation stings. 'For all you know I could be an Agent,' I say, turning around.

'Really?' he says. 'Do you know how stupid it is to say you're an Agent when you're not?'

I cave. Damn, why am I so crap at lying?

'I wasn't exactly following you. I was worried.'

'Stop trying to save me,' Noah cries.

'I'm not…'

He's right up in my face, his breath hot on my cheeks.

'You don't know me,' he hisses. 'You don't owe me anything. What gave you the right to interfere in my life and ruin everything?'

'Excuse me?' Anger explodes like fireworks. How dare he?

'I really pissed off my best friend saving you,' I snap. 'You have no idea.'

'I didn't ask you to.'

'If I hadn't saved you, that dummy would have been dressed as you.' I spit back.

'Maybe that's what I wanted!' he shouts.

We stop, allowing the darkness to put a little necessary space between us.

'Bullshit, nobody loses a game on purpose.' I turn towards the storeroom. 'I'm going back to bed.'

'Kass. Stop. You asked me how I knew?' His desperation makes me stop and the hair on my neck tingle. 'You were right when you said it would have been me.' His voice wobbles. 'That's what I wanted. It should never have been Cali. It was a mistake. Noah Winston was supposed to die tonight. In the electric chair. For real.'

21

I don't understand what he's saying, so I just repeat his words back to him. 'You were supposed to die?' I don't get it. 'What do you mean for real? Like as in proper die?' The words coming out my mouth sound so ridiculous, I giggle, waiting for him to join in.

He doesn't.

I wait for more 'cause I'm sure as hell not happy with that explanation.

Noah fidgets from foot to foot.

'Really?' I say.

After a moment of awkward silence, he grabs my hand and pulls me through the run. 'Where are we going?'

'I need to take you back into the house.' Noah's voice is strong.

'Stop.' I push my heels into the ground, forcing him to stop. 'What did you mean, Noah was supposed to die? Tell me what's going on.'

He throws his arms up in the air. 'It's not real. The game, the house, any of it. It's all fake.'

'Fake? So that's not Cali? This is a wind up?'

'No, she's the only thing that is real.' He's acting weird, half laughing into the darkness and it's scaring me.

'My name isn't Noah, it's Tom. Tom Stockett. I set this all up.'

'What?' Warning bells are chiming so loud in my

head right now I can hardly hear over their incessant pealing.

'None of it's real,' he says. 'It's as fake as the reality it's pretending to be. Even the studio isn't a studio anymore, it closed down months ago.'

'But the game? The cast? How did you…?'

'I'm a TV director. Pippa's worked in TV production for years. *Lie or Die* was a concept I had been working on for a while. It was easy. One little advert and over a thousand applications. We held auditions and crewed the show as usual.'

'Wait, so you're older?'

'Of everything I'm saying, you question that?' Noah says. 'I'm twenty-four. Isla always joked that my baby face would come in handy some day.'

'Isla the director?' I'm trying to keep up.

'Director Isla is an actress, I named her after my twin sister. Isla Stockett.'

I know that name. Isla Stockett was a reality TV star.

'Why would you fake all this?' I say.

'To kill Reality,' Noah says.

'I don't understand.' I wish I could see him properly, this whole weird confession in the dark's freaking me out. I can't tell if he's messing with me. 'You want to kill reality TV? Why?'

'Because it killed my sister.'

Oh. I may not be able to see his face but the agony in his voice is painfully clear.

'People get eaten up by the cult of celebrity.' He carries on talking into the dark. 'Winning a reality show made my sister an overnight star. She made it all the way to the top and it was perfect. Until it wasn't. My sister took her own life. Isla is dead.'

He stops, lost in his grief. I wait. I remember her; her death was all over the media.

'Nobody could have predicted how crazy famous she would be. It was too quick, she wasn't prepared. There was so much attention, the positive and the hype and the fame. Then the good turned to bad. The trolling led to pile ons, and the hate…' His voice cracks. 'So much hate, day after day after day. She was too fragile. They tried to protect her, but it was too much.'

My heart burns as his pain becomes mine. 'I'm so sorry.'

'She was all I had. When our parents died, we only had each other.' His voice bubbles anger. 'I'm doing this for all the others like her. I'm doing this to stop the monster.'

'Reality TV?'

Noah shakes his head. 'No, reality TV is the machine. We love to hate it. We moan about how crap it is, then we sit back and download the next crazy series, pretending not to like it while binge watching it in a weekend. The machine makes the monsters.' He thumps his chest; the sound resonates through the tunnel. '*We* are the monsters.'

'We're the monsters?'

'We follow, we make judgements, we love to criticise.

190

We think we own them. We raise them up and decide when they fall. We get so consumed by the celebrity lie, that we forget the real people underneath the glitz and the glamour. I can't stop the monsters; but I can destroy the machine. We need to wake up. Someone had to die. The media frenzy would be crazy. A public outcry. Broadcasters would be forced to shut down. Reality television would be dead. No more reality stars to bait.'

'What do you mean someone had to die?' *What is he saying?* 'You're scaring me,' I whisper. 'You wanted to die?'

'No,' Noah says quickly. 'It was all a set-up. An illusion. Noah Winston would have a terrible accident, an electrical fault on the chair would cause a huge shock. When Noah was found under the set, he would be dead. He had a heart defect, it's all documented. The shock would have been fatal for his weakened heart. My body would be swapped with the dummy and taken out in a body bag for all the world to witness. Meanwhile Tom Stockett would be on a plane to Canada to start a new life.'

'But why fake your own death?'

'Sometimes you have to do something extreme in order to facilitate change. Reality killed her. They didn't mean to, they tried to help, but as long as the public watch and the sponsors pay, there will always be someone vulnerable, desperate for a chance. We all think we're strong enough – until we aren't.' He stops and after a sharp intake of breath pushes his shoulders back, grief replaced with unwavering resolve.

'We used all her money, everything she gained from fame and sunk it into this. Pippa and I planned it down to the last inch.'

'Why would Pippa ever agree to this?'

'She was in love with her.' Noah takes a beat for me to catch up. 'So, you see? It should have been me in that chair. I should have been electrocuted tonight.'

I can't keep the horror out of my voice. 'Electrocuted?'

'It was just meant to be an elaborate stunt, good enough to fool viewers for long enough to cause an outcry.'

Images of Cali in the electric chair flood my mind. 'But Cali?'

'Something must have gone wrong. What happened wasn't fake, she…'

The realisation hits me harder than an artic lorry. 'That was real? Cali's dead? Like really dead, not TV dead?' I can't breathe. 'We watched. We all stood there and watched.' Bile hits the back of my throat as my brain presses replay. 'The smell. Oh my god, it smelt of burning meat … or flesh.' My brain is in hyperdrive. 'Did I do this?' All the air's knocked from my lungs. 'By playing that card to save you, did I kill Cali?'

Noah pulls me to him. 'Listen to me, this was not your fault. Somehow the chair malfunctioned. It was a prop, it wasn't supposed to really work, it was all effects, a bit of buzzing and vibration, the shock wasn't enough to kill a mouse.'

'Then … how?' I can hardly say the words.

Noah shrugs helplessly. 'I have no idea. I'm still trying to process. I was trying to find a way out, but the smell got my attention.' He shakes his head. 'I found her lying here like this. The chair must have short-circuited somehow. I don't get it; I went back into the Courtroom last night to try to speak to Pippa and the chair looked normal.'

'You think someone covered it up?'

'I need to find Pippa, she'll have the answers, but I can't get out and she's not talking to me in the Confessional. All I know is that this is not my game anymore. The poison. That was a prop, just a bit of fun. It wasn't *real*. Amara wasn't supposed to be killed, nobody was, that's what Dougie was for. And Dougie isn't the right dummy, that's my dummy. We had a different one for him, a normal one, not a super-expensive bespoke film mannikin.'

'What, wait. You think Amara's dead too?' Amara's ashen face and blue lips demand centre stage in my mind. 'No,' I shake my head. 'We all saw her, we all said she was acting… I wanted to check…' I'm choking on my words. '…no one believed me.'

'I'm not certain, but I'm starting to think so. Max called it – two kills in one night,' he says. 'That wasn't my plan. Everything was set up to get me accused of Dougie's murder and into that chair.'

'Why didn't you do something?' I say. My mind is scrolling between Cali and Amara like a digital photo book. I can't make sense of any of it; it doesn't seem real.

'I did,' Noah says. 'As soon as I saw Amara, I went to

talk to Pippa, to find out why she was changing things. I didn't imagine for a minute she was dead. And Cali? When you switched us, I had no reason to think she was dead either, the chair wasn't electrified. I thought she was out, like Amara, I just didn't understand why. I tried to talk to Pippa and when I couldn't, I tried to get out. That's when I found her. If Cali is really dead, what if Amara is too?'

'It doesn't make any sense,' I say.

'Neither does that Necromancer card. I never put that card in play. Someone knew you would use it to save me.'

My brain is whirling so fast it's hard to catch a coherent thought. 'Wait,' I say trying to slow my mind. 'Pippa's the Executive Producer, so she would be watching, right? If someone put a card in play, wouldn't she see?'

'Not necessarily,' Noah says. 'The Confessional sound booth is isolated; it has to be to stop any sound pollution. It was Isla in there, I'm pretty sure of it. She wouldn't question a change; she was just playing her part as the director. Pippa would only see you receiving the card if she was in the gallery, watching the cameras or the live feed. She could easily have missed it. And you kept it quiet until the Courtroom. If she wasn't watching your status reveal she wouldn't know until it was too late.'

'There's another option,' I say. 'She could have been watching and she didn't stop it because she was the one who put it there.'

'No way, Pippa would never. She would never betray

me and my sister.' Noah shakes his head. 'No. Someone is messing with us.'

'Someone other than you and your fake show and your fake death?' Is he messing with me with his big eyes and heart-wrenching sister story? Why would someone want Cali and Amara dead? No way. I shake my head so hard it hurts. 'This must have been an accident. An awful, awful accident.' Even as I say it, I don't believe it.

'Then why are we still playing? The game's done. We only planned it up to the first execution. There *is* no more game to play. You were all meant to be out by now.'

Despite everything, my mind is desperately trying to find another solution, anything better than the one Noah is presenting. 'How can I be sure this isn't a wind-up and you're not an Agent on some kind of secret mission?'

'I get that,' Noah says. For all the crazy, he's way too calm. 'But think for one second. If I'm on some kind of crazy Agent mission we would be on camera, right?'

I nod.

Noah speaks gently. 'Look around. We are not in the game anymore. This is not part of the show.'

My eyes search the black desperately looking for the small red lights that tell me he's lying. But the camera-run's dark. There are no cameras here. Noah's not lying.

And if he is not lying then the body under the set *is* Cali.

'Kass?'

I can't breathe. I jerk away from Noah, stumbling up

the run, my arms flailing wildly in front of me. I need to get out, find Lewis, call the police. Fear and panic have overridden all my senses and I need to leave – now. If Amara and Cali are dead, could I be next? Or Thea?

'Kass, wait.' Noah's following but I don't stop. My flight reaction has kicked in big time, and I desperately search for an exit. My hands hit the door and I come to a halt. It won't open. I throw my body hard against the unsympathetic surface. I bang, pummelling the metal with my fists until they hurt.

Noah's behind me, his breath on my neck. His hands cover mine. 'It's locked.'

I knew that. It's the same door that Henry opened to let me out in the dry run. I kick it and it clunks in reply. 'Whose stupid idea was it to have it only open from the outside.'

I try to catch my breath. I need to think.

'There has to be another way,' I say.

'There's only one way into the studio from these runs, all other doors lead back into the set.' He gestures into the black. 'Back that way leads past the bedroom to the house garden. We could try to get out from there, but the walls are way too high.'

'What about the main house doors?' My voice is strangled by desperation. 'We can go back in and force them open.'

'The main house doors are on the studio security system,' he says quietly. 'They open electronically, and we don't have lanyards. And they're fire doors, too heavy to break down.' He faces me. 'There's no other way out of the set. We're trapped.'

This can't be happening.

'If Cali is dead.' I'm shivering. 'And there's no more game, then what the hell are we all playing?'

My brain is trying to catch up with his words and put them into order, but I can't stop them tearing around my head.

Noah was faking his death.

I played a fake Necromancer card.

Cali died for real.

Amara wasn't supposed to be murdered. And she might be dead too.

My legs give way.

Noah waits while I crouch, hands on the floor and try to calm myself. The camera tracks are cool beneath my palms, and I concentrate on taking deep breaths.

'I need to find Pippa.' Noah's voice is steady and calm.

'What if someone is trying to hurt us?' I am full on freaking out. 'What if I'm next? Or you, or Thea? We need to tell them. We should…'

'No,' Noah says. 'We need to look at the facts. We don't know for sure that Amara's dead, we haven't found a body, only Cali, and that could have been some kind of awful accident.'

'You don't believe that,' I say.

'But we don't know who or how or why. No point freaking everyone out until we get the facts.'

'That doesn't make sense. If someone is hurting us, surely we should warn the others?'

'Kass, please,' he holds onto my hands tightly, his eyes pleading. 'If it gets out about my fake show, I'm in a whole heap of trouble. If Cali's death was an accident I could be charged with manslaughter. If Amara really is dead, it could be even worse. You understand?'

I nod, standing slowly. 'Thea is in there. I'm not going to…'

'Listen to me. I need to make this right. I will find a way out and I will get answers. Keep your head down, get Thea and stay safe. I'll get help.'

A noise hits my ears. A groan, click and a clank.

Noah holds up his hand for quiet. 'Someone's in here,' he whispers.

I'm shaking with cold and terror. The claustrophobic darkness of the run is closing in and it's hard to breathe.

Noah is talking fast, glancing over his shoulder like he's scared someone's going to jump out. 'We can't stay in here.' He slips the microphone back over my head. 'If anything happens to me, tell the others and you find a way out, by any means. Get to the main gallery. Under the desk is my bag, it has my phone. Call the police. Find my laptop, it has everything you need on it.'

I grip his arms.

'You can do this,' he says gently. 'When I met you in the cafe you said you were afraid of being ordinary. Kass Bourbon Kennedy you are anything but ordinary. I need to know you believe me. I need to know you have my back.'

I don't know what to do, every bone in my body is telling me that he's speaking the truth, but my brain refuses to acknowledge it.

'Look, give me an hour.' Noah sounds desperate. 'Let me go back to the Confessional and try to speak to Pippa again. Shit, come with me if you want. Just let me try to find out what's going on, and if I can't, you can shout it into every camera in the house.' He pauses while my brain helter skelters. 'Please, Kass.'

'One hour?' My voice sounds pathetically tiny.

'One hour. I'm so sorry I got you mixed up in all this. I should never have put you in the game. You were so like Isla when I met you, it blew me away. I thought it would be ironic.'

His face is a blur in the dark, but his voice sounds full of determination. My mouth is way too dry to speak. He clips my battery pack back around my waist and as he leans in he whispers in my ear. Taking my hand, we walk towards the storeroom door.

The door closes behind us with a determined click. All my senses are ramped up to high alert. The house is quiet. We creep through the storeroom, tiptoeing into the living room.

'Where the hell have you been?' Tayo and Skye are in the kitchen area.

We both freeze, rabbits in the head lights.

Noah puts his hands up in surrender.

Skye's face morphs from shocked to concerned. 'You okay?' she says scrutinising my face. 'You look like you've seen a ghost.'

'I... I...' I try to get it together, but I can't hide the horror that must be painted all over my face. I drop my eyes to the floor and hope they let it go, I'm not sure I can lie about what I've just seen.

'We're not Agents,' Noah whispers, giving me a beat to pull myself together.

Tayo and Skye look at each other and then back to us. Tayo's long arm fills the space between us. 'Stay back,' he says.

'How do we know *you're* not the Agents?' I adopt a defensive approach.

''Cause we're not,' Skye says, waving a bottle of water in the air. 'I got up for a drink and found Tayo.' She looks at Noah. 'He was looking for you.'

Noah smiles. 'Pass the water,' he says. Tayo throws him a bottle from the counter.

'Here.' Skye hands me hers. I drink greedily, the dry cold of the run has made my throat parched. Noah sips his.

We watch each other warily, no one wanting to make the first move. There's a weird taste in my mouth. I take another swig of water, finishing the bottle in one gulp.

'I was just going in there.' Noah points to the Confessional, moving backwards and leaving me with the others. I follow him then stop.

'Hey?' Tayo's by my shoulder.

Exhaustion hits me like a steam train. The room spins and I reach out for support. The yellow Confessional door closes behind Noah. I should go with him, I want to, but the need to sleep has overridden everything and I stagger towards the bedroom. Skye leads the way. Tayo's hand is on my elbow, guiding me. It's like walking through cement.

'Steady,' he's chuckling gently. 'You're drunk with exhaustion.'

He's right, the stress, the drama and lack of sleep has hit me all at once. I need to lie down. Reaching my bed, I fall forward. Someone's speaking, I can't tell who.

The room is spinning. I just want to sleep.

As my head sinks into dreamland, Noah's whispered words sing in my ears. 'Trust no one.'

22

The wailing siren yanks me out of dream-black safety and back into the nightmare of reality. My head is pounding, my eyes are scratchy from exhaustion and my tongue feels like sandpaper.

It's like one helluva hangover.

'Hey.' Skye's sitting up, watching me. Jumping out of bed she perches on the end of mine, her face screwed up in concern as her eyes flit over my face. 'You were out of it. Snoring like a boss.'

I nod, the motion hurts my head. 'Sorry.'

'Don't apologise. It must have been the excitement.' She squeezes my arm. 'Make sure you drink today, and eat, it's easy to get dehydrated in here.'

I hold my head. I don't feel like I've slept at all, more like I've been run over by a bus. Glancing out the window I can see dummy Dougie hanging from the tree.

I head to the bathroom, splashing cold water on my face, trying to flush out the memories of last night. It doesn't work. She's in my head: my brain colouring in the blackness and the vague silhouette, until I have a perfectly formed dead Cali stored in my imagination for eternity.

I head straight to the boys' bedroom, eager to see Noah.

He's not there.

The boys are heading to the table.

'Man, let us sleep,' Rhodri shouts, but the siren continues its relentless scream. 'My head is thumping already.'

'Too much sleep makes contestants alert and rational,' says Tayo. 'And it's the lights.'

'What is?' says Rhodri rubbing his head.

'Making our heads hurt.' Tayo gestures towards the glaring ceiling. 'Constant artificial lighting. We need some fresh air.'

'Which we would have if we had the key to the garden,' Rhodri shouts into a camera.

'It's torture,' Xander says, his hands over his ears. 'That's what it is. Tor-ture.'

Only Noah's missing. Maybe he's in the bathroom?

The bathroom's empty.

'Kass, hurry up,' someone shouts from the table.

Where is Noah?

I sit at the table. The siren stops wailing immediately. There's a Noah-sized space opposite me.

'Why'd it stop? Where's Noah?' Xander says. Tayo's staring at me, the question hanging from his lips. I shrug a *don't know*.

'You all look like crap,' Max says. Tiredness and strain cobweb our faces, as we regard each other with mistrusting, bloodshot eyes.

Noah's secret is bubbling up my throat. I can't keep it in any longer. 'Guys, I have something to tell you…'

Cohin cuts me off in one holographic heartbeat.

'Morning, contestants, and welcome to Day Two. I trust you slept well?'

A murmur of *yeah rights* ripples around the table.

Cohin continues. 'Last night, while the house slept, the Agents claimed another victim.'

Thea mouths, *'NOAH'*.

Cohin's face morphs into Noah and my pulse races. 'I can reveal that the second victim of the Agents is Noah Winston.'

The Accusation Clock starts its countdown with an audible click. It goes unnoticed.

'Jaffa Cake? No way,' Rhodri says. 'Damn you, Agents, I liked the dude.'

'Bit moody,' Xander says.

'Yeah, from having to look at your annoying face all day,' Rhodri says.

Cohin disappears.

'Wow.' Tayo's giving me a long look.

It's him, it has to be. Tayo was the last person Noah saw before he went into the Confessional. Tayo and Skye. But Skye was with me, I remember.

My head's all fusty; I can't think properly. Noah said the game was finished, so how are we still playing?

'Kass?' I vaguely hear my name over the hammering of my heart. Is Noah dead too?

'Kass?' Louder this time. It's Thea. 'You okay? You look weird.'

Pushing my chair back, I bolt from the table, clamping my hand across my mouth until I reach the toilet.

And I throw up.

I keep throwing up until there's nothing left and the retching eases. Sitting back against the cubicle door, I lean my head on my arm.

'Kass?'

Pushing back the door, I let Thea in.

'Shit.' Her voice is harsh, but the hand squeezing my shoulder counteracts the tone. She grabs a handful of toilet paper and wipes my mouth. Sitting next to me, her arm coils around my shoulder.

'I'm sorry about Noah,' she says. 'He was your friend and you wanted to save him. I reacted like a proper bitch.'

'You didn't,' I say, only half genuine.

'Yes, I did. This place is getting to me.'

We sit in silence for a heartbeat. The whirr of the camera cuts through the quiet. I don't even bother to cover my mic.

'You remember when you broke your arm roller skating?' Thea says. 'I didn't believe you, even when it went blue and disgusting.' She chuckles. 'I guess I don't handle stress as well as I could.'

I remember that day. She got so angry with me for having to leave early. But she also sat with me in A&E for hours, and helped me every second for the next six weeks. There is such an enormous heart underneath all that armour. If I'd stuck to our plan and never played that card, Cali might still be alive.

'It's weird,' she says. 'I have no problem posting on my socials, but here? Knowing thousands are watching everything you do, and you have no control?' She shudders. 'Completely different. Everyone wants to be liked right?' She nudges me. 'It's just a game.'

Panic surges through me and I lose control of my mouth. 'Cali's dead. And Amara,' I say. 'And I think Noah is too.'

'Uh huh…' she says slowly.

'Noah told me something.' My voice is trembling.

Thea turns into gossip mode. 'Ooh, was he the Detective? I wondered, with all that brooding and long looks. Who did he name? Max, I bet it's Max?'

'No, he said that…'

Thea's way too excited to listen. 'Damn, that doesn't mean he's not an Agent only that Noah didn't name him. Could be Skye, I'm getting definite Agent vibes from her.'

She's looking at me expectantly.

'Cali's dead,' I say. 'It's over.'

'Girl, you need a thicker skin,' she says.

'No.' How can I make her understand when I'm struggling myself? 'Noah is gone.'

Her face is one big picture of misunderstanding. 'I didn't realise you were so into him. Accusations are hard but this is the game, it's only gonna get harder. *Lie or Die*, clue's in the title, right? Noah didn't play the game, so he had to die. Plus, I'm pretty sure he's gay.'

'I need to tell you…'

'Think about the money. Sure makes the killing easier. Fifty grand.' Standing, she plants herself in front of the mirror. 'Enough now. You need to get on with it. Besides you're gonna see them both again in a couple of days.'

I stand slowly.

'But I'm right about Noah,' she says. 'Barking up the wrong tree there.' Her attention turns back to the mirror. 'Splash some water on your face, clean your teeth and give it a minute before you come out.' She smiles at her reflection. 'You've got this.' She's out the door before I can stop her. I do as she says, waiting for a beat before I'm ready to face the house. I head straight to the kitchen. It's like sleepwalking through a dream. I'm here but I'm not. I don't know how to process this.

Tayo's by the sink. I grab a glass automatically, filling it from the tap.

'You're not supposed to drink that,' he says, his voice playful.

I raise the glass and drink.

His eyebrows arch in question, as his huge eyes watch me. 'Bit of a shock, huh?'

Looking directly into his eyes, I try to work out if he's fishing for information or being genuine. I'm not reading guilt, just concern. Could he have killed Noah? For real?

Before I can answer him, the lights dim and Cohin appears. Only it's not Cohin, it's Cali.

The glass freezes on my lips.

'I didn't want to be the first one executed.' She's smiling. 'To be murdered first is bad, but to be accused and found guilty, arghh.' She rolls her thickly lined eyes. 'Guess I didn't play the social game as well as I thought.' She's turning her head like she can see us. 'I have the last laugh though. I was a Player.' She holds up both hands and waves. 'Innocent.' She pauses, listening to a question off camera. 'I'd put money on either Kass or Noah. Could that be an Agent alliance?'

Her face morphs into Noah and my heart stops.

'There's only one thing worse than going out first and that's being killed in your sleep.' His face turns, his expression cheeky, reminding me of the boy I met in the cafe. 'So, Agents, shame on you,' he shouts. 'Come on, Players, play the game hard and get the Agents out. And remember. Trust no one.'

The glass falls from my hand and smashes onto the kitchen floor.

'Whoopsie,' says Max.

Tayo moves to the storeroom, returning with a dustpan and brush. He kneels.

'Don't move.' His voice is lullaby gentle. 'There's glass everywhere.'

Max ambles over and plonks himself on a stool. 'That was sick,' he says. 'Innocent. Damn. One more for the Agents.'

'You okay?' Tayo's holding the pan filled with shards of glass.

How is Cali talking on a VT *and* lying under the set? I press my palm to my forehead. And Noah? Far from being dead, he's making jokes about being the Agents' next victim.

'Sorry.' I'm fighting to keep it together. 'Bit shocked by Cali's accusation. Didn't see it coming.'

'We should all see it coming,' Tayo says. 'Complacency leads to death in here.'

'The Detective would be good right now,' Skye says. 'They could give us a clue.'

'Nine times out of ten the Detective gets murdered as soon as they reveal themselves,' says Xander. 'Probably waiting for the right time.'

'Unless Noah was the Detective?' Thea throws me a knowing look.

Rhodri walks up to Xander. 'Is it you?'

Xander stares right back. 'No, it is not me.'

'We have an hour, guys. We need to get this right,' Skye says.

Rhodri turns away from Xander, frowning.

Everything's so normal. Everyone's tired and suspicious but from gameplay, nothing else. Tayo's talking behind me. Xander's disappeared into the girls' bedroom. I need to speak to Thea but she's deep in conversation with Skye. Max and Rhodri join them and the four huddle together, heads down. Thea's got over her dislike of Max in return for finding favour with Rhodri; how quickly things turn in this game.

Confusion's banging on my temples so loud I can hardly think. I can't believe that anyone in here would be trying to hurt us, especially Tayo, he has good guy written all over him. Are Cali and Noah absolutely fine or did Noah even make it out of the Confessional?

My thoughts make me tremble all over again.

There's another explanation. There must be a hundred explanations before the jump to *murder*. Maybe Noah couldn't take the pressure. All that stuff about creating the show so he could bring down reality television? In the harsh light of day, it's more than a little far-fetched. There must be a less sinister explanation. But I can't explain Cali's body in the camera-run, no matter how hard I try. But if it was real, why would she just be left lying there? It's like I'm banging a round peg into a square hole, nothing's gonna make it fit.

My head is cottonwool tired. Tayo's talking quietly. He was there, he was with us. Did he wait for Noah to come back out of the Confessional then stick him with a card? Is he playing the game or did he kill him for real, the thought's just too insane. *Shit*, he's talking to me, how did I not realise?

'I need to talk about last night. I was…'

'Sorry, what?' I interrupt, my attention fully focused. 'Start again.'

'Meet me in the boys' bathroom. Five minutes.' He walks away. Damn. I wish I'd been paying attention.

I follow Tayo towards the bedroom but before I reach the door, I change my mind. Until I know for sure, following a potential suspect, however nice, into a room alone is probably not the best idea. Tayo can wait. I need answers and I know exactly where to get them.

23

Pushing the yellow door open, I walk in, sit down and stare directly into the lens.

'Hello Kass.' It sounds like Pippa. 'How are you today?'

'It's about Noah and Cali.' I jump right in. 'And Amara. I want to know they're safe.'

Silence. I wait.

'We can confirm that they are here,' the voice says, slowly. Is Pippa trying to tell me something?

'Are you sure?' My bottom lip trembles.

'Noah was the Agents' third victim. The Agents were made aware that he broke the rules by leaving the house and tricking you into following him. They chose to act accordingly.'

'He didn't trick me,' I interrupt.

There's a pause. 'The rules state that all gameplay must be conducted inside the house.'

Gameplay?

'And Cali?' She sticks in my throat and I have to spit her out.

'Cali has left the studio, just like Amara.'

But I saw her. I want to shout. *She's under the set. And Amara had blue lips.* A hot tear runs down my face.

'Kass, you're emotional. Can you tell me what's the matter?'

'I saw her,' I whisper.

'Who did you see, Kass?' The voice is patient and calm.

'Cali,' I say.

'Cali was found guilty by the Jury. She has been eliminated from the game.'

More tears fall. 'I *saw* her.'

'What did you see, Kass?' The voice is honey smooth, curling around me like a virtual hug. I'm really tired. 'Did you actually *see* Cali?'

I frown. 'I saw her lying there.'

'And you are certain it was Cali?'

My head's cloudy. 'Yes, it was Cali.'

'Did you see her face?' The voice is soft and reassuring and it's turning me around. My memory is blurry. I was so certain.

'No, I… It was dark. There was a hood.'

'Kass, if the face was covered how can you be sure?'

'I touched her.' Doubt burrows under my skin.

'What did you touch, Kass?'

'A boot.' I pause, I didn't actually touch the body. 'There was a body.'

'Like the one on the tree?'

'Yes… No…'

I didn't see her face. It was covered by the hood. I felt the boots and freaked. My mind has coloured in the details like a morbid colour by numbers.

'It wasn't Cali? It was a dummy?' Relief makes my words breathy.

'And Amara?' The voice is so patient. 'Do you have any reason to believe she wasn't performing a role within the game?'

She had blue lips.

'Kass, Amara got up and walked out of the set. You were there. Did the other contestants give you any reason to think otherwise?'

'No, but…'

'This game demands a lot from its contestants. This is why we only chose the mentally strongest to participate. You came in late and were not as prepared as your castmates. Do you think you can handle the pressure, Kass? Do you have what it takes to be extraordinary?'

I raise my chin to the camera, pushing down the doubt and fear. 'Course.'

'Kass, we are always here to talk.' The voice is calming and gentle and comforting. The sort of voice you can trust.

'Kass?'

Urghh, stop with my name already. 'Yes?'

'Who told you it was Cali's body?'

'Noah,' I say as the last fight dribbles out of me. Noah told me, and Noah is gone. 'He said the game was over.'

'It is over,' the voice says. 'For Noah. But the game is very much in play.'

'Oh.'

'Kass.'

'Yes?' I say.

'You are deep into a murder-mystery game, way outside your comfort zone, and you are operating on a very small amount of sleep. Do you think your mind could be playing tricks on you?'

I try to shake off the confusion. 'I … maybe … yes?'

'Kass, what is the one rule of this game?'

'Trust no one.' I stare into the lens. 'It was part of the game?'

'Sometimes what you think you see may not be the truth.'

My body flushes with relief. It was all part of the game and like an idiot I fell for it. Oh god, I'm going to look like a total moron. There's always one, every show. The one everyone takes the piss out of for being *that* stupid. I can see the meme now. I'm gonna go viral for all the wrong reasons.

'Kass, do you have any other questions?'

My face is burning with embarrassment and confusion in equal measure. Am I so far into this game that I can't tell truth from lies?

'The door is open.'

Shakily, I get to my feet.

'One more thing, Kass.'

I turn back to the camera.

'The removal of your LAV microphone is considered a rule break, as is leaving the house by any means. Failure to comply with the rules will result in immediate elimination. By leaving the house with Noah and removing your microphone you broke the rules.'

My heart leapfrogs into my mouth. 'I'm sorry … I didn't…'

'Kass, we understand that you were tricked into entering the camera-run, but we have no choice but to issue you with a formal warning. Any further rule breaks will result in your immediate removal from the game.'

'Okay,' I say, relieved to be given another chance. Not knowing what to say, I move to the door.

'Remember, Kass, trust no one.'

I lean on the other side of the door, not ready to return to the others, waiting for my legs to stop shaking. If someone is messing with my head, it's working. There are two options.

Option one: There's a dead body underneath the set, and a possible killer running around taking us out one by one or…

Option two: This game has ramped up into overdrive and it's dragging me along for the ride.

I'm so confused right now I can hardly remember my own name. I put on my rational hat. I didn't *see* Cali. Was it a dummy? Was Noah simply playing on my fears and imagination? I have to admit, option two is way easier to swallow.

I bet Noah's in a hotel room right now enjoying room service and a hot bath, laughing at stupid, gullible me.

It wasn't Cali. I hold onto that fact for dear life. *It wasn't Cali, Amara was acting, Tayo may be an Agent but he's not a real-life killer and Noah is a sick bastard.*

Tayo's waiting in the bathroom.

'We don't have long.' He glances over my shoulder making sure the door is closed. Suspicion is buzzing around my head, and I keep my guard firmly up. 'I know you're a Player and Noah was too. I saw you follow him to the storeroom, so I waited for you. He told me to watch you.' He stops my interruption. 'In a good way, he made me promise to watch out for you and have your back. He was worried, but he wouldn't tell me why. I knew something was up when he didn't come back from the Confessional.'

I knew he'd been watching me. I back up to the door. If he is an Agent, he can't do anything until the next Kill Window, so I'm safe … for now.

'How do you know we are Players? How were you so sure last night that we weren't going to card you?'

His eyes keep defaulting to the bathroom door. 'Because I'm the Detective.'

'Oh,' I say.

'I put up Noah's name on the first night in the Confessional and yours last night. They confirmed you're both Players. You were both acting weird and there was that whole "save him" thing, which looked kinda sus.' He pauses, his dark eyes pleading. 'I am placing all my trust in you here, if you say anything to anyone, I'm a dead man.'

'I won't,' I say.

Tayo relaxes a little, his eyes scanning the ceiling for

cameras. 'I don't get why an Agent would kill Noah. It doesn't add up, there are far bigger threats in here right now.'

I'm so desperate to share.

'Skye.' My mind is whirring. 'It has to be, she was with us last night, we were the last to see him.'

Tayo doesn't look convinced. 'Maybe, but she was with me and then with you. I saw her get up and come into the kitchen; she didn't speak to anyone else. She helped you to bed and stayed with you all night. I have another theory. I think it's…'

'Kass? Is everything okay?' Thea's voice outside the bathroom door.

'Someone's coming.' I panic and reach for the door. 'Thanks,' I say to him, massively relieved to know that Tayo has my back.

There's no sign of Thea in the boys' bedroom. Max walks in, suspicion flaming over his face. I hover round Noah's bed, gesturing to his holdall.

'Have to take it to the storeroom,' I say. 'Like the others.'

Max studies me, dark circles underneath his eyes betraying his exhaustion. Tayo comes out of the bathroom. I try to look unfazed. Max buys it. Pulling his T-shirt down, he heads into the bathroom.

'Might wanna clear the area,' he says.

I laugh and pull a face. Noah's holdall is open. Checking I'm alone, I rummage through his stuff, not knowing what

I'm looking for. Stuffed down the side, under a pair of socks is a photo.

It's Isla Stockett. I recognise her immediately, she was a winner of *Get Real*, probably the biggest reality show on TV right now. She was an overnight celebrity, a real rags-to-riches story. The likeness to Noah is remarkable, I can't believe I didn't see it before. I had no idea she was a twin. I watched her win and followed her on all the socials. Her death was a massive shock to everyone and caused a huge media storm against reality shows. Until it didn't. Someone else started trending, everyone jumped on their story, and Isla was forgotten. Another show, another star. Our attention was diverted without ever asking why or how or who was responsible.

I study the photo. She's beautiful, dressed for a gala event in a gorgeous sparkling evening dress. Her arms are bare, there's a mark on her wrist, a dove, like Noah's.

Did Noah do all this for her? To avenge her death and make it count?

Option one? Was Noah telling the truth? Is Option two the lie?

Tucking the picture into my pocket, I zip the holdall closed, carrying it to the storeroom, in case anyone's watching.

The Accusation Clock ticks down. Six minutes left to accuse. I stop, confused.

'I know right?' Rhodri's watching the clock. 'Where the hell did the time go? I swear they've moved the clock forward. It's time. Fry or be fried.' I'm not sure what my face is doing but Rhodri stops and looks serious. 'Chill, it's a joke.'

I pull my face back into default normal. Thea and Skye join us.

'Do you have a name?' Thea crosses her arms like she means business.

'I … I'm not sure,' I say, watching them both. 'We're Players, right?'

'Totally.' Skye looks right into my eyes. She doesn't look like she's hiding something. Thea shuffles under my gaze. 'Course.'

'MAX,' Rhodri shouts. 'TAYO.'

Xander runs in, perching on the table. Tayo ambles out of the bedroom, followed by Max.

The clock's down to four minutes. A sense of excited emergency fills the room. We scrutinise each other's faces, searching for any tell-tale signs of treachery. As the clock hits two minutes the sound of ticking fills the room – 'cause there wasn't enough tension already.

'I nominate Kass.' Xander scowls at me.

'Woah. What?' Thea says. 'Where'd that come from?'

Xander shrugs. 'I don't believe her. She's always wandering around at night. I say she's an Agent.'

'No.' I try to stay calm and not do my automatic guilty face. I deliberately raise my eyes to meet the room. 'I'm a Player.'

Thea folds her arms across her chest and gives him a *so there* look.

'Well, she would say that, wouldn't she?' Xander says.

'You're gonna have to give us a bit more than that,' Tayo says to Xander, his voice calm. 'Why should we believe you, Kass?'

I glance at the clock as it ticks down to zero.

Skye jumps up and tucks her arm through mine. 'I've been with Kass pretty much all the way through this game so far, we shared a bed on the first night and last night she felt unwell so I sat with her all night. She didn't leave the room.' She squeezes my arm. 'If she's an Agent then I must be one too.'

'And me,' Thea says from my other side, and I flush warm with relief that my alliance is holding.

'And I'm Spartacus,' chuckles Tayo.

We all look at him, he puts his hands up. 'It's an old reference. My dad loved the Hollywood greats. For what it's worth I believe her. I don't think Kass is an Agent.'

'Guys, the time,' Max says as the clock hits the last sixty seconds.

'I nominate Xander,' Rhodri says. We wait for an explanation. He shrugs. 'I panicked. He's right in front of me. Besides he's way too vocal.'

One minute...

'That's no reason for you to nom...' Thea says.

'I nominate...' Xander shouts.

'I second for Xander,' Max interrupts as the clock hits zero.

Xander cries, 'That's bullshit.'

'It may be bullshit but it still counts.' Rhodri pats Xander on the back. 'Guess we'll see how good your game is.'

Xander scowls and chews his bottom lip, his pretty face creased with anger.

I've never felt so lost. I may not be facing the electric chair, but my brain is totally fried. I can't get a grip. I'm relieved that the heat was taken off me but terrified for Xander. My paranoia has sent me totally bonkers. I can't tell what or who is real in here. I'm clinging onto the facts like my life depends on it; we are in a game show, none of it is real, nothing anyone says is true.

And no one is *actually* dead… Right?

24

'Xander nominated Cali and argued for her to be electrocuted. He was the only one certain that she was guilty. Once she was out of the way he decided to split up the Tayo-Noah alliance. Cali said she saw him out of bed on Night One. I believe he was looking for the other Agent.'

This is crazy.

I'm in the Courtroom, lights blinding my tired eyes, listening to Rhodri, a tattooed apprentice sparky from Porthcawl, accuse Xander, a cute seventeen-year-old and the baby of the group, of being a ruthless Agent responsible for the murders of Amara and Noah.

He's making sense. I can tell the others think so from the murmurs of agreement. With Amara gone, no one's fighting for his innocence.

So, when Cohin puts on his cap and intones in his *you're gonna die* voice, nobody, not even Xander, is surprised.

That's until the sack is put over his head and the spot snaps on over the chair.

This time I know what's coming.

Cali's body is tattooed onto my eyelids.

Was it all part of Noah's game plan?

That's what the nice voice in the Confessional told me.

The lights dim. Xander bucks in the chair as the buzzing increases, like Cali and I did.

I can't *not* watch: like some crap horror movie, waiting

for the scream and the smell, as the tension rises in time with my terror. I can't move; fear has me frozen to the spot, bound and gagged and powerless.

The buzzing reaches its crescendo and Xander shakes and shivers in the chair. But this is different. This is not like Cali.

It doesn't look real. At one point I swear Xander giggles.

This time there's no smoke, no smell. Just the buzzing, louder and louder in my ears until I can't hear if he is laughing or screaming.

Xander's body jolts one last time and the lights snap to black.

There's a scraping sound, metal on wood, as the trapdoor opens followed by a muffled scream.

Silence.

I wait in the dark, my eyes locked on the space where Xander used to be. A muted sound hits my ears. Shuffling? Struggling? Screaming?

Leaning forward, I listen harder.

The scream is so loud we all press our palms against our ears. It's not real. An effect, exaggerated and produced to the finest degree and played in to deafen us, or to silence something else. My eardrums cry in reply and the ringing in my ears keeps going long after the scream stops.

It's dark for the longest time and we all shuffle uncomfortably. I can just about make out faces in the black.

'Is it done?' whispers Skye.

The lights stay out.

'Do you think they're waiting for us to do something?' says Max.

'Shhh,' says Thea.

The lights snap back on. I shield my eyes. The chair is back in the dock, no sign of Cohin or Xander.

Rhodri jumps off the benches. 'I'm starving.'

Tayo takes the steps two at a time, landing gracefully on the studio floor.

Skye doesn't move, she's visibly paled.

'You okay?' I say.

She nods. 'I feel bad for him. Poor Xander.'

Thea tuts impatiently. 'It's not personal. If you want to win this game, you have to know when to separate emotions from logic.'

'Is that what you do?' Tayo asks, his eyes narrowed in a thoughtful frown.

'Yes.' Thea sticks her chin out, the way she does when she wants to make a point.

'And at what cost?' he asks. 'Do you sacrifice loyalties as well?'

'I want to win. Nothing wrong with that.' She stares him down – David to Goliath.

'Noted,' Tayo chuckles.

Back in the house we splinter into groups. I follow Skye and Thea to the sofas and flop, too tired to worry about looking good. It's late and the lazy summer sun is setting over the garden. Having been shut indoors for over two days, I long to get some air and clear my head, but the door to the garden remains stubbornly locked and despite us all looking, no key has been found.

Thea's watching me. She's worried. She has this tell-tale half-smile half-frown thing she does when she's concerned, and she's doing it right now. I smile an *I'm fine* to ease her mind. Not sure if it works, she keeps casting looks my way.

Cohin appears on the table, wearing Xander's face.

Hologram Xander's laughing. 'I got fried! Thank you, people, total blindside. This baby face didn't fool you, did it? And congratulations, you killed an Agent.' He claps his hands. 'Ah ha, not telling you who my partner is, so you'd best get to work. Agent to win! Loved every minute of it. Love this game!'

Xander morphs into Cohin.

'Congratulations, Players, you have successfully eliminated one of two threats. The game is wide open. Anyone can win. But remember; the more winners, the more to share the prize. Do you want to share?'

'Hell yeah,' says Skye.

'To congratulate you on your successful accusation, you will find a full Chinese feast in the storeroom.'

The room erupts in cheering.

'Remember, when the Kill Clock starts, no one is safe.' Cohin disappears.

Thea runs to the storeroom and I grab plates from the kitchen.

Rhodri and Max do a dance around the table which ends up as some weird kind of twerking.

'We did it, we did it, we only bloody did it,' they sing as they dance and twerk and laugh.

Skye squeals as Tayo spins her off the ground.

'Come on.' Rhodri fist pumps the air. 'One to go.'

'Xander. You sly dog.' Thea's voice is full of admiration. 'Wow, he played that well. I had no idea. Well played everyone.'

The atmosphere's changed completely. Five minutes ago, we all looked like we had the weight of the world resting on our shoulders, but now adrenaline and relief that we, the Players, are finally getting somewhere, has rejuvenated us. And we have the first part of the combination. Stuck inside the bag of food was a card with the numbers 09 81. The meal is helping too, and we all tuck in.

'This game is nuts,' Tayo says reading the numbers on the card. 'Do these have any significance, I wonder?'

'Like a clue?' Max says, taking it from Tayo. 'Interesting.'

'Well played, Rhodri,' Thea coos. 'I have to admit that was great investigating.'

'I seconded,' says Max, still eating.

'You too,' Thea says, smiling.

I nod my agreement.

'Whaaaaaaat? Girl Next Door approves?' Rhodri presses his hand to his heart. 'I've won already.'

He ducks as I throw a fortune cookie at him, but I can't help the grin that's tugging on my lips. Am I actually starting to like Tattoo boy? I shake the thought away before Thea sees. *Chicks before dicks*. He is strictly off limits, no way I'm making that mistake again.

After we've had our fill of Chinese, we veg out on the sofas, stuffed, and relaxed, much more house party and much less reality TV murder-mystery.

'I might go take a shower.' Max stretches on the sofa. 'Need to wake up. Tonight's gonna be tough.'

'It's the third kill night and we're knackered. Anything could happen,' Tayo says.

'One in six, and over halfway through,' Rhodri says. 'I am liking these odds.'

Max rubs his hands. 'Bring it on.'

Thea wrinkles her nose at me. 'You need to get out of those clothes, you've been in them since we came in.'

'It's not so bad. I'll come hold the towel up if you like,' Skye says.

I want to make a joke, but I don't think they're messing. It's been so full-on I haven't even thought about changing. I struggle to get myself up off the sofa and into the bathroom.

Skye stands by the cubicle like a sentry, guarding the door, keeping a beady eye on the camera in the corner. It's ignoring us, there's no red light or whirring as we move around.

The warm water's good against my skin and the doubts and worries of last night begin to wash away with the grime. I can do this, it's all part of the game, sick maybe, but just the game. And I'm still here. I've not been voted out which is a personal best. I must be doing something right. Thea's still in too. My plan is working; she's thawing under the heat of the studio lights and our friendship is back on track.

We're killing it.

'Kass?' Skye whispers through the shower door. It's hard to hear against the rush of the water. 'I can trust you, right? I know the whole premise of this game is to trust no one, but I get a feeling with you. I trust you. And Tayo.'

I turn off the shower and grab the towel, wrapping it around my body before taking off my now-soaking underwear, hoping Lewis has packed more and kicking myself for not checking first.

'Yes,' I say, trying to navigate the towel situation. I stupidly didn't bring a change of clothes into the bathroom with me. 'Of course. And for what it's worth I think you're right about Tayo too, he's solid.' I trust her but I'm not about to tell her he's the Detective.

She's chewing her hair, lost in thought. 'So that leaves Thea, Rhodri and Max.' She frowns. 'I don't trust Thea.'

Reaching for another towel, I dry my hair.

'Gut feeling. There's something about her,' she says.

I screw up my face. 'I don't get that vibe. Don't forget Max is a super fan. He is gonna have some serious moves.'

I'm in front of the sink, watching her in the mirror, trying to keep my face neutral.

'Maybe. You don't get that vibe from Thea?'

'Nope, I trust her.' I don't want to sound too gushing, just need to give enough to get her off Thea's back. It works.

'That just leaves Rhodri and Max.'

'And you,' I say, gauging her reaction. She chuckles lightly.

'Yep, and me. I'm a Player, I swear.' She puts her hand over her heart and smiles warmly. There are no tell-tale signs of lying, no twitches, or flushes of pink on her cheeks or tiny beads of sweat on her forehead. She's telling the truth.

I smile warmly. 'Me too, so it has to be Rhodri or Max.'

'I'm leaning more towards Max,' she says. 'And not because Rhodri's stupidly sexy, it's just a feeling.'

I get it. Nothing against Max, but I'm starting to get what everyone sees in the six-foot Welsh boy.

I dress in my old clothes again to go out to the bedroom. Fifty thousand pounds or not, no way am I going on camera in a towel.

Thea's packing Xander's suitcase.

I smile. 'Shower's free.'

'Still don't believe it,' she says. 'Thought he was for real.'

I open my suitcase. Hardly worth unpacking now. I take out the first T-shirt, grab a pair of jeans and rummage for underwear.

Red lights flash through the living room as the Kill Clock starts its deadly count down.

'Third night,' Thea says. 'We survive tonight and there's just one more night to go.'

I roll my eyes. 'Easy.'

As I'm rummaging, my hand hits a screwed-up bit of paper. Instinctively I push it into my pocket. A camera spins round to me, its red light blinking like a heartbeat. I pretend to unpack while waiting for Skye to come out the bathroom, convinced my cheeks are burning a guilty red. As soon as she's out, I dive back in, my pile of clothes under my arm, mumbling about wanting some privacy. It's not a lie, and they all know that.

Running into the toilet cubicle, I check the ceiling for cameras. Taking the paper out of my pocket, I cough to cover up the crackling as I pull it open.

I recognise Lewis' untidy scrawl.

Something very weird is going on. Came back and all the day-crew were leaving - said Pippa sent them home. No crew came for the night shift. NO CREW IN THE BUILDING. Only Pippa. Worried for you, so hid in the loo. Building locked. Stuck inside - no way out. Be careful.

I reread the note. This was written the first night, forty-eight hours ago? What if the day crew didn't come back? Have we been in here all this time without a crew? And where is Lewis now?

Last night, the camera-run, the body and Noah come crashing back.

Someone bursts into the bathroom.

'Kass? You in here?' Thea's voice is high pitched and breathless.

'Coming.' I stuff the note in my pocket and flush the toilet.

'Hurry,' she says. 'I found a key in Xander's stuff. I think it's for the garden.'

Dressing quickly, I rush into the living room. Everyone's there, Thea's hovering in front of the garden door, key in hand.

'Guess Xander didn't want us to go out there,' she says. 'Let's find out why.'

Tayo appears at my shoulder, he must have been in the Confessional. He gives me a 'look' like he wants to talk, but now is not the time.

231

Unlocking the door, Thea pushes it open. The summer-scented evening air whispers across my face. It's so refreshing. After two days inside we all pile into the garden as the sounds and smells of Wembley assault our senses over the wall. Rhodri and Max are first, heads facing the sky, as we all gulp in the air greedily.

It's dark, an almost full moon lights the garden with its silvery touch.

'I don't think I've ever been so pleased to be outside,' Skye says. Wembley's still busy despite the hour, and I soak in the atmosphere.

Rhodri and Max are messing around near Dougie the dummy. As I get closer my throat tightens. Dougie looks different. The way he hangs, the gentle swing of his legs, his arms hanging either side of his body, pale wrists exposed.

There's a tattoo on his wrist.

I try to warn the boys, but my words are lodged in my throat. Everything moves in slow motion. Rhodri pats the dummy on the shoulder. The body swings round to face us. The floodlights snap on, illuminating the garden with an unforgiving light. For a moment we're all blinded by the sudden flash. Rhodri does a strange double take as his face changes from happy to horror, his body recoiling so fast he ends up flat on the ground.

Silence.

Wembley holds its breath as our eyes adjust to the macabre tableaux in front of us.

Then comes the screaming.

232

25

'Shut up.' Thea's screaming in Skye's face. 'Shut up.'

Tayo engulfs them both in his arms, masking the sight of the body hanging from the tree. Skye's screams subside into hysterical sobs.

'How long has he been there?' Thea's chalk white as she frees herself from Tayo's embrace.

Max looks like he's about to puke or faint, or both. Tayo's a strange shade, like all the shine has drained from his skin, but he doesn't leave Skye, his arms tensed protectively around her.

Rhodri's on the ground, leaning up on his elbows.

My feet walk me to the front of the body, robot like.

'Don't.' Max's hand is on my arm. I shake it off. I can't take my eyes off the body.

It's him.

Noah.

Tom.

His head's down, chin on chest. His bleached white hair is puckered pink. The back of his head is a deep crimson, a huge wet patch of blood stains his skull. Blood has dripped from his head onto his shirt as he hangs like a carcass in a butcher's. His dead hand's clutching a card, round and blood-stained and stamped with the letter 'A'.

My eyes follow the blood trail. Spindly streams meander down his body, seeping into his shirt turning blue to purple, from shirt to jeans, from feet to floor. A small pool of blood collects beneath him, darkened by the midnight moon.

In the centre of the pool something glints, teasing my morbid curiosity. The shiny silver makes the red blood shine as it stretches over the slippery surface. I pick it up.

'Ewww, gross.' Thea's hovering. 'Kass?'

I'm looking straight at her, but I can't see her. All I see is Noah. Not Noah on the tree, the Noah I met in the cafe, my friend.

Tayo's beside me. He takes the object, a pair of cable-cutters, yellow handles stained dark, the shiny metal blades sticky and red.

I'm steered back into the house. A giggle bubbles up through my throat and erupts into the night air.

Thea glances at Tayo, worry strewn across her face. I want to tell her I'm okay, but I can't stop.

Everything Noah told me is true.

Someone is killing us.

And we are all going to die.

We collapse in a heap on the living room floor. Max slams the door behind us, locking it as though that will keep the nasty outside.

While we're in here.

Locked in this set.

With a killer.

My giggle turns to cold realisation as reality kicks in.

Noah.

Amara.

Cali.

Dead.

Certainty replaces paranoia.

And Xander makes four. He must have been killed after falling through the trapdoor. Those muffled cries I heard were real, that's why they played the scream that almost deafened us, to mask what was happening under the set, to cover up his murder.

'Mate.' Rhodri gestures to Tayo who's still clutching the cable-cutters.

Tayo throws them into the corner, wiping his hand on his jeans, leaving a dark smudge of Noah's blood on his thigh.

The floodlights snap off plunging the garden into darkness.

Cohin appears. 'Contestants, assemble at the table.'

Rhodri looks at Cohin and back to us. 'Is this for real?'

We don't move, terrified to get any closer to the grinning, hooded hologram.

'I'm waiiiii-ting,' Cohin sings.

Still, we don't move. Skye's eyes are so wide, she looks like a cartoon version of herself.

Cohin's voice simmers angrily. 'I don't like waiting.'

Tayo strides forwards. 'Who did that to Noah?'

Cohin chuckles; the sound makes my skin crawl. 'The Agents are coming to get you.'

'This is bullshit,' Rhodri shouts.

'Sit. Down.'

We sit.

Rhodri remains standing, fists screwed tight.

Skye pleads, 'Rhodri.'

Rhodri stares at Cohin.

'Mate, sit down, you can't fight him. He's not real,' Tayo says.

Rhodri punches the table, making us jump. He sits.

'What did you do to Noah?' Thea says fiercely. I envy her strength.

Cohin spins to face her. 'I did nothing. You did.'

Thea lets out a sob.

'And Cali?' I choke. 'Xander?'

'All executions were carried out as per the rules of the game. The sentence was death. You knew the rules. And you all voted.'

Tayo leans towards Cohin, his voice hard. 'What exactly do you mean?'

'We were playing the game,' says Max. 'Because it's a *game*.'

'And we saw them.' Skye's hopeful eyes dart around the table. 'Afterwards, on the video. They were alive.'

Tayo's eyes are set on Cohin, his voice calmly cold. 'No, we didn't. It wasn't real, was it? You manipulated the footage to make us think they were still alive.'

The table erupts into angry outcries.

'You're having a laugh,' shouts Rhodri, sounding anything but amused.

Max bangs his palms on the table. 'This is a game. We are on a game show. This isn't real. There are rules.'

'What the hell is going on?' Thea sobs.

Skye's eyes are wide with fear. 'This isn't happening, it's not true.'

Only I stay quiet, silenced by my guilt. I knew. Noah told me. I didn't trust him enough and I didn't trust my instincts. And now he's dead.

Cohin spins, morphing into our faces one by one. 'The rules of the game have changed. Refer to section 7:2 of your contracts. The terms state that production may change the gameplay with immediate effect.'

'They can't do that.' Max's eyes dart frantically around the table. 'Noah's dead. They can't make us play.'

'Players must find the remaining Agent. They must pay for their crimes. When the Agent has been tried and found guilty, the remaining Players will be released.'

The lights change, flooding us with blood red.

'Contestants. The game has changed. You are now playing for your lives.'

'This is a joke, right?' Thea whispers.

Cohin is spinning between our faces, over and over. 'Agent, you are also playing to survive. You have until the Kill Clock stops to make one last kill. Players, whoever survives Night Three will have one last nomination. Choose wisely. If Players do not identify the Agent correctly, all remaining contestants will die.'

He morphs back into Cohin. 'Buckle up, contestants. Reality just got real.'

He disappears.

237

'This is a joke,' Thea says again. 'This is a task, right?'

Nobody answers.

She flumps back in her chair.

No one moves. Skye's face is hidden under her hair. Max is fighting tears. Rhodri's eyes blaze with anger. Only Tayo looks calm, but the twitching of his mouth says he's trying to hold on as much as the rest of us. Thea squeezes my hand.

'No,' Tayo says. One word has never sounded so strong. 'The only way this works is if we play.'

Rhodri's anger turns hopeful. 'You mean refuse?'

Tayo nods. 'What can they do? We don't know who this is but there are six of us. And I don't feel like playing anymore.'

There's a collective shift of mood around the table as hope banishes terror. We feed off each other's strength.

'We can beat this freak,' Thea says, shouting into the air. 'So, stick that in your reality show, mister.'

'Don't piss off the crazy killer,' Skye whispers.

'What do we do?' I ask Tayo, trying to sound as strong as Thea. 'We can't just sit here.'

'Can we move?' Thea says. 'Knowing Cohin could appear at any time is freaking me out.'

We push our chairs back in one big move of solidarity and head into the girls' bedroom, closing the door behind us, shutting Cohin out.

Thea, Skye and I huddle together on Skye's bed. The

bright studio lights inside the house mask the dark of the garden, making it thankfully impossible to see Noah on the tree.

'What did he mean about Amara and Xander?' Rhodri paces up and down. 'Are they dead too?'

'I think so,' I say.

'And Cali?'

'I found Cali.'

Everyone's eyes are fixed on me.

'Where?' Max's voice wobbles, as his eyes sweep the room.

'Under the Courtroom.'

'I feel sick,' Thea says.

Six faces stare at me – confusion and disgust mixing a morbid cocktail of horror.

'I followed Noah into the camera-runs. He was trying to get help.' Everyone's faces are blank. I point to the mirrors. 'You know they're two-way mirrors, right?'

Everyone nods.

'There's an entrance through the storeroom: it's how I found Cali. There's a door at the end of the run.'

Tayo stands up. 'Then I say we get the hell out of here.' Everyone stands.

'We already tried,' I say. 'There's only one door out and it's locked.'

'I bet I could break down the main house doors,' Rhodri says.

I shake my head. 'They're fire doors, they're totally

solid. Noah tried to get out. He went to the Confessional, but he never came back.'

'And we all know what happened to him.' Skye's eyes linger on the garden windows.

'Don't.' Thea flinches.

'I need to get out of here,' Skye says.

'There is no other way out.' I say. 'We tried.'

Skye's about two seconds from losing it. She runs out. Tayo and Max follow.

'Why didn't you tell us?' Thea's tone is sharp.

Rhodri's green eyes turn cold. 'She's got a point. All of this was going on and we had no clue.'

'I thought it was part of the game,' I say. Rhodri huffs and walks to the window. 'I thought I was being paranoid.' I turn to Thea. 'I tried to tell you, in the bathroom. You didn't listen.'

'You should have made me,' she says, hurt creeping into her eyes. She joins Rhodri at the window.

'What are they doing?' Thea says, as the shouts for help reach us in the bedroom. 'Are they in the garden?'

Rhodri pushes his face against the glass window to stare into the garden black. 'Looks like Max is trying to get onto Tayo's shoulders, they're going over the wall. Come on.' He rushes out and we follow.

Max is struggling to climb onto Tayo's shoulders. After a struggle he ends up collapsed in a helpless heap.

'They're not tall enough,' Skye cries.

She's right. There's no way Max on Tayo will reach

the height of the wall. Even if they could, the top is covered in rolls of barbed wire.

'I need to get out.' She's spiralling. 'I need to get out.'

'Hold it together, guys,' says Thea, her voice cracking.

Skye runs to a camera. 'Please. If you're watching, get us out. We're not playing. This is real. Help us.'

Rhodri holds Skye's shoulders, talking calmly. 'Hey. We'll figure this out.' Skye's eyes keep drifting to Noah's body. She can't help it. I know 'cause it's taking all my strength not to turn around and see his body hanging in the dark.

'Look at me,' Rhodri says to her. 'Keep looking at me.'

The Welshness of his tone is surprisingly calming.

Skye lifts her chin to him. 'We need to do something.'

Tayo stands straight, helping Max off the floor.

'You could stand on Max,' Rhodri says to Skye. 'A human pyramid. Like in the circus.'

I grab hold of his desperate enthusiasm. 'You're tall and weigh like nothing, it could work. We'll hold you up. Think cheerleading.' I turn to Tayo and Rhodri. 'Could you do it? Could you hold them.'

Looking at each other they shrug. 'We can try.' Tayo nudges Max, who's staring at the grass, arms folded, his body tense as a bow. 'Buddy?'

Max just shakes.

Skye shudders as she raises her eyes to the wall. The impenetrable rolls of wire sit on top, hundreds of razor-sharp shards sparkling in the moonlight, daring us to try.

'I'll do it,' Thea says.

'Skye's taller,' Tayo says, an apologetic smile hovering on his lips.

The garden floodlights snap on, bathing us in bright white light. We all freeze like rabbits in the headlights. The cameras in the garden turn with a whirr, their little red lights snapping on. 'Guys?' Max says. 'We're being watched.'

'Then we need to be quick,' Skye says, prompting us all to move.

Rhodri and Tayo link arms to form a base, bracing themselves for the weight. Thea and I help Max up. Soon, he's balanced on their shoulders, leaning against the wall. It's not enough, even with his arms outstretched he can't touch the top.

'With Skye on his shoulders we could do it,' I say.

Tayo and Rhodri support Max, fierce concentration splashed across their faces.

'Blimey, mate, you need to lay off the snacking,' Rhodri says through gritted teeth.

'Get lost, Welsh boy, I comfort eat when I'm nervous,' Max says, struggling to balance.

'Fair dos,' says Rhodri.

Skye climbs up Rhodri's bent knees, and with our help he lifts her high.

'Wait.' Thea runs back into the house returning with a duvet. 'Don't want to cut yourself to pieces on the wire.'

'Come on,' Max puffs as Skye climbs onto his shoulders. Thea and I hover at the bottom of the pyramid, supporting from all sides. The four-man pyramid shakes as Tayo and Rhodri strain under the weight.

Crowd noise blasts from the speakers. Max wobbles, Skye's arms helicopter in the air as she tries to balance. Rhodri and Tayo struggle under the extra strain as the crowd noise fills the garden, drowning out our desperate cries.

'Shit.' Max fights to balance while holding Skye. 'I can't.'

'Hold on, mate, we got this.' Rhodri can't keep the desperation out of his voice.

'Contestants to gather at the table.' Cohen's voice punctuates the crowd. 'Don't make me angry.'

'Oh god,' Max cries.

'Ten...' Cohin starts a menacing countdown. 'Nine...'

'Oh god, oh god.' Max's panic makes him wobble even more. 'What's he gonna do?'

'Hurry,' I shout.

Thea's face drains of colour. 'Here.' She throws the duvet up towards Skye's open hand. Catching it, Skye tries to throw it over the wire snagging herself on its sharp spikes. She whimpers and a small line of blood trickles down her arm as the wire tears at her skin.

'Eight...'

'Quick,' I say. Thea takes a step back towards the house.

The pyramid sways. Tayo and Rhodri struggle to hold them.

'Seven…'

'Go,' Tayo shouts. 'I've got them.'

Rhodri refuses to move. 'She's almost there.'

'Six…'

Skye wrestles to get the duvet over the wire, the metal spikes spin dangerously with every touch. She cries out in pain and frustration. 'I can't reach.'

'Five… Four…' Cohin's still counting.

Max swallows a cry. His legs start to shake. 'I can't.' He wobbles more. 'I'm sorry. I don't want to make him angry.' Max launches himself off the pyramid, leaving Skye hanging from the wall and making Rhodri and Tayo collapse to the ground.

Landing with a thud, Max scrambles quickly into the house. Unable to hold on, Skye falls backwards. Tayo jumps up to break her fall, but she crashes clumsily on top of him and he lands on the hard ground with an almighty thump.

'Get inside,' Max shouts from the door. I pull Rhodri up and, grabbing Thea, we run into the house. Tayo and Skye stay stuck in the garden.

'Two…'

'He's hurt,' screams Skye. The impact of her falling on Tayo has winded him and he's struggling to stand. Skye tries to help him up.

'One.'

Rhodri tries to run back outside but the door closes with a sharp click. The lock slides into place, locking us in and Skye and Tayo out.

Rhodri pulls at the handle, screaming through the glass. 'I can't open it.' He bangs on the window. Skye's still struggling to help Tayo to his feet.

The window shutters descend. Skye runs to the door.

'Let us in.' She's screaming, her small fists pounding on the glass as the shutter lowers. 'Let us in.'

The crowd noise pumps into the house. The garden floodlights snap off, swallowing Skye and Tayo in darkness.

'Do something,' Thea screams. Max is slumped at the table, head buried in hands.

Rhodri tries to stop the shutters but fails. As they reach the floor the lights flash brightly, casting a strobe effect around us.

'What's happening?' I shout to Rhodri, his face a ghoulish white in the flashing light. Thea clings to me and we stand, terrified, in the middle of the living room. I close my eyes as the strobe becomes unbearable.

The crowd noise reaches an ear-shattering crescendo.

Rhodri throws his fists against the shutters.

Silence. The room fills with a deadly hush. I blink, my eyes still strobing from the effects, the thumping of my heart replacing the crowd noise.

Max whimpers.

The shutters rise with a metallic screech. We fall to our knees to see outside but it's too dark.

Rhodri's still pounding on the glass. In one quick-thinking movement Thea runs to the light switch and turns off the inside lights, helping our eyes adjust to the night dark. The shutters pass over the door handle with a click. Rhodri throws it open, and we run into the garden.

Tayo is laying in a heap on the grass, his whole body shaking as he gasps for breath. I fall by his side.

'Hold on, man.' Rhodri's beside me. 'He's hurt, bring towels.'

There's so much blood. Tayo's once white T-shirt is seeping red. His hands claw the grass, squeezing mud between his fingers as if to absorb the pain. Sticking out of his lower back, just below his ribs, is a knife. He's panting, short, ragged breaths. Instinctively I know that to pull it out will kill him.

My hands close around his, warm and clammy.

Thea reaches us with towels. We wrap them round the knife and press.

'Keep the pressure up,' I say, my hand clutching Tayo's.

'Do something,' cries Thea, kneeling opposite me, both hands wrapped around the towels.

'Oh god, oh god, oh god.' Max rocks back and forth.

'Where's Skye?' I say. Thea's eyes dart frantically around the garden.

We find her in a shadowed corner, curled so small it's like she's trying to push herself into the wall. Her face is blank, eyes wide with fear. Her hands are covered in blood, scratched and torn skin seeps more. Thea runs to her. My one hand presses against the towel, warm with Tayo's blood, as I try to will the wound shut. My other holds his hand tight, squeezing away the pain.

Tayo moves his head, his eyes searching for mine. I lean in close so he can see me.

Rhodri runs to the cameras. 'Help us. Somebody, help us.'

We are rewarded with more crowd noise blaring into the garden, swallowing up our cries for help.

'You bastards,' he screams. It's no good. He grabs the duvet from the wall and covers Tayo's shaking body, kneeling in Thea's place, wiping his eyes with his arm.

'Hey mate, how ya doing?' He speaks softly and gently, his Welsh lilt calm against the screaming of the crowd noise. He takes the pressure on the towel, leaving me free to hold Tayo's hand. 'We're here.'

Tayo coughs and splutters as he tries to speak.

'Steady, mate,' says Rhodri. 'Easy now.'

Tiny bubbles appear at the sides of his mouth as he tries to form a word. He's struggling so much my heart contracts with his pain.

'Stay with me.' I hold his hand tightly and will him to live. 'Stay with me.'

'My name is Tayo Asaju, and I live in Kentish Town.' Tayo's voice blasts from the speakers. Confused, I look up into the house. Tayo's piece to camera is playing on the table.

Skye and Thea cry out in horror, but they stay frozen in the corner.

'Stop it.' Max spins to face the house. 'Stop it.'

'Stop it now. You sick bastard,' Rhodri screams to the corner camera.

'This is MY game.' Tayo's VT flickers out and Cohin appears, hooded and anonymous. 'I make the rules.'

Tayo is gulping for air, his eyes round and terrified. I squeeze his hand. 'Stay with me, please Tayo, stay with me.'

Rhodri presses against the towel, blood staining his hands and wrists.

I have never felt so helpless.

The image on the table flickers from Cohin to Tayo and back again.

'Watch out, I am playing to win,' says Tayo's image.

'Failure to comply with my rules will lead to immediate termination of contract.' Cohin screams.

'Bumblebee.' Max runs up and down screaming at the cameras. 'Bumblebee.'

Tayo's trying to speak. I lean forward. His lips open and close.

'You will play my way,' Cohin screams.

Tayo's hand reaches out, fingers straining to point. Looking up, I see Thea.

Tayo whispers in my ear.

Two words that break my heart.

'Killer Agent.'

His eyes close, his hand falls limp in mine. As a final jagged breath leaves his lips, his laughter spills from the hologram.

'Stay with me, stay with me.' I clutch his hand in mine, tears blurring his face. 'Please, Tayo … stay with me.'

In the middle of the garden, in a reality television game show set, beautiful Tayo Asaju dies.

26

A stunned silence fills the garden, punctured by soft sobbing from Skye.

I'm still holding Tayo's hand. His face is peaceful, all pain washed away by the state of permanent sleep. He died trying to save us.

The floodlights snap back on and my stomach churns as their cruel light illuminates the horror surrounding us.

Max is crumpled on the floor, leaning against the wall, head in hands. He's not moving, not crying, a hundred per cent still. Rhodri's pacing like a restless lion, his hands shiny red with Tayo's blood.

He stops and turns to Tayo, gently covering his face. The duvet's not big enough to cover all the blood and a trail of red pokes out underneath, making an abstract crimson pattern on the grass. My eyes follow the pattern of dark against light. Something glints in the grass. Reaching out I grab a small vial, just like the poison bottle found in Noah's chair. This one reads: SLEEPING POTION. Without thinking I slip it into my pocket.

Thea's by my side. Her arm curled around my shoulder does nothing to stop the shaking. She takes my hand, gently unwrapping my fingers from Tayo's.

'You need to come away now,' she says. It only makes the tears fall faster. 'We need to take Skye inside.'

It takes a minute to coax Skye back into the house.

She sits on the sofa next to Rhodri, his long arms cocooning her, keeping her safe, just like Tayo did before. We surround her in stunned silence.

'What happened?' Thea says gently.

'It was so fast.' Her eyes dart from one of us to another. 'It happened so quick. We were at the door, trying to get in. Then he was there. I saw the knife.' She shivers.

'Do you know who he is?' Rhodri asks.

Skye shakes her head. 'It was too dark.'

'You didn't see his face?' Fear and urgency make my question harsh, and panic fills Skye's already terrified eyes.

'He was big, not Tayo big, but big. It was dark. I ran at him; he went for me. He pushed me and I fell.' She holds out her arms and the gashes of red sliced through her skin confirm her story. Thea runs into the kitchen and returns with kitchen roll and a bowl of water. 'Tayo was helping me up … he came up behind him…' Her breaths are jagged, words disjointed as she relives the horror. 'I couldn't do anything… There was so much blood.'

'It's okay.' I reassure her quickly. 'It's okay.'

Skye sobs.

'Shhhh.' Thea washes her wounds. 'See? You're gonna be alright.'

I love Thea's optimism, the slashes from the knife look pretty deep to me, deep enough to scar, I reckon.

'Where did he come from?' Rhodri asks. 'Where did he go?'

Skye takes the kitchen roll from Thea and presses it against her arms. 'The door in the garden.' She gestures to the garden, the end of the camera-run. 'He ran back in when Tayo fell…' She sobs. 'I should have stopped him. I should have done more.'

'No.' Rhodri squeezes her in his arms. 'You did the right thing.'

We all murmur our agreement.

'I'm such a mess,' she says, with a shaky smile.

'You look fine,' I say, immediately kicking myself for such shallow comfort.

Rhodri catches my eye. His eyes are a deep emerald green, darkened by pain and fear. He frowns, jumping up from the sofa, he paces again.

'Look.' Thea points at the Kill Clock. 'It's stopped.'

'Guess there's no need to kill,' Rhodri says. 'At least he's sticking to some of the rules.'

Max's head is bowed between his knees. 'He's going to make us play until we are all dead.'

'That's not what he said,' says Rhodri. 'He said if we get the Agent, we'll live.'

Max sobs. 'The Agent should reveal themselves and everyone can go home.'

'Not everyone,' Thea says. 'The Agent will die.'

'But the rest of us will live,' he says.

'So, you want to sacrifice one for the good of the four?' Rhodri says. 'Way to be a hero, Fanboy.'

'I never said I was. I'm not brave. I want to live.'

251

'So did Tayo,' says Skye.

'So, we play. We stick to all his stupid rules and then what?' Max carries on. 'You think he's gonna let us go?'

'What else are we supposed to do?' asks Thea.

'Who is he?' says Skye. 'And why is he doing this?'

'Who knows?' Rhodri says. 'Did nobody play with you at school?' He's staring into a camera, challenging the killer to come back. Thea walks over and whispers in his ear. Whatever she says works, his shoulders sag and he slumps on the sofa.

'Noah was working with Pippa,' I say. 'He was going to find her and get help. He said the Necromancer card was not part of the game, that it was planted, but if she was watching, wouldn't she have seen it? Why didn't she stop it?' My eyes default to the window. I squeeze them shut.

'We think this is Pippa?' Max says.

'No. Sorry, but she's tiny. No way could she lift Noah onto the tree,' Rhodri says.

'It was definitely a male,' Skye says. 'Even in the dark, I'm sure of it.'

'Then she's working with him,' Thea says.

'Never liked her,' Rhodri says.

'What are we going to do?' Max says.

'What can we do?' Thea says. 'We can't get out, but they can get in. If we try to escape, they kill us. We're totally trapped.'

No one answers her. What is there to say?

I'm so tired. Numbness has crept into my bones and

252

my brain is offline. It's like fear has hit a limit point and what was once terrifying is now the norm. Is this what shock feels like?

Tayo's death has taken the fight right out of us, replacing it with a paralysing terror. There's no choice but to play, so some of us can get out alive. But to play is to pass a death sentence. Looking around the room, it's clear the others feel the same.

Time passes. We don't move. We don't talk. We don't eat. It's like we died with Tayo. We know we have to play, but we can't bring ourselves to do it.

The floodlights stay on all night, a terrifying reminder of our actions. Only when the sun's morning rays appear do they stop their relentless vigil. I never knew the moments before sunrise could be so quiet. We stay silent and unable to move as morning spreads its warming fingers over the garden and into the house.

An alarm sounds.

Cohin appears.

'Contestants, assemble at the table.'

There is no pretence of politeness.

There's a sharpness to his voice I didn't notice before, a barely concealed hatred spilling through from the virtual to the real. Whoever is behind the hologram must have a lot of hate to do what they are doing.

'Welcome to Day Three. Tayo Asaju has been found brutally murdered.'

'Freak,' Rhodri spits. I get it. I'm angry too but I wish he would stop poking the bear.

'The Agent responsible for the murder must be found and brought to trial. They must pay for their crimes.'

Thea makes a terrified cry. 'The Agent isn't responsible. You're the murderer! This is so twisted.'

Cohin turns. 'Contestants are reminded of the rules of the game. Any attempt to leave the confines of the set or to remove microphones or inhibit or damage any equipment or structure will be regarded as a major rule break. Break the rules and you will pay. Tayo broke the rules.'

The sound of indrawn breaths resonates around the room as we all take in Cohin's warning, his meaning crystal clear. If we try to escape, we die. We have to keep playing.

He flickers in and out. He's glitching. Something else is flicking on as the images merge into each other.

Music blasts over Cohin. It's a Taylor Swift video. After a few beats Cohin reappears, his words jumbled and disjointed. Back to the music, a different video, but still Taylor. Cohin. Taylor. Cohin. Taylor.

Blank.

'What was that all about?' Max says.

Thea's eyes are fixed on mine, and I know exactly what she is thinking.

Lewis.

I replay the music in my head, trying to identify the songs.

Max thumps the table. 'This is bullshit. I'm not sitting here waiting to be killed off one by one.'

Panic bleeds over Skye's face. 'We have to play the game. Tayo refused, that's why he…'

'So, we carry on?' says Thea. 'Find the Agent and then what? Kill them?'

Nobody answers.

'Great plan,' she says. My whole body flashes cold as I remember Tayo's last words. Is Thea the last remaining Agent?

'There must be something we can do?' Thea says. 'I would rather fight like Tayo than do what this psycho says.'

'Me too,' says Skye.

Max starts to pull his microphone over his head.

'No.' Skye's cry stops him. 'That's a rule break.'

Max leaves the mic round his neck, helplessness splattering his face.

I'm half listening, my head filled with Swift songs. There were three songs. Lewis is trying to send a message, hundred per cent. He must still be in the building. Thea's eyes are gleaming. I'm certain she's come to the same conclusion.

I just need to figure out the titles.

I make an excuse to go to the bathroom. Thea follows.

We cling to one another. Hidden in the cubicle, we talk quietly, our mics wrapped up in towels.

'You heard them too? Swift-isms?' Thea says.

I'm nodding way too much. '*End Game* and *The Other Side of the Door*.'

'Yes, yes,' Thea says. 'I didn't get the last one.'

'*Sweet Escape*,' I say. 'Although technically it doesn't work as it was a cover.'

Thea's smiling. Under the circumstances it's so not appropriate. 'What?'

'When you see Lewis, you tell him exactly that.'

'That's what he's trying to say.' I'm having a eureka moment. 'He's still here. He's waiting on the other side of the door.'

'Which one?'

'He'll be at the end of the camera-run. My sweet escape from earlier. It's the only way into the run from the studio and he can open it from his side.' Lewis wasn't even here when I got stuck in the run, but I have to believe in something. Thea watches while I cling onto imaginary straws. 'I'm sure of it.'

My desperate optimism must be catching, 'cause she full-on beams back.

We hug again. It's not a happy hug, but at least it's hopeful.

'I'm so sorry I got you into this.' Her voice is muffled against my shoulder. 'It's all my fault.'

I hold her tighter. 'Nobody forced me to play. I'm a big girl, I make my own decisions.' I pause. 'And I'm sorry about Noah, and not telling you. I was protecting you.'

'Doesn't matter,' Thea says.

I hold her at arm's length, my hands shaking on her shoulders. 'I know.'

She looks confused. 'Know what?'

My heart sinks. 'Tayo told me.'

Thea's face is the perfect picture of innocence. I press on, desperate to know the truth. 'I won't say a word, I swear. Just tell me the truth.'

Her hair swooshes madly around her shoulders. 'I've no idea what you're talking about. I…'

'You're the Agent.' My fingers grip her shoulders. 'It's okay. I won't say a…'

'Woah.' Thea pushes me away, clutching her mic, her eyes flying up towards the cameras. 'Why would you say that? Why would you even think that?' Her reaction throws me, and my conviction wavers. 'Tayo was wrong. I'm a Player.' Her face flushes corpse-white as she flicks her hair with her hand.

Am I wrong? Did I mishear Tayo's last words?

'You have to believe me.' Her voice rises. 'Saying that is a death sentence. Please.'

Her eyes dart up over the cubicle door as the familiar whirr of the camera fills the bathroom.

'Okay,' I say quickly.

Backing into the corner of the cubicle, Thea scrambles to cover her mic with her top, her fingers shaking. 'Shit.'

I've never seen Thea lose it, she's always so controlled. After a minute she dabs her fingers under her eyes and sticks out her chin defiantly. 'Do you think Lewis is okay?'

I go with the change of subject. 'After that I do.' I squeeze the microphone tighter in my sweaty palm conscious that this conversation could kill us. 'We're going to get out of this. I'm gonna find Lewis and get help.'

'I'm coming too,' she says.

'I'm taking Rhodri.' Her face falls and I quickly try to explain. 'Please don't think I'm putting boys before you, I'm not. He needs to do something. He's so wound up he's gonna piss Cohin off and I'm scared he'll end up like…'

'Tayo?' She finishes for me.

'Noah said he had a phone in the main gallery. That's behind the Courtroom somewhere.' I say, remembering back to the dry run. 'If I can get there, I can get help. I need you to hide us, pretend we are still in the house, so the cameras don't notice we're gone.'

'Showers,' she says. 'We can cover the doors with towels. It won't hold forever, but it gives you some time.'

'You're not the Agent?' I say. 'Swear? On our friendship?'

'I swear.' Thea half smiles, half frowns and flicks her hair. 'Be careful.' And she's gone.

I take noisy big breaths to calm my thudding heart and shake the betrayal now lodged in my chest.

Thea's denial was totally convincing, but the tell-tale flick of her purple-tipped hair and her nervous half-smile tell me everything I need to know.

Thea's the Agent.

And she lied right to my face.

27

'Which way?' Rhodri took very little persuading. His bloodshot eyes stare down the dark camera-run, wild but determined.

I point right. I'm regretting my decision, big time. But there's no going back, even if Lewis is not on *The Other Side of the Door*, we still need to try to get to the gallery and Noah's phone.

'Come on.' Rhodri pushes ahead. 'Can't be in the shower long, my new tats will scab.'

Our breathing's way too loud in the cold quiet. Rhodri low whistles, stopping at the crawl space.

'What's this?'

I grab him before he ducks down. 'This way.' Pulling him away, I take the lead.

'If this is the camera-run, where are the cameras?' Rhodri says as we grope our way in the dark. 'Or the crew?'

'Both excellent questions.'

'What the hell did we get ourselves into?'

We keep going in silence until we reach the door.

Pulling the handle towards me, my heart plummets. It's locked.

'What now?' Rhodri whispers.

My confidence shatters into a million pieces. What was I thinking? This isn't a happy-ever-after. There's no Prince

Charming on the other side waiting to sweep in and rescue me. Any rescuing is gonna have to be done by yours truly and a six-foot Welsh boy suffering from severe shock.

And I'm terrified.

I bang the cold metal with my clenched fists, each hit echoing through the run.

'Way to get the killer's attention.'

I fall against the door. As I'm about to drown in my despair, there's a faint knock. 'Lewis?'

He confirms with a tap. There's a grunt, and the door opens.

Standing in the doorway is my Lewis.

I breathe in his familiar Lewis smell as I crush him in a super bear hug.

'You're in danger of squeezing me to death,' Lewis says. 'Which, to be fair, wouldn't be the worst way to go, right now.'

'How?' I stammer. 'When?'

'I raced to yours and back pretty quick. Pippa announced over comms that the day crew were done. Everyone went home, but no night crew came. Didn't feel right, so I hid in your dressing room. When I tried to get out I couldn't, all the doors were locked. The "how", I kept my head down and prayed. I've prayed a lot, to every god I could think of and to Taylor.'

'As lovely as this reunion is, we've a serial killing lunatic after us and we're supposed to be in the shower,' Rhodri says. 'Need to hurry this along.'

'The shower?' says Lewis.

Before I answer, Rhodri grabs the lanyard hanging around Lewis' neck. 'He's got a bloody key.' He drops it, looking smug. 'I say we use it on the main doors and get everyone the fuck out of here.'

Lewis raises his hands in a slow, silent clap. 'I would never have thought of that.' Sarcasm drips from his words. 'Code's changed. It's useless. We are just as trapped out here as in there.'

'Why are you still wearing it then?' Rhodri hisses back.

I'm nervous of time. 'We need to get to the main gallery.'

'Follow me,' Lewis says. 'It's on the next level.'

I freeze. We are in his domain now; the killer could be anywhere.

Lewis takes my arm. 'It's safe. We have a small window of time. Trust me.' He leads us around the corner. I recognise the passageway. There's the sink in the corner, the yellow hazard tape covering the wires running over the floor like spaghetti. I recognise the rolls of cables, hanging doughnut-like on the walls. The claustrophobic feel of the runs is blown away by the hangar-like airiness of the studio. The stairs are in the corner. We tread softly to mask the tapping of our shoes on the hard metallic steps.

From the gangway the set looks ominous, a dark impenetrable prison.

Lewis ducks inside a door. I hold my breath, alert for any noise that signals danger. Hearing nothing, we follow him inside.

It's dark. A desk spans the entire width, five chairs set at it. Banks of monitors stacked one above the other fill the room with a kaleidoscope of light. Each monitor shows a different angle of the house. The bedrooms, kitchen, living area, garden. Different images flash in front of my eyes. I scan the rows until I find Thea, standing in the bathroom holding up a towel. My heart double-beats with love. She's been there this whole time, pretending I'm in the shower. Max is on another monitor, doing the same for Rhodri. It's working. With the towels and the steam why wouldn't you think someone's taking a shower? But we can't stay in there forever, we need to be quick.

'You're fine,' Lewis says. 'If he's not in here he can only see the main feed.' He points to a monitor labelled Main TX. It's showing the lounge area. 'He can only see this unless he changes the feed to the main TX, and to do that he needs to come in here and use this.' His arm sweeps across a huge board filled with coloured buttons and mixers.

'I can't see Skye,' I say, searching the monitors.

'There,' Rhodri points. 'She's in the Confessional.' He whistles. 'There must be at least twenty monitors in here.'

'Twenty-two,' says Lewis. 'I've been watching you, on and off, while hiding from Mr Bogeyman. He's in here a lot, mixing the images into one feed. That's what's been playing out on the monitors in the dressing rooms. I guess he's streaming his own sick reality show.'

'You've seen him?'

'Only from a distance, and in the dark – don't dare get too close. He watches and vision-mixes then moves between the galleries and the Confessional.'

'So, it's definitely a he?'

'I'd put money on it.'

'We thought it was Pippa,' Rhodri says.

'Definitely not Pippa. Forgot to mention. I found her,' Lewis pulls a face. 'Brace yourselves.' He moves away from the desk to reveal a body slumped in the shadows. I recognise the red bobbed hair. She's hidden in the corner chair, facing the monitors. Her arm's resting on the desk like she's watching the action and taking notes. It's only when you look closer you notice the weird angle of her head, the lack of a pen between her fingers … and the large syringe sticking out the back of her neck.

Her laptop's open. Lewis swipes the touchpad and the screen springs into life showing the *Lie or Die* page on YouTube. The *Lie or Die* logo's frozen on Friday's show.

'How long do you think she's been here?' Rhodri says, his jaw clenched tight.

'Found her Saturday morning.' Lewis presses his fingers under his eyes, looking up at the ceiling. 'Urghhh, I promised myself I wouldn't cry again.'

'What about Amara?' Rhodri says, ignoring Lewis' discomfort. 'Could she be working with him?'

'Also, dead.' Lewis points to the monitors. 'I watched. He put the shutter down so you couldn't see him take her out. There's a door in the bedroom, end corner.'

Rhodri leans over Pippa's body, staring into the laptop.

'Over one million hits. We've gone viral.'

'Everyone's asking for the next post,' I say, reading the messages.

'He stopped the playout.' Rhodri gestures to the top left monitor. The countdown clock's stopped ten seconds before the top. 'No one's watching.'

We fall silent as we process Rhodri's words. We're completely on our own. No one's coming for us.

'There was never going to be a playout,' I say, slowly. 'Noah planned to fake his own death. Pippa was in on it too. The show was supposed to stop after the first electrocution. Instead, the story about the real-time death of a reality show contestant should have flooded the media. It was going to be the death of Reality.'

'That's messed up,' Lewis says.

'But you saved him,' Rhodri says. 'So, Cali…'

'Somebody electrified the chair. Instead of faking it, Cali really died.'

Rhodri looks like he may puke. He turns into the shadows, hiding his face.

'Why is he doing this?' Lewis stutters.

'To stop Noah?' I say. 'Maybe he's a mad fan of reality television and didn't want it to end?'

'Why not just kill him?' Lewis says. 'Why play with us like this?'

I can't answer. I've no clue why this is happening. But something doesn't add up. 'It was Pippa in the Confessional. After Noah and Cali, I spoke to her. I'm sure of it. But she's been up here dead the whole time. How is that even possible?'

'That I do have the answer for.' Lewis' hands brush over another rainbow-coloured keyboard. 'This beauty can do anything,' he says. 'It's incredible. If you have a source sound or image it can replicate the voice pattern or manipulate the image to make anyone do or say anything. It can even bring them back from the dead. Saw a demo at BSC Expo. It uses the latest in audio and visual algorithm and AI technology. Think deepfake on another level.'

'Cohin,' I say.

Lewis looks over at Rhodri. 'Deepfake's a way of manipulating video and audio to make the subject do or say whatever you want. It's all-over social media, like Ariana Grande dancing around her house with Greta Thunberg, only they're not.'

'I know what deepfake is,' Rhodri growls. I catch his eye. He nods an *I'm fine* back, rubbing his eyes fiercely.

'You think it's Cameraman Jeff?' I ask. 'He was very bitter about the whole state of TV, and he would be out of work if Reality was cancelled. We all did those pieces to camera.'

Lewis shrugs. 'Maybe? I've never seen his face.'

'That explains our dead contestants talking,' Rhodri say. 'Whoever it is is manipulating the footage and literally putting words in our mouths.' Rhodri bangs the table in frustration. He turns on Lewis. 'You didn't think to ring for help? Or leave?'

'Actually, I did.' Lewis goes into full attitude mode. 'While you were all playing you're little TV games and jumping on podiums, I was trying to get a message to you. And yes, I did think about taking him out, for about a nanosecond because,' he sweeps his arm across his body, 'hello, me. And the phone lines are dead. And no. No way was I gonna leave my girls in there.'

'Your girls?' Rhodri snorts.

The tension of the last few days is metamorphosising into a testosterone-filled showdown.

'We don't have time for this,' I say.

'Where's your phone?' Rhodri says.

'Locked in the production office safe, and yes I tried to find the combination.'

'Noah's phone.' That gets their attention. 'It's in a bag in here.' There's no bag. I move Pippa's chair.

'Man, how did I not see that?' Lewis cries.

I grab the rucksack underneath the desk. 'To be fair, it was hidden by a corpse.'

'Look in the pocket,' Lewis says.

'Got it.'

'What's the password?' Lewis says.

'No idea,' I say. 'It has fingerprint ID.'

'We all know where his fingerprint is,' says Rhodri.

'That's not even funny,' Lewis snaps.

'I can call emergency numbers without it.' I press the phone screen and pray.

'Emergency services. Which service?'

'Police,' I say.

'Putting you through now.'

Holding the phone to my ear, I send a reassuring look to Rhodri and squeeze Lewis' hand. Help is coming. It's almost over.

28

'We can't stay here,' Lewis' eyes keep defaulting to the
door where Rhodri's keeping watch. 'He'll be back soon.'

I tuck the phone into my back pocket. The police are
coming.

'Come on,' Lewis shuffles me out of the gallery,
through a different door.

I hesitate. 'We should get back. We've been in the
shower way too long.'

'It doesn't matter,' Lewis says. 'Wherever he is, he's
not watching the house right now; your cover's safe.'

'Help is coming.' Rhodri's eyes dance with hope.
'We'll be out of here soon.'

I stop for my eyes to adjust to the sun's early morning
light. We're in a long corridor. Huge windows run the full
length of the passage. I'm looking out on Wembley, the
busy crossroad, the cafe where Noah and I met. It's early
and the roads are still empty and quiet. It looks like any
other normal day.

Tearing my eyes away from the teasing glimpse of
freedom, I follow the boys into a room at the end.

The room's smaller, with whirring machinery and
blinking lights. There're more monitors, all showing the
external perimeter of the studio.

'We can watch from here.' Lewis taps the monitor
showing the car park. 'We'll see them come in.'

Rhodri keeps the door ajar, and we all listen for the soft thudding of feet.

It takes four agonising minutes for the police to arrive.

'Guys,' Lewis says, as a police car pulls into view.

'One car?' Rhodri shouts. 'One bloody car?'

'Shhh,' Lewis whispers. 'That's all this view is giving us; there could be more.'

'Fuck this.' Rhodri pushes into the corridor. 'Give me your lanyard.'

'I told you, it doesn't work,' Lewis pulls it over his head.

Grabbing it, Rhodri runs to the door at the end. He pushes the lanyard onto the pad again and again, harder and harder but the door remains stubbornly closed. He throws his shoulder against the door with a thump.

'They're fire doors,' Lewis says. 'Too heavy. You won't open them.'

Rhodri presses himself against the window. 'I can see them. It's one car.' His fist thumps on the window.

'Rhodri, come back,' I loud-whisper.

One of the monitors shows the reception desk and the main entrance. Two officers are outside the glass doors. They try the door. It's locked.

'Break it down,' says Lewis. 'Break it down.'

A figure appears and unlocks the door. He's male, wearing a black hoodie, hood up. His back's to camera making him impossible to identify.

Lewis is fumbling with the sound on the monitor.

'Morning.' The figure sounds friendly. 'Bit early, haven't unlocked yet.'

'Is that him?' Rhodri says.

Lewis and I *shhh* him.

The hooded figure's holding the door open.

'Yesss,' says Rhodri.

'Come on,' says Lewis.

'Can't we go down there?' I say, desperate to leg it to the nice safe-looking police officers, screaming for help.

Lewis pulls a face. 'There are three doors between us and them and they're all locked. This is going to work; they just need to do their job.'

The officers are in reception. The sound quality's crap and we strain to hear. 'There's been a report of violence. Possible incident involving a fatality?'

The figure laughs. Even through the muffled monitor the sound makes me shudder.

'There have been many murders,' he says. 'This is a murder-mystery show. Look.' He points to something in the corner.

'Shit,' Lewis says. 'We forgot about the flatscreens that show the studio output. He's showing them the house, he's showing them how normal it is.'

'What about Tayo and Noah?'

'They're in the garden, they can't be seen,' says Lewis. 'The main feed's set on the lounge cameras.'

'And the guys are all acting normal as they're covering for us,' I say.

'Fuck,' says Rhodri.

'I need to change the main TX feed to the garden,' Lewis runs out of the room.

The officers stare at the monitors for an excruciating amount of time.

'Reality,' one officer says. 'Don't get it. My kids love it though.'

'Lewis, quick.' I run into the main gallery.

'I can't,' Lewis is hovering over the vision mix desk, completely frozen. 'There're so many buttons. What if I hit the wrong one?'

'They're leaving,' Rhodri shouts from the corridor. I run back to the security room to check the monitors and listen to their muffled voices.

'We used to get hundreds of prank calls in its heyday, usually fans trying to evacuate the place so they could see their latest fancy man. Thought the studio was closed though.'

'I believe we are the last show,' the figure says calmly.

'It's sad. There's a lot of history here,' the officer says. 'When did you say you were done?'

'Show raps tonight. You should watch, we're planning something really special,' the figure says, swiping a lanyard against the door pad. 'Set de-rigs overnight, then that's it for Central Studios.'

The officers make for the open doors.

'No,' cries Rhodri. 'No, no, no!'

The door slides shut behind them.

Rhodri rushes to the windows and pounds on the glass.

'Up here,' he shouts. 'We're up here.'

I join Rhodri at the window, all caution gone, as our chance of escape is about to drive away. I thump the glass over and over until my fists are red.

One officer stops. Shielding her eyes, she looks up at us.

'Yes,' I scream. *Why can't they hear us?* 'We're here, help us. Help.'

The officer climbs into the car.

'No.' Sobbing, Rhodri strikes the glass as he speaks. 'Fucking.' Thump. 'Sound-proofed.' Thump. 'Mirror glass.'

Lewis appears in the gallery doorway. 'I'm sorry, I panicked. I didn't want to show him the showers in case he realised you weren't there.'

'Where is he now?' I say, as panic projects me back into the security room. 'Is he coming?'

'Doesn't matter.' Rhodri sounds broken.

'Guys.' I can't believe what I'm seeing on the monitors. The hooded figure is stood in front of the camera in reception. Slowly taking down his hood, he lifts his chin, revealing his face. Raising his hands, he makes two tight fists. He holds them together then pulls them apart quickly, fingers splayed in the air like an explosion and mouths something into the camera.

My brain connects the face to the voice. And my body stiffens.

It's Henry.

29

'It's Henry?' Lewis' face drains of colour. Rhodri is the opposite, fire to Lewis' icy pallor. 'How did I not see it?'

'That bloke who sorted out the dressing rooms and shit? Why would he want to kill us? No way.' Rhodri jerks his head. 'He's an idiot.'

'What did he mouth to the camera?' Lewis asks.

'Looked like boob,' Rhodri says. 'Pervert.'

I can't stay still. My mind's trying to make sense of what my eyes saw. I need to see that everyone's safe inside the house.

'It would be a huge mistake to underestimate him right now,' Lewis says to Rhodri. 'He's killed five people.'

They follow me back into the main gallery. 'Six.' My eyes default to the body slumped in the corner. 'You forgot Pippa.'

'Shit, it's like a murder conveyor belt,' Rhodri says. He pulls himself up tall and puffs out his chest. 'I can take him.'

'You may think he's no threat, but he happily put a knife in Tayo's ribs,' Lewis says.

'Give me five minutes in a room with him.'

'Okay, while I am loving this masculine show of aggression, I don't think it's helping,' says Lewis.

'It's better than your plan, Mr *I hide in dressing rooms and listen to Taylor Swift.*'

'That's so out of order.'

'What's out of order is you not pressing the damn buttons.'

'Now it's my fault, is it?'

'Yes, it is your fault.'

'At least I'm not running around hitting everything and saying FUCK.'

'GUYS,' I say.

They stop.

'Look. Pippa's wearing a lanyard. Lanyards open doors. Maybe this one will work?'

Rhodri leans into Pippa. 'How did we not see this before?' I can't watch as he takes the lanyard from her neck.

'What is this?' He holds it up for us to read, his face riddled with confusion. My excitement vanishes. It's fake, someone has made a roughly drawn card and attached it to the ribbon. It shows a cartoon 'boom' above a black bomb.

'Bomb building for dummies.' Lewis reads the words scrawled underneath. 'Don't get it.'

I do, and the realisation terrifies me. 'There's a bomb in the house.'

Rhodri's confused. 'The one with the money? It's a prop. It's part of the game.'

'Like the poison and the sleeping potion?' I say. 'What if it's not. What if it's real?'

'What sleeping potion?' Rhodri says.

Shit, I forgot. I pull it out of my pocket. 'I found it on Tayo.'

'And when were you going to tell us?' Rhodri grabs it. I resent the insinuation.

'I just did, didn't I?' I catch a spark of mistrust flashing in his eyes. 'The night Noah disappeared I felt weird and passed out. What if someone was drugging us, just enough to make sure we slept?'

'Someone inside the house?' Lewis says.

'I don't know. Maybe? I'd just found Cali and I was freaking out, there was no way I would just go to bed and fall asleep. What if someone didn't want me to make a fuss? What if someone wanted to shut me up?'

'There's a lot of what-ifs in that statement, Nancy Drew,' Lewis says.

'Think about it. It would explain why we didn't hear anything the night Amara was killed. Xander was sleeping right next to her, and he didn't hear a thing. And we've all been getting headaches.'

Rhodri shakes his head. 'No way.'

'Trust no one. Noah told me that and then he...'

Rhodri crumples to the floor.

Lewis sits beside him.

We don't speak.

'Henry's messing with us,' Rhodri says. 'He knew we were coming up here. He could have easily overheard the conversation; he can see and hear everything remember?'

My mind is rerunning the conversation with the police. Something doesn't add up. 'Henry just told the police that the show finishes tonight.'

'So?' Rhodri says. 'Means nothing, no one's watching. It's not playing out.'

Lewis straightens as he comes to my realisation. 'He's moving the end up.'

'Dude, you're not making sense,' Rhodri says.

'The show was supposed to run for four nights and four days, that's what Isla the Director said.' The thoughts fly into my head at double speed. 'Of course, it didn't matter then as Noah was only planning one night and one day, but if the show was running in real time we wouldn't finish until Tuesday.'

'I have no idea what day it is right now,' says Rhodri.

'It's Monday,' Lewis says impatiently. 'Day Three.'

'Still not getting it,' Rhodri says.

'He said he was planning something special.' A new fear leaves me breathless. 'Guys, I think he's gonna do something big. Tonight.'

'Boom.' Lewis gasps. 'That's what he mimed, just now, like an exploding bomb.'

'Fuck,' shouts Rhodri. Lewis and I jump in panic. Rhodri's eyes gleam with frustration. 'Sorry.'

'We broke the rules.' I'm so close to losing it. 'He's angry. The last time we went against him…'

'Tayo…'

'You don't think he would set off a bomb?'

276

My eyes dart frantically from Lewis to Rhodri. 'We've been too long. We have to go back.'

'We don't have much time.' Lewis jumps up. 'Now would be a really good time for a plan.'

'We'll get the others and bring them up here, it's got to be safer than down near the bomb. We'll wedge something in the camera-run door so we can get back out.' I press my hands onto Lewis' chest. 'Watch Henry, make sure he doesn't catch on.'

'We have Noah's phone.' Rhodri stands. 'And his fingerprint.' He waits for us to catch up. When I do, I wish I hadn't. I gag at the thought of using Noah's dead hand.

'Shouldn't we just call the police again,' Lewis says.

'And say what? We told them, they came, they let Henry persuade them it was a prank call and they left. We don't have time to convince them.' He shakes the phone in Lewis' face. 'If the police won't help, we can try others.' Rhodri leaves the gallery. 'Quick.'

I follow Rhodri, my mind helicoptering.

'Watch Henry,' I say to Lewis as I follow Rhodri. 'But please be careful.'

'Careful is my middle name,' Lewis smiles sadly. 'Tell Thea…'

'I'll tell her you'll see her soon.'

Lewis nods.

'Be safe,' I say. 'Love you.'

'Love you too, hun. Hey,' Lewis says. I stop halfway down the metal stairs. '*Forever and Always.*'

277

Before I have time to say one back, he pushes the gallery door shut and disappears.

I run down the stairs. Rhodri's grabbed the large brush by the sink and wedged it in the door. Having had a taste of freedom my mind and body mutiny. My flight response has ramped up and every step back into the camera-run is a battle against my brain.

But I won't leave Thea. We've only made the situation in the house worse. We need to get them out.

'Crap.' Rhodri stops, patting his pockets. 'The phone. I don't have it.'

Pulling it out of my pocket, I hold it up. I understand how he's feeling, there's so much panicked adrenaline surging through my veins right now it's like I'm turbo-charged.

I reach for his arm and look straight into his eyes. 'Don't stress,' I say as calmly as I can. He puts his hand over mine, his green eyes darkening as a thin smile brushes his lips.

'Thanks.'

His response makes me flustered. Letting go of his hand, I push past him, willing myself back to Thea. I don't see the camera track stacked against the wall and hit it straight on. My body thumps against metal, knocking it over in one almighty crash. Metal screams as it hits metal and bounces along the floor.

We freeze, statue-still, my pulse racing. Rhodri's eyes flash wildly in the dark. One of us has to move.

I step forwards, avoiding the tracks now scattered all over the ground.

Rhodri startles, looking behind us. 'The door,' he whispers and before I can stop him, he's running back up the run. I follow him. The door out of the run is shut tight. Rhodri's leaning against it, his head bent forward on the shiny surface, shoulders slumped.

'Lewis,' I say. 'He's watching. If Henry closed the door, Lewis will open it. Just wait. He'll be fine.' I can't stop the shudder sprinting down my back.

Rhodri's not convinced. Even in the dark I can feel his despair. 'What if it wasn't Henry?'

'You think it's someone in the house? How? They would have to come past us.'

'You think the storeroom is the only door into here? There could be loads of secret doors.'

He's right, but I don't want to believe it could be one of us. 'No way, Lewis will come,' I say, stubbornly sliding my body to the floor. He has to come. Without him there's no way out.

We wait.

The runs are cold, but my shivers are from more than the chill.

Still Lewis doesn't come.

'Do you really think there's a bomb?'

Rhodri make a strange half-laugh noise. 'Who knows?

This bastard's a fruit loop and you can't second guess a madman. We should go…'

'Just wait.' I grit my teeth and wait. *Please let Lewis be okay, please let Lewis be okay.*

Rhodri kneels in front of me, his words gently persuading. 'Lewis would want us to stick to the plan. Maybe he's stuck somewhere and can't get away without Henry seeing him. If we don't move, he's gonna think something happened to us. Let's get back inside. Lewis will see us on the cameras.' Jumping up, he holds his hand out. He's right, we have to get back to the others. Taking his hand, I let him pull me to my feet, his grip reassuringly strong. His eyes flash angrily.

'He's not going to win.' He strides down the run, pulling me along. I've no idea what his plan is but moving is better than sitting and hope is way better than despair. 'We are getting out of here alive. This ain't my day to die.'

30

'Where the hell have you been?' Thea runs up as soon as we walk back through the storeroom door. 'You were ages.'

Max and Skye appear from the bedrooms.

'It's Henry, Pippa's assistant. He's doing this,' I blurt out as soon as I see them and watch as fear and confusion quickly replace relief.

'No way,' Max shouts and rants, throwing his hands in the air he paces the living room. 'I don't believe it. Henry? Why? Why would he?' Rhodri takes his arm and pulls him to one side, talking to him calmly.

Skye and Thea stay quiet as they take it in. Skye covers her microphone and leans in. I smother my mic in my palm.

She whispers, 'Did you do it? Did you get help?'

I shake my head. Thea's small intake of breath speaks volumes.

Skye's face is full of questions. She opens her mouth again but is silenced by Cohin.

'All contestants to assemble at the table.' His voice is hard. 'Immediately.'

There's no time to explain.

'Lewis?' Thea mouths without Skye seeing.

I shrug a helpless *don't know* and her hand flies to her mouth to smother the cry. Skye's by her side, blinking rapidly.

'Angry tears.' She flaps her hands in front of her eyes. 'So unbelievably scared.'

'What's this?' Rhodri's staring at the clocks while he guides a slightly calmer Max to the table. Both the Accusation and the Kill Clock are counting down together.

'They started at a hundred,' Max says as he sits, rubbing his eyes furiously. 'No clue why. It's freaking me out.'

'Guys.' Skye beckons us to sit.

Rhodri hesitates, his eyes wandering to the window. I get it, he's gonna try to get Noah's fingerprint. But how, with cameras watching our every move?

I sit between Thea and Skye, my back to the garden. It doesn't work, Noah and Tayo are in my head, upfront and centre stage, whether I'm looking at them or not. Rhodri wavers. He changes his mind and sits.

The ghosts of our dead housemates haunt the empty spaces round the table, cementing our fear, a constant reminder of our fate.

'Congratulations. You have survived to the final day of *Lie or Die*,' Cohin says.

'No,' Max cries, his voice echoing the panic in his face. 'That's not right, we have one more night and one more day. Four nights and four days, that's the game. This is Day Three.' His terrified eyes sweep over us all, pleading. 'We have more time.'

Rhodri puts a comforting hand on his shoulder.

Max turns to him. 'He can't do that; we have more time. He can't do that.'

Rhodri's jaw's so tight, the tendons in his cheek are pulsing.

'You've had your fun, now let us go,' Skye says to the hologram.

Cohin chuckles. It's not a funny sound. 'The game will end when the Players have uncovered the identity of the last Agent.'

Rhodri jumps up, knocking his chair flying. 'I'm not killing anyone. You can't make me. You can kill me, but you can't make me.'

Cohin seems to grow bigger. 'Sit. Down.'

'Rhodri, please,' Skye says.

'Sit down, mate, you're gonna get yourself killed.' Max's head is buried in his hands. 'Just don't.'

Rhodri stays standing, fists clenched. With a small cry of frustration, he picks up his chair. Banging it down on the floor with a crash, he sits.

Cohin morphs into Tayo. We all look away.

'Players. The game has changed.'

The clocks have reached sixty minutes and have stopped.

Tayo morphs back to Cohin. 'You have one hour to accuse *and* convict the last remaining Agent. If you are unsuccessful in this task, all remaining contestants will be eliminated.'

A horrified intake of breath explodes around the table.

A metallic clicking starts, like a speedy robotic heartbeat.

The glass area containing the money and the cartoon bomb lights up.

Cohin speaks again. 'The bomb is now active and will detonate when the clocks reach zero.'

Fifty-nine minutes and counting down.

'The bomb can only be disarmed with the Agent's code. Failure to disarm will lead to immediate termination.' Cohin's hooded head turns as if he's talking to us all. 'If Players successfully reveal the Agent and stop the bomb, the prize money will be theirs and they will be free. If the remaining Agent survives, all remaining contestants will be terminated. Kill the Agent and live, or all die together. The choice is yours.'

'He's bluffing,' Skye says. 'He's hardly gonna blow up the entire place.'

'He's not bluffing,' I say and Skye's eyes widen. 'We were coming back to get you out.'

'Well, let's go,' Thea cries, her eyes wild with panic. I grab her hand under the table.

My eyes are filling with hot tears. 'We can't, the door's locked again. We can't get out.'

Thea's hand is shaking in mine. I squeeze it hard and don't let go; there's no way I'm gonna let anything happen to her. Stick together no matter what, that was our plan.

'May the best contestant win.' Cohin disappears.

Nobody moves.

Our horrified eyes flick madly around the table, searching for answers. *I can't think. There's not enough time.*

Rhodri pushes his chair back with a loud screech. 'We're not doing this,' he says. 'We're not playing your sick game.'

He picks up his chair, for a minute it looks like he's gonna smash it through the window. Instead, he opens the garden door, wedging it open with the chair.

'Come here,' he says to Max. 'MAX.' Max shuffles reluctantly from his chair. 'Sit on this and whatever happens do not move.'

Max sits. The rest of us stand, watching. He doesn't speak but I get it. He's gonna use the chair to stop the shutters, giving him time to get back inside. Rhodri turns to me; his eyes filled with trust and holds out his hand.

Noah's phone is tucked in my pocket. Taking her hand from mine, Thea wipes her eyes. Looking at me, she nods. I lift my lips into what I hope is a reassuring smile. Standing, I take Rhodri's hand and let him lead me into the garden.

'Guys?'

I can't answer Max as I walk past, all my focus is on not throwing up as I get closer to Noah's body.

'Guys?'

'They have Noah's phone,' Thea says, sharp as always. 'Reckon they're gonna unlock it.'

'How?' Max says, his voice heavy with doubt. 'They need his password, or his fingerprint and they haven't…' He goes quiet.

The warm summer sun kisses my skin but does nothing to warm the chill that's shivering through my bones. I can't look at Noah, so I focus on the dove on his wrist. The phone screen lights up in my hand and double beeps a warning.

Shit.

The battery's low. I didn't even think to look. I should have turned off the screen after I used it. Panicking, I hold the phone out to Rhodri. 'Ten per cent.'

He clenches his jaw. 'Best get on with it then.'

I stare at the fingerprint shape on the screen. I can do this. Holding my breath, I pull the Agent card from Noah's fingers and take hold of his hand. It's cold and clammy and stiff.

'I don't know which finger,' I say.

Crowd noise pumps through the speakers. A metallic groan is followed by a whirring as the window shutters start to fall. I drop Noah's hand. I can't do this.

Rhodri grabs Noah's wrist, pressing his thumb on the screen.

'Start with the thumb, it's always the thumb.' Ignoring the shutters, he keeps going, pressing the stiffening thumb onto the keypad, waiting for the phone to unlock.

Bile stings the back of my throat, but I stand my ground. It doesn't work. With an impatient tut, he drops Noah's wrist and grabs his finger, his face screwed up with concentration.

'Uh guys?' Max crouches as the shutters hit the chair. They groan and grind against the high plastic back. Max beckons us back inside. 'This chair won't hold for long.'

Dropping Noah's hand, Rhodri holds the phone in the air in triumph. We all cheer. 'Shit, no signal.'

Rhodri jogs around the garden holding the phone high in the air looking for a signal.

'Go,' he says to me.

I dart back inside, bending under the chair as it strains against the weight of the shutters. One of the chair legs snaps with a shattering crack, followed by another and shards of plastic hit my legs. The chair crumbles and the shutters continue their descent.

'Rhodri,' I shout.

As Rhodri turns, his eyes fall on Tayo, his dead body covered by the duvet. He stops, staring at the camera-run door, his intent way too obvious.

'Don't, there isn't time.' I bend low under the descending shutter. Rhodri turns his back to the window and walks to Tayo. I scream. 'Rhodri.'

'What's he doing?' Thea asks. We're on our knees, cheek to floor as the shutter almost reaches the ground.

'Stop the shutters,' Skye cries, trying to hold them up.

Max tries to help. 'It's no good. Look.' Rhodri's pulling the duvet off Tayo. Leaning over his body he pulls the knife out of his back.

'He's gonna fight Henry.' I pound on the shutters to get his attention. 'Rhodri, NO.'

Rhodri turns towards the window. As the shutters fall into place, I catch one last glimpse of him standing next to Tayo, his face determined, a bloody knife in his hand.

31

'No, no, no.' Thea's banging the shutters. We try to lift them, but they're too heavy. Rhodri's shut outside. I'm pretty sure he's gonna fight Henry to try and put an end to all this.

'Can he do it?' Skye says. 'Can Rhodri beat Henry?'

Thea shakes her head. 'Henry knows he's coming. He'll be prepared. Rhodri's got no chance.'

'We don't know that.' I pace up and down, willing the shutters open. 'What we don't need right now is more panic.'

Skye flushes pink. 'I'm not panicking.'

Max has his ear glued to the shutter. 'I can't hear anything.'

'That's good right?' Thea says. 'We would hear them fighting.'

'Or Rhodri's dead,' Skye says unhelpfully.

There's nothing we can do but wait. The bomb sits on top of the pile of money, backlit and TV-shiny. The clocks count down, the minutes running by at what seems like double speed, while the clicking of the time bomb fills the terrifying silence.

Finally, the shutters groan and shake and rise. Scrambling to the window, our hands curl under them, pushing them up.

Rhodri's sat on the grass, the knife by his side glinting

in the midday sun. There's no sign of Henry. My eyes run frantically over Rhodri's body, looking for the tell-tale signs of blood. There're none. As soon as the shutter is high enough, I squeeze out into the garden.

'It's dead,' he says quietly. I hear *he* instead of *it* and hope that Henry has come to a fatal end, and it's over. Hope flickers for the briefest instant before I see the phone cradled in his hands.

He stands. Lifting his arm, he lets out a brutal scream and launches the phone against the wall. It shatters against the hard surface. Rubbing his face with his arm he walks back into the house, still clutching the knife. We all follow behind him, a sombre procession of despair.

Rhodri throws the knife onto the table, where it sits, stained with Tayo's blood. No one speaks.

There's nothing left to say.

The clicking of the time bomb gets louder.

And the clock counts down.

Skye's watching the bomb. 'What are we going to do?'

No one answers.

'We're running out of time,' Skye says.

Rhodri's head snaps up. 'What are you saying?'

'I'm not saying anything, but that clock's ticking down and I don't want to die.' Skye's voice is one big wobble.

We stand in an awkward circle.

'I'm not accusing anyone,' Skye says eventually.

'Then you will die.' All eyes snap to Max. 'You heard him. If we don't do this, we all die. If we choose someone…'

'To die… For real,' Thea says. 'Say it.'

Max takes a huge breath. 'The rest of us have a chance to live.'

Squirming under our mutually disgusted gaze, his face darkens.

He points out the window at Tayo and Noah. 'If we don't, we all die. If we want to live, the Agent must die.'

'Max is right,' Skye says. 'We have no choice but to do what he wants.'

'Unless one of us is already doing what he wants,' Rhodri says, quietly.

'You think one if us is in on it?' Skye asks.

'Why not?' Rhodri says. 'Makes sense. Who says it wasn't one of us that killed Amara?'

'No,' says Max. 'I don't believe that.' He tugs on his T-shirt, pulling it down across his bum, his tell-tale tic.

Rhodri's face flashes angry. 'Someone was in the run with us, someone closed the door.'

Thea's face flashes guilty red. 'I was in the bathroom with Skye, holding up the towel.' She points at Max. 'He was on his own.'

'I was in the boys' bathroom the entire time,' Max cries.

Skye's eyes grow wide. 'How do we know? You had plenty of time to slip out.'

'Yes, but I didn't,' Max splutters.

'Henry's been one step ahead of us at every turn,' Rhodri says.

'Maybe 'cause he can see and hear everything?' Max says.

Rhodri turns on him. 'You've managed to stay completely under the radar this whole time. Not one nomination. Why is that?'

'Dude, you were the one who went all Rambo and broke the phone, our only chance of getting out of here.'

And you were the one who said the door in the run was closed. I didn't hear it shut. You got there before me, you could easily have pushed that broom out of the way. For all I know you could be working with Henry. I think but don't say. *I am putting a lot of trust in you, Rhodri from Wales.*

Rhodri's right up in Max's face. 'You made the pyramid fall. You ran inside before Skye could get over the wall.'

'I'm a coward, not a killer,' Max says, taking a step back.

'Prove it,' Rhodri says.

'This isn't helping,' Skye says. Rhodri turns on her.

'What really happened when you were outside with Tayo?'

Skye's eyes flash with hurt. 'You think I killed Tayo? I told you what happened.'

'But you weren't with Thea,' I say as my brain catches up. 'We were watching from the gallery. Thea was the only one holding up the towel in the bathroom.'

Skye's face is calm. 'I'm not lying. I was by the door. Maybe the cameras didn't see me?'

'But you went out,' Thea speaks quietly. 'I remember, you left for a while.'

Skye rolls her eyes. 'I'm so sorry. I did. I went to the Confessional. I thought I could help, maybe talk to them. It didn't work.'

'She's right, we saw her.' Rhodri looks at me. 'Remember?'

Skye spins round to me. 'Kass is the one who's always creeping around in the night. She's the only one that saw Cali *and* she found Amara in bed.'

'That was Xander,' I say. This is getting out of hand. 'Guys, please.'

'We have to find the Agent,' Max says. 'Is it you?' He pounces on Thea. 'You were on podium nine.' He points a shaking finger at her. 'Most deceitful. That was you. And you were very quick to second Cali's accusation.'

'Noah was on nine.' I correct him.

'Just then, when we were talking about the Agent, you were really quiet.' He points his finger at me. 'And you had that card, the one that saved Noah. Xander said it was you, he thought you were the Agent.'

'Because Xander *was* the Agent,' Rhodri says. 'Why would he take out one of his own?'

'Because he wanted the money,' Max shouts. 'And now we are all going to die.'

'Enough!' Thea covers her ears.

We all take a breath, spreading out to different corners of the room, processing Max's words. Nothing he said was untrue.

We all look guilty.

The clock counts down mercilessly. We eye each other with suspicion as paranoia and fear take hold.

'Pick me,' Rhodri says quietly.

'No.' Thea's eyes are fierce. 'No one is sacrificing themselves.'

'Why not?' Max says. 'If he wants to then who are we to stop him.'

'Do you realise what you're saying?' Thea says.

'He could be the Agent,' Max shouts.

'Stop it,' Skye cries.

Max backs off.

'I don't think Henry would allow it,' I say, trying to calm everyone down.

Rhodri tries to speak again.

'Don't.' Skye puts her hands on his arm. 'Tayo wouldn't want you to throw yourself under the bus.'

'But I screwed up, I thought I could fight Henry. I wasted time and let the phone battery drain down.' Walking away from Skye, Rhodri stands with his back to us. 'Accuse me already.'

'It was Kass who had it in her pocket,' Skye says. 'She didn't even notice it had low battery.'

'I…' before I get a chance to defend myself an image flickers on the table. Thea gasps. Everyone turns to the table.

It's me, or rather my audition tape. I'm smiling at the camera. Pippa's voice is heard off camera.

If you had to choose between betraying a friend on television or losing the game, which would you do?

I love Mafia, and I am ruthless. I would be fantastic on your show.

This is not how it happened.

Pippa speaks again. *In your application you say, and I quote, 'I screwed over my best friend for a boy I liked even though she had only just finished with him.'*

'Brutal.' Max walks right up to the table. 'Girl Next Door is a bi-atch. Who knew?'

'I was just messing.' The frenzied panic in my voice is making me sound guilty.

All eyes are on me.

'It wasn't like that,' I say. 'It's been edited.'

Thea turns away.

The image flickers as the recording plays again. Pippa's voice plays over my smiling face.

So, Kass, how far would you go to win?

All the way. Who needs friends when you have money and fame?

The room goes quiet.

'We should at least let her explain,' says Skye turning to me. 'Did you say this? Are these your words?'

'No. Yes.' It's hard to think straight when panic's stolen all my thoughts. 'I said them, but not like that.' My cheeks are burning a guilty red as I search their faces for allies.

'Wow.' Rhodri eyes glint with betrayal as he stares directly at me. 'I mean. Wow.'

It sounds bad. *I* sound bad. No one will look at me. And who can blame them. I've totally screwed everything up. Why don't I ever think? I send Thea a silent *help me*, but her face is hidden behind her hair.

'Oh, come on,' I shout at her.

Thea looks up, her face passive, and moves closer to Skye. It's as though she doesn't even know me.

Thea? I silent scream for her help, but she's terrified.

'I… I…' The clip looks way worse than it ever was and makes me look way worse than I ever could be. But the people round this table don't know me well enough to know the difference and with no other reasons to nominate, I'm in trouble.

'Guys.' Max gestures to the countdown clock. 'We are running out of time.'

'It was a joke.' I try to catch Rhodri's eye. 'I was joking. I didn't know it would be used. It was before…'

'I nominate Kass,' Max says.

'Max, no … I'm…' I cry out, desperately trying to form words in my defence.

'Seconded,' Skye says.

It's like a full-on sucker punch. The room's spinning. I grab the table for support as I try to steady my breathing.

There's no time to recover before the images move again. This time it's me and Thea in the bathroom.

Remember the plan: lie, lie, lie, stick together and pick them off one by one, I say.

Watch everyone, Thea says. *I proper don't trust Amara and Xander or Max.*

The video shows Thea getting into bed and me creeping out of the bathroom a few minutes later.

'Way to turn the room against you.' Max's face is one big picture of hurt.

Thea's cheeks have drained of colour.

'That's not right, that's not what we said,' I say quickly.

'But the words are coming out of your mouths?' Rhodri's voice is heavy.

'Yes, but…'

'You can't blame the deepfake if you said the words.' The hurt in his voice is knife-like and just as sharp.

Music plays loudly into the house. It's that Beatles song, *With a Little Help from my Friends*.

An image appears. It's the picture of the three of us Thea took in the toilet, right before we came into the house.

Thea's head snaps in my direction, her cheeks flushed angrily.

'How could you?'

'What?'

'That picture was taken on *your* phone, you showed them.'

'No … showed who?' I stammer, floored from the force of her words. 'I didn't show anyone anything.'

'Did you trade?' She spits the words at me. 'The picture for an advantage? Is that how you got that Necromancer card? The card you used to save some boy you'd just met?'

She's got this all wrong. 'No way,' I say. 'I would never betray you.'

'I've heard that before,' she spits.

'Thea, please, you have to trust me,' I plead. 'They must have hacked my phone. Why would I? I'm in the picture too. Why would I incriminate myself?'

Thea sits slowly, uncertainty sweeping across her face. But not before I see the mistrust in her eyes. The old guilt comes tumbling out as that one JB kiss comes back to bite me on the arse again.

Skye's lovely face is screwed up in confusion. 'You two are friends? Like on the outside?' Confusion turns to betrayal. 'You *lied* to us?'

Thea shrinks into her chair. 'We thought you would vote us out if you knew.'

'Ya think?' says Skye, betrayal turns to anger. 'You had a huge game advantage and didn't think to tell? That's cheating.'

Rhodri turns away from the table.

'No.' Thea shakes her head, her hair flying round her face. 'Pippa knew. Someone left and Kass came in last minute.'

'We… It wasn't planned. We didn't know,' I splutter.

'But you kept lying to us, even after everything. We've all made mistakes and we all look guilty, but that was a deliberate decision.' Skye's eyes turn hard. 'We don't know you at all. How can we trust anything you say?'

'The public were right, you are the most deceitful,' Max says.

'Oh my god, were you both trying to set me up just now?' Skye asks, clinging onto Rhodri's arm.

'I nominate Thea,' Rhodri says quietly.

Thea's eyes flit from the clock to us and back again.

'Seconded.'

My eyes search the face of the seconder and see only sadness in Skye's eyes.

Thea cries out in despair.

The clicking of the time bomb increases, louder and louder, metal on metal.

Rhodri bangs his fist against the glass wall with an anguished thump.

My mind is screaming for me to save us, but I can't think over the noise.

I'm too late.

It's done.

32

I get it. I'm a crap friend. I violated every friendship code with my lying and scheming. I lied to the house about not knowing Thea. I lied to Thea about my status as the Necromancer. I wasted my advantage on a boy I'd just met. I kept quiet when I knew something was wrong. But most of all it was my words and actions that helped get Thea nominated. I should have deleted that photo. I should have kept my big mouth shut.

And I'm not even an Agent.

The rapid clicking of the time bomb fills the Courtroom, never letting us forget that we are running out of time.

Max is behind the lectern. He's talking quickly, every word sticking in his throat as he condemns me to death in one terrified rush. I want to tell him it's okay, that I don't blame him for nominating me, but my thoughts are getting lost in all the terror.

Thea's in the other dock, face hidden behind her hair.

'She's the Agent.' Max stares down at his shaking hands. 'Maybe more, maybe she's working with you,' he shrugs. 'I don't know. She lied to us. And she had the phone,' Max says. 'Maybe she wasted the battery on purpose. I don't know. That was our chance to get out...' His voice breaks. He looks at me with frantic eyes. 'I don't know.' I send him as much reassurance as I can. Wiping his face, he turns to the cameras. 'Happy now?'

Cohin's between us. A spindly finger points at me. My terror doubles.

'Do you have anything to say in your defence?'

Through the pain and the fear, a rage sparks. Like I'm gonna give Henry the satisfaction of begging for my life. The remaining Players stand on the bench. Three days ago, I was in this exact same spot, looking at a group of strangers, quick to envy and even quicker to judge. Now I'm lucky to call them my friends.

What can I say? If I can find the words to save myself, I condemn Thea. How could I ever let that happen? She could be more and do more than I ever could. She's not like me. My best friend's one of the shiny people. She has everything she needs to live that celebrity life she wants so bad. Ever since I can remember, she's had my back, and now it's time for me to have hers. I get it now; I get how much I hurt her. I remember what Tayo whispered as he died, and I know what I have to do.

Whatever I say, one of us will die today. And I won't let that be Thea.

Max's words give me an idea. Henry doesn't care who the Agent is, he just wants to see us play his deadly game. If I can persuade them that I'm guilty, then maybe he will let them go. It's a long shot, but I have to try.

'It's true.' I stand straight. 'Everything Max said is true.

I've been lying to all of you all along.' *Here goes.* 'I'm the Agent.'

'Kass, no,' Thea cries. I ignore her.

I talk quickly, eager to get it all out before I lose my nerve. There is only one way to end this, with the death of the Agent. I can only hope this will satisfy Henry's bloodlust.

'You were right,' I say to Rhodri. 'I knew you were watching me in the biscuit task, so I double bluffed. I played you all. I put the poison and the biscuits in Noah's chair to frame him. Cali suspected, so I used the Necromancer card, not to save Noah but to eliminate her.' Rhodri's shaking his head manically. 'Then everything got bad, and I didn't want to play.' The look of scepticism passes from face to face; they're not buying it. The words tumble out of my mouth, so quickly I struggle to keep up. Desperation replaces thought as I race to save my friend. 'I've been talking to Henry in the Confessional. He told me to leave the phone on, and I did. I knew it would drain the battery. He said if I betrayed you all, I would live.'

A shocked gasp fills the room. I can't look at them. The hurt on Rhodri's face almost stops my lie. Instead, I focus on the back wall. I stick my chin out, channelling strong and defiant. 'I betrayed you all and I betrayed my best friend. I got carried away with all the glitz and the glamour. I wanted to be one of the beautiful people so badly I forgot who I was. I'm not one of you; I shouldn't even be here. I'm just the ordinary girl next door. I only got to play because someone was ill and there was no one else. I'm a fake. You need to vote for me.' I turn to Thea and mouth, 'I love you.'

Thea's expression of shock and love takes my breath away. I sit before my legs give way, gripping the bars of the dock.

The silence in the Courtroom is thick.

And still the clicking of the bomb, counting down...

Rhodri walks behind the central lectern. Placing his hands on Max's shoulders, he gently moves him out of his way. Max returns to the bench, next to Skye. They're all on the bottom now. The back row is empty.

Rhodri lifts his head, his eyes jet black with rage.

'You may begin your accusation.'

Rhodri stares at Cohin, his face set.

Cohin speaks again. 'Failure to give a reason for an accusation will be considered a rule break and all contestants will be punished.'

Rhodri still doesn't speak.

'Rhodri.' I force him to look at me. 'It's okay.'

His hands grip the lectern even tighter, knuckles white. His gaze moves to Thea, eyes pleading. She nods.

'Thea lied to us and pretended she didn't know Kass when they were friends on the outside. So, we can't trust her and that's my reason to nominate her.'

Rhodri takes a haggard, painful breath.

'That's all you're getting, you sick freak.'

I'm surprisingly calm, considering. I'm so tired of being terrified that now I know my fate, I'm okay. Thea deserves this much more than me. They will vote for me, they have to. They have way more on me than Thea. My best friend will be safe, and my friends will live.

It's almost over.

Thea doesn't wait for Cohin. She speaks directly to the bench, her voice strong. 'Kass is trying to protect me and save you. I think we can all agree that she's a crap liar.' She smiles at her joke, but nobody laughs.

Shit, this is not how it's supposed to happen.

'I'm the Agent. I kept quiet because I was scared. I'm also a coward.' She turns to me. 'I wasn't brave enough to do the right thing, but I am now. I won't let you take the fall for me.'

I jump up. 'It's not true. She's lying. You saw the clips, it was me, it was my plan.'

Cohin turns to me. 'Sit down.'

Thea turns back to the bench. 'Tayo was the Detective. He caught me coming out of the Confessional on Night Two. He knew what I was, and he told Kass before he died. He totally backed Kass as a Player too, right before Rhodri nominated Xander. It was Xander's idea to card Cali. She saw him. She told you, but you were all so caught up with Noah and the Necromancer save, that you forgot. Think about it. Kass couldn't have been an Agent and the Necromancer, that doesn't make sense. She's pretending to be an Agent and if you get it wrong, Henry will kill us all.'

She's totally destroying my argument.

'Kass is loyal to the core. She would never work with

303

Henry and betray you. She's lying to protect me. You can trust her.' Thea turns to me, her eyes full of love. 'I know I do.'

'Don't.' My cries sound helpless as my one chance to save my best friend disintegrates to dust. 'Please.'

'Accused number one.' Cohin warns me. 'Sit down.'

'You underestimate yourself, Kass Kennedy, you always have done. I'm a bitch. It's in my DNA. But you? You are headstrong and brave and loyal and clever. You got all the smarts for both of us. I was never massively pissed off with you about the boy thing. I was jealous, so I made you feel bad so you would come with me and do this. See? I'm selfish and manipulative and a bitch.'

The clicking is louder, forcing us on.

She turns back to the bench. 'I was wrong. It's what you do when no one's watching that counts.' She points to me. 'She gets that. Everything she's done in this house has been for the team. She's proved how strong she is when the cameras *aren't* recording. She's one hundred per cent real. Don't you dare fail her now. This is the only way. I am not lying. I am the Agent. Kill me and the game is over. Kill me and you will live.'

Thea stays strong, her voice steady as she gives them permission to send her to her death. 'Let me do this for my best friend.'

The lights dim. I'm standing in a pool of bright light.

Cohin lifts his head. 'It is time to vote. Remember, this is the last chance to find the Agent.'

The wait is brutal. My heart's thumping so loudly in my chest it's gonna break my ribs.

'The votes have been cast and counted.' Cohin's voice booms beside me. I can't breathe. 'Thea Anne-Marie Holland you have been found guilty of the murder of Tayo Asaju and have been condemned to death.'

NO!

I grab the bars as my legs buckle beneath me.

The room falls deathly silent.

Thea walks from the dock to the electric chair.

Standing in front of the chair she turns to face me, eyes set determined, mouth curved upwards in a sad smile, the black hood clutched in her hand. 'This is my choice.'

She steps up onto the chair and sits, never taking her eyes off me. Her smile breaks my heart.

'Have a full life. Live the shit out of it. For both of us. Look after Lewis. He's gonna need you.' She pauses. 'Strong like mountains.'

'Strong like steel,' I say. 'Always.'

'I love you.' She puts the hood over her head.

The tears waterfall down my cheeks. 'I love you more.'

The lights turn to black. One solo spot over her chair. I break out of the dock and run towards her. Strong arms pull me away, holding me tight. I can't watch. I bury my head in Rhodri's chest as the buzzing starts. Thea makes no sound. The buzzing rises to its horrific crescendo.

Louder.

Louder.

The sound of the trapdoor.
Silence.
A single gunshot shatters the quiet.
Reality dances a slow-motion waltz.
Pain explodes like fireworks.
Arms hold me tighter.
I scream so fierce, it will tear me in two.
It's done. It's over.
She's gone.

33

They carry me back to the house. A panicked frenzy surrounds me, but I don't care, I'm completely numb. Let the bomb go off, what does it matter?

She's gone.

'Three minutes,' cries Max.

The metallic clicking of the bomb is getting louder and quicker.

'Where is it?' Rhodri is shouting. 'Where's the code?'

They all search wildly. She was the Agent so the code should be here. That was the deal.

That's what she died for.

The countdown hits sixty seconds.

'I've got it.' Skye runs in from the Confessional. She's waving a card with a four-digit number. She passes it to Rhodri, who's already inputting the numbers from Xander's Agent card, spinning the numbers on the dial too quickly in his panic.

'Twenty-nine... Twenty-eight... Twenty-seven...' Cohin counts down the final seconds making Rhodri's hands shake even more.

'Steady.' Max hovers by his side.

'Eighteen... Seventeen...'

Rhodri punches in the last number and steps back. Everyone waits, holding a collective breath, staring at the bomb through the glass.

'Ten… Nine… Eight… Seven…'

Cohin stops. The metallic clicking stops. There's one last tick as the numbers on the wall stop counting down. Rhodri drops to the floor with a relieved cry.

A loud hissing replaces the clicking.

'Look.' Skye's pointing at the bomb. The string is fizzing and spitting like a sparkler, burning quickly towards the big round bomb.

Cohin starts again. 'Six… Five…'

We run to each other in horror and confusion.

'Four… Three…'

'Stop it,' Max screams at the camera. 'We did what you wanted.'

'Two… One.'

'No,' Max screams.

A loud pop, like a champagne cork. The bomb splits in two with a pathetic splatter, exposing a Lichtenstein-style 'BOOM'.

Henry's playing with us.

'YOU BASTARD,' Rhodri screams into the camera.

The heavy silence is replaced by talking.

A video.

It's Thea.

Skye and Max form a human shield in front of me. 'Don't look.'

My name is Thea. I'm seventeen. I am at college right now. I'm an influencer. My plan is to go viral and create a social media empire bigger than the Kardashians. I know I've got what it takes to win. You can put me down, but I'll get up again and again. There is no stopping me, I'll always come back fighting.

I try not to look, but the sound of her voice draws me to the joy and hope lighting up her face.

I hope I'm an Agent. It's always more fun to play the bad guy. And the Agents always win. And I'm playing to win. Essex girl through and through and we are tough as nails.

Grief explodes harder than an atom bomb, obliterating any fight left in me. It's all-consuming. The pain in my chest is so real I can't breathe. Huge ugly, body-shattering sobs hijack my body.

She's gone.

They leave me on the sofa, tiptoeing around me, quiet whispers mask quieter sobbing. Caught up in their own fear they leave me be. I couldn't save her. I tried to have her back, instead she had mine. She has done since we were little kids; I just didn't see it until now.

I have no clue how long I stay cocooned in my grief; time moves on without me.

Strong arms fold round my shoulders.

'Hey.' The word gets suffocated by my pain. 'Kass?'

I twist away, I'm not ready to talk.

'Look.' Rhodri's Welsh lilt is soft and calming. 'I'm not very good with this sort of thing, never got the words to say it right, so I'm just gonna say it and then piss off, if that's okay?'

I say nothing. The calmness of his voice punctures the pain and soothes my broken heart.

'I know it's hard, I can't pretend to know what you're going through, but we need you, Kass, and we need you now.'

I don't respond. We can't beat Henry. Noah, Tayo, Thea, that's what happens when you fight him.

'I know you don't feel like fighting.' Rhodri reads my mind. 'But we don't have a choice. By the time people miss us, it will be too late. I need to get out of here. I have people who depend on me. My sister's eleven and she's a wild one, proper strong, mad into horses. She wants to be a nurse when she grows up and I know she'll be great, she's so caring, see? Her name's Carys, it means love in Welsh and I love her to bits. I have to live for Carys.' His hand squeezes my shoulder gently. 'And you need to live too. Thea may be gone but Lewis needs you.'

Just when I think my heart can't break anymore it cracks again. I don't even know if Lewis is alive, but what if he is? I sniff loudly, wiping my nose unceremoniously with the back of my hand. Rhodri keeps talking, soft and gentle, his face close to mine, his breath warm against my cheek.

'There's a saying my dad used to say when I was young, *Ar ddiwedd y gân daw taliad*. It means *At the end of the song comes payment*. I never got it till now, but Dad's right. This song is nearly over, and Henry needs to pay.' He tilts my head up gently, so his green eyes are staring straight into mine. 'I want to make him pay.' He wipes a tear from my cheek with the tip of his finger. 'But I need you. If I have to cope another minute with Max, I may end up killing him myself.' He chuckles. 'And the thought of cwtching him better.' He stops. 'That's a hug by the way – just a hug.' He shudders. 'The boy needs to shower. Please, I'm begging you.'

Rhodri's small act of kindness pulls me back to the now. The pain in my belly solidifies into fire and anger. He's right, Henry should pay for what he's done.

I remove myself from his arms and walk up to the nearest camera, brushing away the tears burning my cheeks. I won't let Henry see my pain.

The others move towards me.

'Henry.' I don't recognise my own voice. 'It's over. We did what you wanted, now let us go.'

He doesn't respond.

A hot rage explodes through my veins.

'Henry, you coward, show yourself. We've won. We found your Agent. We stopped the bomb. You've had your fun. LET. US. GO.'

'Would Max come to the Confessional.' Cohin's voice booms into the room.

'No,' Max cries.

Skye's by his side, her arm under his elbow, pushing him towards the Confessional. 'I'll come with you.'

Cohin appears. 'Players, sit.'

Rhodri sits. 'It's over, Henry.'

Cohin spins around, his face hidden by the hood. 'I can confirm the Players have eliminated one threat from the game. Thea was identified as an Agent and has been taken out of play.'

I swallow my cry.

Rhodri jerks upright, a frown growing on his exhausted face. 'What do you mean eliminated one threat?'

Skye and Max walk straight back in. 'Found this in the Confessional.' Max puts a small satin pouch on the table.

'The game has changed.' Desperate eyes widen as we absorb Cohin's words. 'A new threat has been confirmed. One of you is a Double Agent. You must all take one stone from the bag. Do not reveal it. Whomever draws the black stone is now an Agent. Players you must eliminate this threat to earn your free—'

'NO.' Rhodri grabs the bag and throws it across the room. It smashes against the wall. 'We have played your sick game and jumped through your hoops. Enough of us are dead.'

Terrified, we all hold our breaths. Rhodri paces up and down.

'Sit down.'

'Rhodri, please,' Skye begs.

The room turns red. Skye lets out a dismayed cry as we all reach the same conclusion.

Henry's never going to let us go.

And Thea died for nothing.

34

An imaginary ticking thuds against my temples.

Screw you, Henry.

'No one else is gonna die,' I say, surprised by the strength in my words. 'But no one is coming for us, so it's up to us.'

'He has a gun,' Max says weakly. He looks strange; his dishevelled hair made even blacker by the unforgiving red light.

'Guys, think, you were picked out of hundreds. You're here because you're the best,' I say.

'Yeah, right,' Max scoffs. 'Best at being a gigantic nerd.'

'They saw something special in all of you. I need you to *be* special right now,' I say, catching Skye nodding enthusiastically out of the corner of my eye. 'So Max, you'd better grow a pair, 'cause I swear if you so much as get a paper cut, I'll kill you myself.'

'Good pep talk,' Rhodri says. 'Not liking the imagery but loving the sentiment. Actually, fuck it. You're so right. We are the best. So, bring on the imagery and Max, grow a fucking handful. We need you to have balls bigger than the Hulk and play like you're Geralt of fucking Rivia.'

Max stands straight and a determined expression flashes across his face.

Skye walks up to the camera. 'Screw you, Henry,' she

says. 'And I never swear.' She turns to me, hands firmly planted on hips. 'We could overpower him, there are four of us and one of him.'

'He's out there somewhere,' Max says, his courage short lived. 'We are safer in here than out there.'

'There are three of us and Max,' Rhodri says. 'No offence, man.'

'None taken,' Max says.

'Besides,' I say. 'He's one man and a gun. Not liking the odds of us all getting out in one piece, which kind of goes against my "no one else is dying" strategy.'

'How did he get hold of a gun?' Max throws his hands in the air. 'This is Wembley, not downtown LA.'

'Easy if you know the right people,' Skye says. 'And I reckon Henry does.'

'Noah set up a whole fake game,' I say. 'We are working way outside of the boundaries of possibility. And Max is right, we're safer in here. We need him to come to us.'

'Easy, we just need to piss him off,' Rhodri say. 'Like Tayo.'

'And we're right back to someone dying,' Max says.

'No one else is going to die.' I will my words to sound convincing. Looking at everyone's faces, I'm not so sure it worked.

'Still doesn't help us get out. The doors are locked,' Max says, gesturing to the main house doors.

'Then we need to figure out a way to unlock them,' Skye says.

Rhodri's hanging around the boys' bedroom door giving me the weirdest look. I catch his eye and his head moves the smallest amount. He ambles casually toward the bathroom.

I count to ten elephants before I follow.

Walking into the bathroom he puts his finger over his mouth and gestures to his mic, rolling my T-shirt around mine we crouch over the sink, turning the tap on full.

'He's got all the power,' Rhodri says. 'We need to take it back.'

I pull a helpless face and he grins a grin completely lacking in funny.

'Got a plan. You were right when you said we are safer in here,' he says. 'When we were in the run, you tripped over camera tracks. It's given me an idea. Fucking crazy one, but it could work.'

I mouth an *okay*, this is too big to risk Henry overhearing.

'The camera track runs all the way around the house, even in the garden. That's a whole metal circuit surrounding the house. I can run cable from the fuse box to the track. If I can connect the two together, I can make a high voltage circuit. We lure Henry onto it and fry him. He won't see it coming. Worst case, the power will trip and knock out all the cameras, so he won't be able to watch us. More importantly it will trip the door locks. The emergency override will kick in and they'll open. They have to, it's all

315

part of health and safety, giving us a fighting chance to escape.'

I can't help but giggle at the absurdity of health and safety right now.

'How do we set up a high voltage circuit?'

'Uh, hello. High voltage sparky here. It's what I do.'

Damn, I've never been so glad to have forgotten something.

'The fuse box is in the kitchen, remember? We need to make a circuit, metal on metal, and attach a cable from the fuse box to the track. It's a three phase, two-hundred-amp supply. That's enough to take down an elephant.'

I'm nodding so enthusiastically my head may fall off.

'Only problem. The back-up generator. If we don't turn it off too, we'll only have minutes before it kicks in, doors lock, and we're trapped again.'

Shit.

'I saw the controls in that room upstairs.'

'The gallery?'

He shakes his head. 'No, the smaller room Lewis took us to.'

Lewis. My mind fills with a eureka moment. 'Lewis could do it.' A sharp pain stabs through my chest. We haven't heard from him since the gallery. My optimism is quickly replaced with grief. I bury it quickly, just like the rest. 'We don't even know if he's alive.'

Rhodri adopts my enthusiastic nodding. 'Lewis is fine. He managed to hide from Henry before, didn't he?' I bite my lip to stop the quivering. 'Disabling the generator is easy. But we need to get a message to him.'

I'm blinking back hot tears.

'We need to distract Henry while I set it up. I'll need a roll of cable; we passed some outside the run. We won't have long but it could work. But Lewis will have to open the run door, so I can get to it.'

'Why can't we all come with you?' I say.

'Won't help, we'll get stuck at the next locked door.' Rhodri's eyes flash with anger. 'This needs to be over, once and for all. It's him or us.'

'Okay then,' I say. 'Let's do it.'

He catches my arm, his accent making the words soft. 'I'm so sorry about Thea.'

I can't talk about her, not yet. I push the grief deep down.

'This is risky, Kass,' he says. 'And dangerous. And I've done a lot of stupid things today.'

His eyes have darkened to a deep seaweed green.

'The song's about to finish, right?' I say.

'And Henry's about to pay,' he says back.

We smile dorkishly before embarrassment sets in. I tear myself from his gaze.

I leave the bathroom hopeful. One way or another we're gonna get out of here, on our terms, not Henry's.

But first I have to get a message to Lewis. I duck into the girls' bedroom. Skye's sitting on the bed. Max is buried under a duvet again. I count the cameras. Six.

How the hell do I get a message out without Henry seeing?

I stare at myself in the mirror. It's hard not to when it runs the whole length of the room. God, I look rough. An idea bounces off me and my reflection knocks it back.

I make a show of pacing around, arms folded across my chest. The others are pretty motionless so, luckily for me, I'm the most interesting thing in the room. The cameras whirr, their small bellies rotating in my direction. Once I'm sure all the red lights are on, I sing, praying Henry isn't a Swiftie or I'm dead. I don't even know what I'm singing, it doesn't matter. 'Unlock the key to my heart, boy, why don't you unlock the key to my heart and let me ruuuuun.'

'You okay?' Skye asks, as I circle past. 'Stupid question, I know. But are you?'

I make sure all the cameras are on me and speak clearly. 'Sorry.' I fake embarrassment. 'When I'm nervous I sing. It totally helps.' Skye's giving me the weirdest look. 'Only Taylor Swift, no one else does it.' I look directly at the camera. '*The Boy Behind the Mirror* is one of my favourites. I find the lyrics really get me, so haunting.'

Skye pulls a face. 'Way too white-girl, candy-floss pop for me.'

I laugh. It sounds wrong after everything that's happened. 'My friend would tear you to pieces for saying that. He's a Taylor super fan.'

'I hope I meet him one day.'

And that stops that conversation. What else can we say? Glancing at the camera, I hope I've done enough. Sitting on my bed, I wait.

Rhodri strides over to Max's bed and pulls off the duvet. 'Dude, you stink, you need to wash.'

Max moans and turns over, pulling the pillow over his head.

Rhodri grabs the pillow. He pauses, then kicks him. 'Come on.'

It takes forever for Max to get out of bed and into the bathroom. Rhodri risks a wink as he passes me. Talk about dead man walking, Max has completely given up.

I focus on the mirrors and wait. Soon a shadow appears on the other side. Jumping up I pretend to preen, pressing my face closer to the glass. *Wait there*, I mouth. The shadow moves closer and I'm staring into Lewis' eyes.

My relief at seeing him alive almost gives me away. Turning back into the room, I clock the door on the back wall. I get eye contact with Skye, just enough for her to know something is about to go down. She moves to the end of Amara's bed.

Max bursts out of the bathroom, straight into the living area, screaming.

'Get lost, Rhodri. There's no way I'm getting in the shower. I don't care. We are all going to die.' He runs to a camera, waving his arms, and screams. Rhodri slips into the storeroom.

'He's gonna pick us off one by one until there is no

one left.' Max turns to another camera. 'I'm right, aren't I? Hello? HELLO? Bumblebee, BUMBLEBEE.'

The cameras whirr and turn to capture Max's very visible breakdown.

He coughs and splutters and cries and screams. 'Let me out. LET ME OUT.' He throws himself into the garden, running around the walled grass, waving his arms, and screaming. All the cameras turn outwards towards him.

Now's my chance.

I dash to the door in the bedroom wall. There's no handle, no lock on this side. I knock quietly, my body pressed against the door. I open the door slowly but something heavy is pushing against it. The door bursts open and Amara's body falls into the room.

Skye's by my side. 'Put her back. Quickly. Put her back.'

Lewis' hands appear from the dark as he grabs Amara's arms and pulls her back inside the run. We help, praying Max is diverting the cameras. We push the door back. The whole thing takes less than a minute.

I lean against the mirror, my heart banging.

'She must have been there the whole time,' Skye whispers.

Grabbing my washbag, I pretend to do my make-up in the mirror. Skye hovers against the door, keeping it open a crack, just enough for Lewis to hear.

I pull the microphone cable out of my pack and speak quickly and clearly into the mirror. 'We have a plan. We're going to lure Henry out. Rhodri's going to trip the electrical system and open the doors. We need you to stop the generator from kicking in. There's an override button in that room next to the gallery. When the power goes out, turn it off. Lock yourself in, so he can't get in to turn it back on. You need to keep the camera-run door open for Rhodri.'

I reconnect my microphone. My heart's thumping. I long to run through the door and give Lewis the biggest hug ever. I do my hair in the mirror. I can just make out Lewis' face, his black eyeliner streaked down his cheeks in jagged zigzags. His palm presses against the glass and I press mine to it. Even through the glass the pain in his eyes is so intense, I bite my lip to stop from crying out, as Thea's ghost stands between us.

I make a thing of putting my washbag back in my suitcase. Skye leans casually against the secret door as I go past, closing Lewis back in the run.

I gently push Thea to the deepest part of my consciousness. Skye nudges me, the cameras are starting to whirr back around to the house.

Rhodri needs more time.

We leg it out into the garden and join Max, screaming at the top of our lungs. 'HELP, PLEASE HELP US. WE ARE TRAPPED IN HERE.'

We get one shout in before the crowd noise deafens our cries, but we don't stop, raising our voices to be heard over the artificial sound. The crowd noise increases.

Coupled with the noisy evening traffic there's no chance of being heard, but the cameras stay fixed on us. Noah's still on the tree and Tayo's on the ground. None of us have to act. It feels good to let it go and tell the world how terrified we really are – even if we know the world's not listening.

35

'All contestants assemble at the table,' Cohin shouts as we tear around the garden. Our one small act of rebellion.

Exhausted, Max has fallen in a heap on the grass, sweat peppering his forehead, but still he shouts and cries and distracts, and I love him for it.

'Contestants to the table.' Cohin's tone is terrifyingly angry.

'We've done a top job of making him angry,' Skye says. 'I'm glad.'

Rhodri appears. Catching my eye, he nods.

That's it. The circuit's live. We're on.

My emotions are all over the place. The once infrequent sensation of terror-filled despair is mixed with a surge of overwhelming love for these people. Rhodri, strong and determined, with a heart the size of Jupiter hidden underneath all those tats. Skye, beautiful, brave and loyal. And Max, sweet, geeky Max, wearing another oversized *Star Wars* T, clinging onto a broken chair like a lightsabre. We're bonded by something stronger than anything I've ever felt. Then there's the anger, so hot and fierce it's painful, and it's getting stronger, feeding off the unbelievable pain of grief.

Whatever happens, this ends today.

As we move towards the table the red wash of light disappears. We don't sit. Instead, we form a circle. Taking Rhodri's lead we sit on the floor, facing out.

'Contestants must sit at the table.'

'No.' It's amazing how calm I sound. The others are looking at me, fierce determination and trust tattooed onto every face.

The air is super-charged with tension.

Cohin screams. 'You don't tell me no.' Everyone tenses. 'I make the rules. You will sit at the table and play my game.'

I wait for a heartbeat. 'No.'

We answer one by one.

Skye, 'No.'

Max, 'No.'

Rhodri, 'No.'

One by one we unplug our microphones and place them in front of us.

Cohin flickers. 'This is my game. I make the rules. This is my game.'

'I think Cohin is an only child,' Max says, and I am surprised at how easily we laugh.

'SIT AT THE TABLE NOW.' Cohin's voice is distorting as much as the image.

'Or what?' Rhodri's voice is perfectly calm. 'What exactly are you and your hologram going to do?'

'I will end you.' Cohin spins through the images of the dead: Amara, Cali, Noah, Xander, Tayo and Thea.

Noah's image appears. *I've got your back.* I fight to keep my reaction neutral.

Xander's appears next. *You are my people.*

Bore on. Amara grins.

Tayo's calming chuckle fills the air.

I bite my lip.

Cali laughs. *Jammie Dodgers. Excellent choice.*

'He's trying to get a reaction.' Rhodri's voice wobbles. 'Shut it out. He can't hurt us if we stay united.'

Thea. *I love you.*

Blood floods my mouth as I bite my lip too hard. It's too much, I can't hold it together. My chest heaves, huge sobs bubble and threaten to explode.

Without a word Skye stands. Calmly picking up the cable-cutters, she walks in front of Cohin. She raises them high, their yellow handles still stained with Noah's blood, and brings them crashing down on Cohin's virtual head. And she doesn't stop. Again and again, she hits the spot in the centre of the table; the small dome where Cohin appears. Cohin flickers in and out. As glass scatters across the table, he disappears.

The room is graveyard quiet. Skye throws the cable-cutters, and they land in the corner with a clattering thump. She sits back in the circle. Always calm, always lovely. Even now.

'We've changed the rules, Henry.' Skye addresses the cameras. 'This is our game now. You want to finish this, then come down here and face us.'

Our breathing's fractured, our chests rise and fall in a rapid gallop.

'We can do this,' I say.

'I love you guys,' Max says. 'No matter what happens.'

I rub my eyes with the back of my hand. Rhodri catches my eye and smiles. I smile back.

We start our vigil. Not knowing where Henry will enter, we all watch a different part of the house.

I pray Lewis made it back to the generator room safely and is standing by.

And we wait.

'It was that dating show,' Max says. '*Dump or Date.*'

'You okay, mate?' Rhodri says.

Max turns excitedly to Skye. 'That's where I've seen you before. I knew it would come back to me.'

Confusion flashes over Skye's face for a quick instant. 'Guilty,' she says with a cute smile. 'You got me.'

Rhodri chuckles. 'You pick your moments, Fanboy.'

Max turns back, his face triumphant. 'I watched…'

Skye cries out. 'He's in the garden.'

We all turn to face the outside.

'It really is Henry,' Max breathes.

Henry's huge form stands in the garden dressed all in black, a hood covering his head, his hand gripped tightly around a small black pistol.

'Why isn't he moving?' Skye says.

'He needs to come closer,' Rhodri says. 'He needs to step on the track.'

Still Henry doesn't move.

'He's not in any rush,' Max says. 'It's not as if we have anywhere to go, or any actual weapons.'

'This is a bad idea.' Skye's voice quivers.

'Keep it together, guys.' I inject as much confidence as possible into my words while ignoring my screaming flight response. Max's attention is fully focused on the cable-cutters in the corner. 'Stay still,' I say, praying Max's courage holds for a few more seconds. 'If this works, we won't need weapons.'

'Come inside, Henry, we're ready for you,' Skye screams like a warrior princess.

Henry steps onto the track.

Nothing happens.

'It's not working,' Max cries.

'Shit,' Rhodri squeaks. 'His shoes.'

Confused I look down at Henry's feet. He's wearing black Doctor Martens.

'Rubber soles,' Rhodri says. 'Damn boots are insulating him from the current. Who wears DMs in the middle of a heatwave?'

'He's coming in.' Skye jumps up.

Henry grabs the door handle. He's about to step off the tracks and into the house.

Rhodri springs to his feet and grabs the knife from the table. With an ear-splitting war cry, he runs at Henry. As the door opens, he dives forwards and throws the knife between the tracks under Henry's feet.

A huge splintering crackle hits our ears as the metal blade connects the two tracks and the power flowing through the circuit explodes.

Sparks fly as Henry is thrown backwards into the garden.

A gun shot fires across the fireworks and Rhodri's body jolts across the floor. The lights go out. The house crashes to black.

I run to Rhodri.

The tracks sizzle and snap.

'Don't touch him,' Max cries.

'He's not electrocuted,' I say. 'He's been shot.'

Rhodri's on the floor clutching his arm, blood seeping through his fingers. Skye rushes forward, wrapping her cardigan around the wound.

'I'm fine,' he says. 'It only grazed me.'

'Uh guys?' Max says. 'Where's Henry?'

'No way,' Rhodri shouts as we peer into the empty garden. With the house in darkness the garden fills with moonlight. 'There's no way.'

'Players one; Henry one,' Max says. 'And this is what they call a stalemate.'

Certain the garden is empty, Skye closes the door.

'At least we stung the bastard,' she says. 'That shock must have hurt him.'

'Not so much if he got up and walked out of the garden.' Rhodri gasps as the pain kicks in. 'Damn. I was sure that would work.'

'It did.' Skye points up to the cameras.

She's right. The room is black. Not one camera is blinking red, there's no whirring, no movement. The only light in the room is coming from the moon. No one is watching.

'The electrics are out.' Skye's voice rises with relief. 'The doors are open.'

'Let's get out of here.' Max jumps up.

'Wait,' Skye cries. 'Henry's still out there.'

Max shrugs. 'So?'

'He's not gonna let us walk out, is he? He has a gun.'

Everyone looks at me for answers. I look to Rhodri, but pain is distracting him. What would I do if I was a psychopathic killer with nothing to lose?

'I would get the power back,' I say. 'If I was Henry, I'd be desperate to get back control. This game is everything to him. He's gonna try to get the power back on.'

'How?' Skye's trying to stem the flow of blood. I'm not sure the bullet only grazed him, her pastel yellow cardi is seeping crimson red, and Rhodri is losing colour. He needs a hospital, fast.

'The generator,' I say. Rhodri nods.

Lewis.

I am not losing both my best friends.

'Is the circuit still on?' I ask Rhodri.

'No.' His pain is so clearly painted on his face. 'It's short-circuited.'

Max and Skye get him up on his feet and make their way to the main house doors. I pick up the knife from the tracks and grab the cable-cutters.

'You need to get him out and get help.' I catch up with

329

them, conscious Lewis is on his own and Henry's had a head start.

Max stands in front of the main doors of the house, taking the handle in his shaking hand.

'Here we go.' He pulls the handle. The door opens.

Words can't explain the relief flooding through my body, it's a total rush. The expressions on everyone's faces say the same as we stumble out of the house that has been our prison for days. Finally free, and almost safe.

36

'Here,' I say to Skye as we stand on the studio side of the set. Emergency lighting has kicked in, giving a soft glow to the black, enough to light the way out. The house looms behind us, a shadowed reminder of the horrors shut within. But we're not safe yet, we can't breathe easily until everyone of us if out of this studio.

'Cutters or knife?' I hold them out for Skye to choose. 'Which one are you, Miss Scarlet or Mrs White?'

'I always wanted to be Professor Plum.' Skye takes the knife.

'Bet you did,' I say.

We walk slowly. Rhodri leans heavily on Max, his movement painfully stilted. We pass the camera-run door, wedged open by the doughnuts of cables stacked on top of one another. Rhodri rests against the studio wall.

Max smothers me in a huge bear hug. 'Stay safe.'

'Rhodri was right about the shower.' I screw up my nose.

Max grins. 'What ya gonna do?' His smile fades. 'Sorry about the nominating and everything. I didn't mean…'

'All good,' I stop him before my mind goes to places I'm not ready to face. 'Everything's good.'

His smile is full of sadness as he turns away.

'You sure about this?' Skye says and I'm glad of the distraction.

I force a confident nod. They're gonna need each other to get out, they still have to get to reception and if I'm wrong about Henry, he could be waiting there.

'Okay then. See you on the other side.' Skye hugs me awkwardly before following Max to the studio door.

Rhodri hangs back, his dangerously pale face popping against the blackness. My heart sinks. Is he planning some brave hero move like Tayo and demanding to come with me?

'Look, you need to get help, fast.'

He smiles painfully, his good hand clutching his bad arm tight. 'Give me a minute. I want to say something.'

'There's no need to say—'

He cuts me off.

'Jeez, shut up already. Can't you see when a guy is trying to have a moment?'

I clam up quicker than an oyster.

Rhodri leans against the wall. His breathing's shallow and he's finding it hard to talk.

'I wanted to say thank you,' he struggles. 'You've been amazing through all this. Your strength gave us strength. You're not like the rest of us. You're extraordinary. You're the girl guys like me write songs about.' He takes a haggard breath and chuckles into the studio quiet. 'I wish you were the girl next door to me.'

I snort, waiting for the punchline. It doesn't come. He stops. His eyes are dark and soulful, more serious than I've ever seen.

Oh.

His eyes meet mine.

My heart does a little flippy thing.

The pain in his arm makes him wince, propelling him out of the moment.

'So don't die.' He grimaces. 'It would really piss me off.'

'Back at ya.' I try to be cool while the warm glowy feeling pulsating through my skin makes me feel invincible. Not knowing what to say, I default to a joke.

'The loss of blood's making you almost human, Welsh boy,' I say. 'Who knew?'

'I'm obviously delirious,' he says.

'Obviously,' I say.

A small chuckle dances on his lips before the pain chases it away. Max appears from the dark and hovers at his shoulder.

'Gotta go, big guy.'

'Ahhh, perfect timing. I was angling for a cwtch.' Rhodri pushes off the wall, leaning heavily on a very confused Max. 'Not from you, Fanboy. Stand down.'

Rhodri smiles and turns away, Max steering him, hand resting gently on his elbow, arm thrown around his waist. My stomach flips painfully. As they disappear through the studio door, I realise I may never see either of them again.

37

I walk in the opposite direction from the boys. Action is way easier than words right now. My head is full of a grumpy, arrogant, six-foot Welsh boy, who has somehow managed to burrow well and truly under my skin. I can't think about this now. It's way too much to process.

The emergency lighting reassures me. While it's dark, the generator is off, and Lewis is safely locked in the generator room. As I climb the stairs, I'm torn between willing my castmates out of here without a mad attack from Henry, and the frantic need to have my boy Lewis safe.

I reach the top of the stairs and pause, allowing my eyes to adjust to the dark.

A body hits me so hard I almost fall back down the stairs.

'Lewis.'

'You're alive.' He mumbles into my shoulder.

Pushing him away, I punch him on the arm. 'I told you to stay in the generator room.'

'And wait for Horrid Henry to come and kill me? No, thank you.' He shudders. 'I got out of there as soon as.'

As happy as I am that he's safe, I can't ignore the fear coursing through my veins. 'Henry will know we're out.'

'So?' Lewis pushes his hand through his hair. 'Reckon he's legged it. Besides, what's he gonna do?'

'Try and stop us?' I say, as the panic bubbles to the surface.

'Hey,' Lewis makes me look at him. 'The others are in reception. Thought they were Henry, shat myself. They said you'd gone back for me.'

'Rhodri?'

'The Welsh dude? He's gonna be okay. The cute gamer is helping him. They're out. They'll get help.' Relief rushes through me, as Lewis talks. 'Brilliant, I thought, everyone's safe. And then I noticed *you* weren't there.' He looks at me expectantly. 'Why aren't you there, Kass?'

'I'm saving you.'

'Oh, I think I'm saving you.' He nudges me. 'Idiot, you should have gotten the hell out.'

'Wasn't leaving you behind,' I say.

'Aww babes.' He grabs my hand. 'Come with me, there's something we need to do.'

I resist. 'We need to go. Now.'

'Trust me. You need to see this.' I try to argue but he interrupts. 'If we don't, Henry could destroy it. He's gonna want to cover his tracks or whatever serial killers do when they know they're about to be caught.'

'That's exactly what I'm afraid of,' I shudder.

'We must stop him destroying evidence, Kass. I'm taking no chances. He's not gonna get away with anything because of some random loophole we don't know about. Help's coming, we'll be quick.'

Escape is all I can think of. 'Lewis, please, we need to…'

'For Thea?' Lewis' expression breaks my heart.

'Quickly,' I say, desperately trying to find a last flicker of brave. He pulls me into the corner of the gangway, up another flight of stairs and through a door. The room is full of racking, columns of hard drives stacked together, rainbow-coloured fibre optics weaving out the back, lights flickering on and off on the front like something from a weird sci-fi movie. On top of each column is a monitor.

'Wait,' I yelp, as dread creeps up my spine. 'How is the power on?'

Lewis shrugs. 'Maybe this floor is on a different supply?' he says. 'It would make sense to keep these machines separate.'

I try to shake off the fear and go with it. None of this makes sense, but I follow him to the corner where a laptop sits open on a small desk. Lewis moves his hand across the keypad and the screen bursts into life.

'It's an editing system.' He reads my confusion. 'Post-production.' Like that clears it all up. He points to the pictures on the screen. It's footage of us, in the house. 'Henry's been editing the live stream down into an hour-long show. Look.' He points to a monitor. There's a clock, like the one we saw down in the gallery.

The screen reads:

Programme title: LIE OR DIE (Final Edit.)
Duration 57min 30sec

There's a sticker on the keypad, a small dove. Frowning I minimise Henry's screen, searching the laptop's home screen.

'What is it?' he asks.

'This is Noah's laptop. Henry must have taken it.' I scour the desktop. 'There.' I point to a dove icon hidden amongst the others. The title makes my pulse race:

Isla's story.

'This is what Noah was working on. He wanted to expose reality TV. He told me to find his laptop, said it had all the answers.'

Lewis snorts. 'Does Reality make the monsters, or the monsters make Reality?' he says.

'Noah's story needs to be told. We can't let it be forgotten in all this mess. Lewis?' Lewis is distracted. He's walked into the row of racks.

'The whole show is on these machines. Every camera.' He runs his hands across the racks. 'Everything Henry did, all the murders, will be on these.' He turns to me. 'I'm downloading the files onto the laptop, but there's a lot and it's slow.' He points to the USB cable running from the laptop to the racking. There's a bar on the top of the home page; forty-three per cent downloaded.

'We need to go,' I say.

Lewis shakes his head. 'We need this. This is proof.' Lewis is absorbed with the monitors. 'I think he was desperate to become a celebrity. Let's face it, Noah's plan was a perfect foil for a psychopath to piggyback. Maybe

337

he didn't want Noah to succeed. If reality shows get stopped there's no chance of fame for him. When he found out what Noah was doing, I guess he got triggered. Ooh look, this one is labelled Confessional.' He fast forwards the footage.

'We need to go. We don't know where Henry is right now,' I say, my heart's stuck so far into my mouth I can taste it. The download's only fifty per cent. I get what Lewis is saying, but I'm shitting myself.

Lewis is shuttling through the footage on the machine labelled Confessional.

'Skye… Noah… You… Xander… Skye…' he says, hidden by the racking.

My fingers drum on the desk as my eyes remain glued to the small bar on the laptop: fifty-four per cent.

'Tayo… Tayo… that must be when he was the Detective,' his voice breaks with grief. 'Skye… Wow there is a lot of Skye on here. D'you think she realised she was talking to a serial killer? How messed up is that?'

'It's sick,' I say over my shoulder, half listening as I will the numbers to reach one hundred.

'Man, there is so much on here,' he says. 'I am sure if he…' Lewis makes a strange noise.

There's a shuffling coming from the racks and a thud. Someone's here. The laptop's still downloading. I shut it quietly, pushing it off the back of the desk. It falls into the mess of black cables. My fingers reach for the cable-cutters and, shaking, I turn to the racks.

Lewis is crumpled on the floor.

And Henry's standing over him.

His face is hidden under his hoodie, Cohin-like. He's holding a piece of scaffold pipe, thumping it repeatedly in his hand.

'Hello Kass,' Henry says. 'Consider this a rule break.'

In one quick motion he lifts the pipe high and slams it into the monitor with a shattering crash.

Splinters of glass fly into the air. I cover my face from the needle-sharp shards.

Crash. The racking falls like dominoes as Henry brings the heavy pipe down again and again.

Turning, I run to the door. The terror surging through my veins makes me clumsy. My body's moving faster than my brain and as my foot hits the metal steps I slip, flying headfirst down the stairs. I land with a heavy thwack. My head smashes against the railing and sharp pain ricochets through my skull. The cable-cutters bounce across the gangway with a metallic clunk.

A hand grabs my neck and I am hauled up to standing in one strangling move. A weird gurgling leaves my lips, my hands grab my throat, my nails clawing against his skin.

Henry pushes me against the rails.

'Before you die,' his mouth's right next to my ear, 'I want you to ask yourself why you didn't run when you had the chance.'

Adrenaline and terror flood through me like a

supercharge. Instinctively I push against him. Taken by surprise, his giant form rocks backwards and I break free. I run, my broken body begging me to stop, my brain screaming to go faster. It's too dark. All escape routes are swallowed up in the black. A metal handrail bars my way. The lazy tread of Henry's shoes against the steps tells me he's following. He's in no rush. The pipe scrapes against metal, a slow screeching that makes the hairs on my skin all rise to attention. My head's throbbing. Touching my forehead, my fingers feel sticky and warm. My eyes frantically search the darkness. In the half-light a small, narrow wooden walkway appears to my side, snaking out over the lighting grid and disappearing into the black. Dipping under the railings, I climb onto it. It wobbles frantically beneath my feet. The huge bulk of the house looms beneath me.

'There's nowhere to run.' Henry's laughter chases me into the darkness. 'I said stop.' He stops laughing. 'You know I have a gun.'

I stop.

'Turn around.'

I turn, the walkway dancing erratically under my feet.

Henry stands on the gangway, the pipe glistening with Lewis' blood.

He drops it. It crashes to the floor below with a piercing clatter.

'Why are you doing this?' I contemplate jumping. It's too high. Even if I didn't kill myself falling on the set, I'd break my neck on impact. I edge back, one foot behind the other, as the walkway judders and jolts under me.

'Why?' Henry screams his anger into the black. 'This was my chance. My turn. *You* ruined everything.' He spits out my trope like it's poison. 'Girl. Next. Door.'

Henry leans against the railings. His left hand's clutching his thigh. *So he was affected by the electricity.*

'I didn't know…' Lewis was right, Henry wants to be one of the shiny people.

'Shut up.' He wipes his forehead with his gun hand. 'Everything was planned perfectly. It was my turn for celebrity. MINE. It was easy to take out a contestant, there was no one to stand in my way.' As he shouts a thin line of drool drips from his mouth. 'Until you turned up.'

'You hurt Bryony so you could get on the show? You took her EpiPen?' I can't keep the horror out of my voice. Henry's face flashes with a crazy anger. 'And when I got on instead of you, you just went ahead and killed everyone? Why?'

'Because the world doesn't need any more two-bit nobodies pretending they're somebodies. You're all the same, with your social media and your followers and your fame. You make me sick.' He points the gun at me.

I throw up my hands. 'Don't do this. Please. We can get you help. We can…'

A shot fires. I drop down, grabbing the narrow walkway as it rocks back and forth.

341

Henry grumbles under his breath. Ducking under the railings he steps out onto the wooden walkway.

He can't get a clean shot at me while the walkway's moving. Using my body weight, I swing the whole walkway harder. He edges closer, trying to aim as his arm swings back and forth. Frustration fills his face.

It's working.

'Stop,' he shouts. He takes a few steps closer then stops, concentrating on his aim.

'Henry, please. Don't do this.'

'You think you're so special.' He laughs. 'You think you're so much better than the rest of us.'

'I don't, I really don't, that's the whole point. Please, I…'

'To think I can't get a chance while people like you get all the breaks. I would have been spectacular…'

'Please don't do this. Henry, please.'

Henry laughs. 'To think your friend sacrificed herself so you could beg and cry. What a waste. You're pathetic.'

You promised me you would live. Thea's voice, inside my head.

Something inside me shifts. By mentioning Thea he's crossed a major line. My fear hardens into anger and my rage builds.

Henry's grinning, the smug smile of a man who knows he's won. No way is he gonna see me broken. A movement behind him catches my eye. Someone's there. Lewis? Relief is soon followed by fear. I have to distract Henry. I need to keep him talking.

342

'Why?' I say, amazed my voice sounds so strong. 'Tell me why you killed them, Henry.'

Henry's face is filled with loathing. 'People like you, beautiful people, make me sick. It's all about your hits and likes and followers. You're nobody. I'm just as good as you. You have no right to fame and wealth. I refuse to allow more useless idiots to have power and influence just handed to you when you have absolutely NOTHING to say. You disgust me. It was my turn, my time.' He's waving the gun all over the place. 'I have something to say.'

Someone's walking up behind him, sure and steady on their feet as they balance on the small walkway.

It's Skye. Henry turns his head. I shout to get his attention. 'Nobody thinks they are better than you, Henry.' He turns back to me, gun pointed. I daren't shake the walkway in case Skye falls so I brace myself and keep talking. 'There are no shiny people. That's the thing. We're all struggling to fit in. That's the whole point.'

As Skye creeps closer my fear and anger solidify into something else. I remember Rhodri's words. I'm someone extraordinary, he wants to write a song about *me*. I stick out my chin and breathe in strength. 'But you're wrong, Henry. I do have something to say. I may not be like all the shiny people, but I am strong, and I am beautiful, and I am brave, and you will never take that away from me. I am happy with my trope. Everybody loves the Girl Next Door. So, kill me if you want to, I can't stop you, but I want you to know that I…'

Henry gasps, his body juddering. His face changes from angry to shocked to scared as he struggles to breathe. I recognise the fear in his eyes.

Tayo had the exact same look.

Dropping his arm, the gun falls. His breath is short and quick, blood bubbles appear at the corners of his mouth. His hands reach out for support but find nothing. He lunges toward me.

'Kass,' Skye screams.

Henry turns around to Skye and shakes his head, his voice surprised. 'You?'

Now's my chance. I kick out, aiming for his bad leg. I push my foot into his injured flesh as hard as I can.

He screams. His foot misses the walkway, dangling for a second in the mid-air black. He tries to find his balance but it's too late. His arms reach out desperately, his eyes fly wildly from Skye to me as he falls backwards into the abyss. A knife handle glints like a falling star, lodged firmly in his back, right under his ribs. He hits the ceiling of the set with a splintering crack. A cloud of dust mushrooms upwards, filling the air with the smell of wood and blood.

The walkway squeaks frantically. I hug the planks, my heart crashing against the wooden surface. My brain refuses to accept the possibility it's over. Skye's clutching the walkway too, smiling triumphantly.

It takes all my effort to pull myself back to the safety of the gangway. We collapse together.

'How did you…?' I can't control the shaking that's hijacked my body and my voice.

Skye smiles. 'Figured you may need some help. Never underestimate the pretty blonde. Totally didn't see me coming.'

Henry's blood is all over her hands. I bite back vomit with small shallow breaths.

'Gross,' she says, wiping them on the gangway. Unlike me, she's calm and in control.

A blinding flash hits our eyes as the generator kicks back in and the rows of hot heads and studio lights burst into action. Peering over the railings we have a bird's eye view of the house. It takes a moment for our eyes to adjust and take in the scene below.

Beneath the huge hole in the set ceiling lies Henry. He's landed face up, wide eyes open, staring up to the lights now focused solely on him. He's on the table, his arms and legs splayed chaotically across the very place where Cohin appeared.

'I still can't believe it was him. He seemed quite normal when he was looking after us. Grumpy, but normal.' My voice sounds weird with its new shake and wobble. I need to find Lewis.

Skye jumps up. 'He didn't look after me. I had the girl, what was her name?' She pumps her forehead with her palm. 'Arghh, can't remember, the one who went in the ambulance with that contestant.' She huffs. 'No, it's gone.'

'You never met him?' I pull myself up, my legs are so weak I struggle to stand.

Skye shakes her head, her hair swooshing prettily around her shoulders as she leans over the railing. 'Why would I?'

'*Dump or Date*. He worked on it.' Puzzled, I scrutinise her face.

'No, never met him.' She looks directly into my eyes. Her face is a smiling blank, no tics, no signs of lying, no hint of remorse or freakage.

The moment's gone in a second.

'Sounds like you were his trigger.' She shudders. 'He thought he was gonna step in after Bryony left the show...' Her hands fly to her face. 'Oh my god, he did that?' Her eyes grow even wider. 'He deliberately put krill oil in her food so she would die, and he could take her place. He created chaos just so he could get on the show and be famous.'

'That's so sick.' I can't take my eyes off him. I'm too scared he might jump up again like in every horror movie I've watched.

'That's fame,' Skye says, her voice calm. 'It's intoxicating. Doesn't everyone want to be remembered? For something? Even something bad?'

'I...' I really don't know what to say. I grip onto the railing worried that my legs will give way.

'He was weak and stupid.' She's leaning over the railing, knuckles gripping the shiny grey metal. Her face is hidden behind her hair, I can only assume the horror that must be churning through her veins right now. 'Most men are. So easy to be brainwashed with a kiss or a fantasy. He didn't question it because he wanted it too much.' She's leaning over too far, her feet poised on tiptoe. My fingers coil around her shoulder pulling her gently back.

'I think you're in shock,' I say. She doesn't answer. 'Skye?'

Her head flips up with a sweet giggle as she pushes herself off the railing.

'I'm fine.' She steps back, feet firmly planted back on the walkway. The pretty smile dancing on her lips doesn't warm the coldness in her eyes.

'Will someone please tell me that lunatic is dead.'

I leap up the steps into Lewis' arms. He staggers back from my enthusiastic greeting. A large gash on the side of his head is bleeding down his super-white face, the congealing blood sticking shards of purple-blue fringe to his forehead. Tucked under his arm is Noah's laptop.

'It's done,' I say. 'It's over.' I help him to the floor where he sits, leaning against the railings. Ripping off a piece of my already torn T-shirt I press it gently over his wound to stem the bleeding. I turn to Skye, but she's gone.

'We're proper superheroes. Like for real.' His eyes are dancing but his pain sits heavily on his face. I squat down next to him.

'We really are,' I say. There's a sharp stinging over my eye and my temples are pounding.

Lewis pulls the laptop up onto his lap and opens it. It springs to life immediately. I've never been so happy to read the words DOWNLOAD COMPLETE. Lewis' fingers run over the keyboard.

'Checking it's all here,' he says, wincing. 'Henry destroyed the hard drives.' Lewis spits his own blood into his hand and wipes it on his jeans. 'Girl, no judgement. It's been a day.' His hand reaches up and takes the bloody cloth from me. 'No. It's been a weekend. I haven't changed my boxers for days.'

The giggle I've been trying to swallow full-on explodes from my lips as hysteria and relief override all emotions. A busy noise fills the space below.

'In here,' a voice says. 'They were in here… Whoopsie.' I peer through the railings, watching as armed police and firefighters spill into the studio, ant-like and just as busy, their voices loud and clear and confident. The stream of gold, green and black disappears into the house, like we did three whole days ago. I shudder, knowing the horror they will find.

Max is leading the paramedics. He looks up and sees us. 'We did it, Kass! We bloody did it.'

'Come on.' I will my body to stand, and turn to Lewis. 'You need a hospital.'

'Give me a minute,' Lewis says, still tapping away on the laptop.

I look down at Henry. Surrounded by police and paramedics, he finally has his audience.

Adrenaline pulses through my veins. Breathing out painfully, I finally let the fear go.

'Game over, Henry.'

A shout, followed by another and a policeman appears at the camera-run door. Max runs to the officer, who's talking rapidly into his comms. Max recoils like he's been tasered. My pulse restarts its frenzied gallop. Max looks up, finding me in the chaos. His expression stops my heart in one bewildered beat.

Joy, shock and overwhelming happiness are all fighting for pole position on his exhausted face.

'Lewis.' I don't need to say anymore, he's standing by my side.

Max cups his hands around his mouth. 'They've found her,' he shouts. 'They've found Thea. She's alive.'

38

A rush of uniforms swarm into the run as Thea's small body is carried out in the arms of a firefighter. He's moving urgently across the studio, shouting ahead to the waiting paramedics.

So many emotions are racing through me right now I can hardly hold onto them. Lewis and I cling to one another, watching as our friend is resurrected from the dead.

'She would love this,' Lewis chuckles through the sobs. 'Being rescued by a hot fireman is totally Thea's M.O.' He holds his head. 'Woah, dizzy, need to sit.'

'I can't see Skye,' I say, helping him back to the floor.

'Probably needs a minute.' Lewis wipes his eyes with a dirty sleeve, smudging more eyeliner down his cheek. 'She killed a man. Probably doesn't want us to see her freaking out.'

'Maybe.' Something's off and I can't put my finger on it.

'You don't stick a knife in someone's back and feel fine. I can't even imagine.'

I scour the studio floor for Skye. 'She said she was fine.'

I'm desperate to see Thea, but I won't leave Lewis and he's in no state to rush anywhere. He snorts, distracted with the laptop files. The deep gash on his forehead glistens ruby red in the studio lights. 'She's taking a moment. Even Kass *mind-reading* Kennedy can misread the tells sometimes.'

The hairs on my neck all jump to attention as my brain leaps into overtime. 'She didn't have any tells.' Lewis throws me an *ehh?* 'She didn't have any tics.' My mouth catches up with my brain. 'Everyone had a tell, everyone. Cali twiddled her earrings, Max pulls down his top, Rhodri swears, Thea pushes her hair around – a lot. Everyone did something when they felt bad or uncomfortable or were downright lying.'

'So?'

'So, Skye didn't. She didn't react at all when Henry died, not until she caught me watching her. And she lied right to my face about knowing him. They did a show together, *Dump or Date*, there's no way they wouldn't have met, or at least had a conversation about it and...' The penny drops like a boulder. 'She knew about Allergy girl.'

Lewis looks blank.

'She knew the runner had gone in the ambulance with Allergy girl, she told me, she said he put krill oil in her food. That's fish oil. How would she know that? Pippa kept it a secret from the contestants. And you just said it, she put a knife in Henry's back, in exactly the same place as Tayo.' I'm talking so fast I keep tripping over my words. 'What if she killed Tayo? We all assumed it was Henry. Noah thought there could be someone working in the house, what if it was her? What if Skye was helping

351

Henry or…' I take a deep breath, her words screaming in my head. *He didn't question it because he wanted it too much.* 'What if Henry was working with Skye?'

Tayo's face fills my head as his dying words replay in my brain. *Killer Agent.*

'In the garden, Tayo said Thea was the killer Agent. He pointed to her.'

Lewis shrugs. 'I don't know; I wasn't watching.'

I shake my head. It wasn't a question. 'I just assumed he was telling me Thea was the killer Agent.'

'Which she was.'

'Yes, but Lewis, Skye was *behind* Thea, what if he was pointing to her, too? What if he was saying Killer *and* Agent?'

'You think he was telling you Thea was the Agent and Skye stabbed him in the back?' It takes a minute for Lewis to process. 'Why?'

'Why what?'

'Why would she do it? What's her motive?'

'Apart from being a complete psychopathic nutter?' I pause. 'Tayo was too strong, he was refusing to play her game. He was giving us the strength to say no, she had to get rid of him to control us.' All my conversations with Skye are fast forwarding through my mind in triple time. I repeat her words out loud. '*Totally didn't see me coming.* She said that to me just now, I thought she was talking about Henry but what if she was talking about me? And in her MIV.' My hands gesticulate wildly as I remember back to the prerecords. 'She said something about being underestimated because she was blonde and pretty.'

'That's a hell of a lot, Kass. If you're right… Oh shiiit.' Lewis is staring at the laptop. He's paused on Skye in the Confessional. 'I did not just see that.'

He rewinds the footage. Skye's in front of the table, the easel next to her, draped with the black cloth. I recognise the biscuit box. She puts a card inside a black envelope. Tucking the envelope into the hatch she places the biscuit box inside. She smiles at the camera.

Lewis pauses the footage. 'Is that?' He taps the screen.

'My name.' I nod, recognising the white envelope on the table with KASS KENNEDY in bold black. We both stare at the screen, processing.

'Did she just put…'

'The Necromancer card in the hatch.' I finish his sentence. 'I think she really did.'

'But wouldn't Pippa have seen it? Wasn't she watching?'

'That's why I thought Pippa was guilty, that and talking to her in the Confessional. How could she be watching and not stop it? But I think she did try to stop it, and I think that's the moment when Henry killed her.'

'So, it was Henry who sent the crew home, not Pippa?' Lewis asks.

'It wasn't just us he was manipulating with that deepfake machine thing.'

Lewis fast forwards through the footage, his fingers

tapping impatiently. Finding what he's looking for, he stops with a triumphant cry. It's Skye again, this time sat behind the table, talking into the camera. He plays. Skye's pretty face jumps to life.

It's almost over. She's talking to the camera lens like it's her boyfriend, her voice soft and seductive, her head at a half tilt, lips pursed in a pretty pout. *This is what you wanted, Henry. You showed them. You showed them all.*

Henry's voice fills the room. *But why do we need to…?*

Skye interrupts, her voice silky smooth. *You've done so well. You figured out Noah's plan, dealt with Pippa all by yourself, and the way you're working Cohin is genius. You deserve everything you're gonna get. Just this one last thing then we are done. We can disappear.*

Silence. Skye leans into the lens. *Don't you want us to be together?*

You know I do. Henry sounds flustered. *Just no more killing. We never agreed to Tayo being…*

Skye interrupts, her face stern. *Tayo was necessary. He gave them hope.* She leans back in her chair and laughs. *I had no idea it would feel like that, slipping the blade in under the ribs, what a rush. And when I almost got caught putting the garden key into pretty boy's suitcase, so exhilarating.*

I let out a jagged cry, Lewis squeezes my hand.

I know you liked it too, the killing. I could see it on your face.

I stuck to the plan. Henry's voice wobbles. *I did it for us. Because I love you.*

You are too far in this now, Henry. You need to finish what you started. Skye takes a long pause, her tone changes again, soft and persuasive, she purrs into the camera. *It should have been you on that show, you deserve all the fame. And when the time is right, we'll show the world what you did, and everyone will know your name.*

She's staring right into the lens, talking right to us. I can't stop shivering as my body turns to ice.

No more killing, Henry again.

A quick flash of anger is covered by a wide-eyed smile. *Don't you see? If we want to be together, we have to finish what we started.*

Why can't we just let them go?

Skye's face becomes hard as she stares down the camera lens. *Don't you want to watch? It's all so deliciously fascinating. They talk the talk of heroes but in the end, they all want the same – not money, power, fame, not even love. When the time comes, human nature says they'll bargain everything away for another chance to live.* Her face changes back to sweet and pretty in one terrifying heartbeat. *I want to see how far they will go to survive.* She laughs a giddy laugh. *I've outsmarted them all.* She shrugs daintily. *Who knew?* She leans into the camera, her eyes wide and mesmerising. *So, start the Ticking Time Bomb, Henry, I want to watch them dance.*

Lewis closes the laptop, thin streaks of dried blood against his chalk white cheeks. 'I think you're right.'

'Skye came up here to cover her tracks.' My voice

doesn't sound like mine as I struggle to breathe away the hysteria. 'She wasn't saving me from Henry, she was killing him to shut him up. She was the one.' I turn my face to Lewis just as the paramedic reaches us. 'Skye is the killer and we've just let her go.'

39

Six weeks later – Boredomville

'Are we actually doing this?' Lewis takes a shaky breath. ''Cause we know the shit will hit the fan if we do, right?'

Two pairs of worried eyes are staring at me right now, but I'm calm and completely sure.

Noah's laptop rests on my knees. I've no clue how Lewis managed to smuggle it past the hordes of police, but I love him for doing it. Besides they got everything they needed from the racks, despite Henry's attempt to destroy every shred of evidence.

'It's what Noah wanted.' I correct myself. 'What Tom wanted.'

'Can't get used to Noah being Tom,' Lewis says. 'It's too weird. I'll always think of him as Noah the Jaffa Cake.'

My phone pings, I ignore it.

'You okay with this?' Lewis turns to Thea. 'This is gonna impact you as well.'

Thea nods. Six weeks after being shot by Henry, she's out of hospital and home. She's still healing, but thanks to Henry's crap aim and her quick thinking, she's still with us. I shudder as I think of her hiding under Xander's body, passing out and bleeding out. I stop myself from going to that place I keep revisiting in my nightmares – what if they hadn't got to her in time?

She squeezes my arm. 'Why should Skye get all the attention?'

Lewis shrugs. 'Still can't get my head around it.'

I know exactly how he feels. Skye didn't just mess with our heads she messed with our bodies too. I was right about the sleeping potion. They found traces of benzodiazepines in our blood, they'd been drugging us through the water, just enough to make us sleep heavily so we wouldn't hear them inside the house. That explains why Xander never woke up when Amara was murdered and why I collapsed on my bed that night Noah confessed. I try to tell myself it wasn't my fault, there was no way I could have saved him, but it doesn't help the guilt that's lodged itself in my stomach next to the overwhelming mountain of grief that threatens to swallow me whole. We really were her puppets, dancing to her every whim. But why? No clue. Every time I try to rationalise Skye's actions, I come up blank. Maybe that's the point, maybe we'll never understand why she did what she did. We were all just rats inside her twisted social experiment, even Henry.

'Noah was right, Reality really does make monsters,' Thea says.

'Think you'll find I said that way before Noah,' Lewis mumbles.

'But it also makes heroes.' Thea's eyes shine.

'Aww, stop.' Lewis grins. 'Besides, reality TV didn't make her a monster, that was all on her.' He shudders. 'I can't even think about her still being out there.'

We go quiet, lost in our own nightmares. Turns out Skye Greenhill doesn't exist, a pseudonym made up for the purpose of getting on the show. She was having conversations with Henry through the Confessional the whole time, directing and manipulating – the ultimate omnipresent game-narrator. There's no doubt in my mind that she seduced him, that she was the brains behind the whole operation. Henry, the failed wannabe reality star, turned down from so many shows for failing to pass the psych test. How easily she fed his fantasy and preyed on his weakness. It was all there, on camera: her plan to push us as far as we would go, to see what she could get away with.

'I can't believe she was in there with us the whole time and we had no clue,' Thea says. Whenever she mentions Skye, her voice trembles. One of the many new tics she's developed since the game. 'And what she did to Tayo.'

'I guess this is what happens when you lock a crazy person in a house with the world watching.' Lewis can't keep the bitterness out of his voice or the anger from his cheeks.

'Especially one fascinated with psychology and criminology,' Thea says.

'They'll catch her.' I smother the fear with a dollop of false confidence. 'They have to.'

'That's my girl.' Lewis smiles. 'Always looking for the happy ending.'

'I don't want to talk about her.' Thea's gone pale. 'Especially now.'

Our heads bob in agreement and we take a unified deep breath, eliminating all thoughts of Skye in one long exhale of grief.

'Max is on board; I spoke to him last night.' I steer the conversation away from Skye.

'Anyone spoken to Welsh?' Lewis asks.

'Nope. And his name is Rhodri.' I concentrate on the laptop, clicking to open the file, ignoring the look Thea and Lewis exchange over my head.

Isla's story

'Are we doing this?' I say. They mumble a 'Sorry'.

Lewis' arm curls around my shoulder and Thea squeezes my knee. I press 'post'. There's a few seconds delay before the ping signals it's loaded.

Pressing the triangle, the picture buffers for a second before Noah's face bursts onto the screen and my heart squeezes painfully. We hold onto one another.

Hi I'm Tom. Many of you know Isla Stockett, winner of Keeping it Real *and my beloved sister. I was the creator of* Lie or Die, *the reality game show set in the world of murder, mystery and intrigue. But that's not what it was designed to do and through the next hour I want to explain to you why I did what I did, for my sister … Isla.*

I press pause. The views are already piling up as 'Noah' immediately goes viral.

'Listen.' Lewis puts his hand to his ear. 'There goes

the final nail hammering into the reality television coffin.'

After the media storm of our *Lie or Die* weekend, this will be enough to honour Noah's last wish.

'Isla has her voice,' Thea says. 'He can rest now. They both can.'

Tears are streaking down my face. I close Noah's laptop, wiping my cheeks with the back of my hand. Lewis sniffs loudly and Thea daintily blots her eyes with a tissue.

The game may be over, but we are all still trying to process. The media attention has finally died down, our five minutes of infamy for being on *that* show is over. It's getting easier. Helped massively by the fact we have each other.

'*Shake It Off*,' Lewis says but without his usual Swift-ism enthusiasm. It's become our mantra, our way of dealing with the unwanted and relentless attention. He jumps off the bed, pats his thighs and busies himself in my wardrobe. 'Man, you are gonna need a whole new wardrobe for uni.'

I pull a face. 'Right back at ya and your artsy-fartsy film school.' He sticks his tongue out at me. I throw a cushion at him before realising Thea's watching. We stop.

'Guys, it's okay,' Thea says. 'I am totally fine with you leaving. Hell, as soon as I get the all-clear I'm leaving too. Besides we still have a year.' She goes quiet, staring down at her hands. 'And I nearly died, so I'm not gonna feel bad about you leaving, and neither should you. We won't let her win, remember?'

Lewis and I wrap our arms around her in a gentle Thea hug.

My phone pings again.

'What *is* that?' Lewis says, lifting tops out of my drawers, shoving them back as if he's looking for something.

'Spam,' I say.

Thea grabs my phone. 'Ooooh,' she coos. 'It's a certain tattooed Welsh boy.'

Lewis feigns surprise. 'Oh? Tell me, Thea. What does he say?'

'Guys, not funny,' I say, putting Noah's laptop carefully on the desk. I haven't spoken to Rhodri since, well since that last day. I wouldn't do that to Thea. I don't get why they're laughing at me.

Lewis folds his arms. 'You should tell her.'

'Tell me what?'

Thea pulls a face. 'Turns out I may have … spoken to him.' My heart dances a little jig before being squashed into the carpet by my conscience. Of course she has, we all thought we had lost her, and now she's back, there's no way I'm gonna let anything come between us ever again – especially a boy. She's still talking. 'We had a lovely chat, and it turns out he may be my type on paper but I'm not into him.'

Lewis fake coughs, 'Bullshit.'

Thea nudges him. 'More importantly he is very

obviously into someone else – he totally friend-zoned me.'

'I always thought he was a dick,' Lewis says, pulling out my favourite black top. 'That whole musician thing did nothing for me.'

They are both staring at me, eyes dancing.

'What?' I say.

'Well, it turns out he's coming to London for a meeting or something with a music college so I suggested he could pop in and say hi.'

Lewis is clapping his hands and bouncing up and down.

Thea waves my phone in my face. 'He'll be here in twenty minutes.'

What the actual?

'Well, come on, girl, we have twenty minutes to transform you, although, to be fair, if he fancied you in that awful sushi T-shirt for two days straight, the bar's not set very high. You know I did pack you some fabulous stuff.'

'Never got round to it,' I say. 'No big.'

Lewis shakes his head. 'When will you learn?' They both stare at me.

'What?' I say suddenly self-conscious.

Lewis pulls me off the bed. 'You can thank me later.'

'What's happening?' I say, as the top is pulled over my head.

'Uh, I think Thea just organised for a hot tattoo-covered Welsh boy to come and whisk you off your feet.'

Lewis shakes his hands in the air. 'And yes, I am well aware you are perfectly capable of doing the whisking, it's just a turn of phrase.'

'Isn't that what best friends are for?' Thea giggles.

My stomach churns with excitement. I have the very best friends in the whole world.

And I'll kill anyone who disagrees.

Metaphorically, of course.

EPILOGUE

January

'You're trending again.' Three words I never expected to come from my dad's mouth, followed by, 'World's gone mad'.

Mum gives him her look and I silently will her not to do the *I told you sos* again. There are so many bad things about this whole situation, and the passive-aggressive bickering from my parents isn't helping.

Dad waves his phone in the air. 'Why now? Why can't they leave it alone?'

My stomach churns guiltily. I know the answer but I'm not about to fess up. Ever since Isla's story went viral our phones haven't stopped pinging. The first episode of *Lie or Die* is trending again, and we and our fellow contestants have become morbid celebrities overnight.

'It never stops,' Mum says. 'It's Thea I feel for, and the poor parents of those who died. This must be a living hell for them. How's Thea doing?'

'She's okay,' I say, but it's a lie. Thea has probably had it the worst, with nearly dying and everything. But we're all struggling. And then there's the new videos, copycats popping up all over the place, our faces pasted onto bodies, faces of those we lost. It's relentless. It's like people have forgotten we are real people with real trauma and real grief.

Someone, somehow got hold of Henry's version of the show and released it. Who knows how many views it had before it was taken down.

Turns out there is something worse than being in a reality show that's taken over by a psycho killer, and that's having to relive the experience over and over.

'It's fine,' I say, my insides dancing to the now familiar anger-to-fear-to-anger tune. I've a pretty good idea of who would put it out there. Despite a huge ongoing investigation the police have no clues. Skye's disappeared like a virtual ghost, while we are left holding our breath, waiting an eternity for closure.

The doorbell goes and I jump up, glad of an excuse to leave the room.

'Have you seen it?' Lewis is standing in the doorway, his face even paler than usual.

'I'm taking a leaf out of Thea's book and ignoring all social media.' I sound way more chilled than I feel. 'The Henry thing will die down. We just have to…'

Lewis shakes his head impatiently, 'Not that. Check your phone.'

It takes a while for my phone to switch on. Lewis is quiet the whole time, leaning against the door, chewing his nails. My phone lights up, pinging with notifications, one after the other.

'Check your messages,' he says. 'Your actual phone messages.'

I've got a text.

Casting Call

LIE OR DIE – Series Two

Big Brother meets Werewolf

Following the success of the first series, we are looking
for more CONFIDENT, COMPETITIVE &
INVESTIGATIVE contestants to take part in
this extreme reality TV game show.

BIG CASH PRIZE.

Do YOU still have what it takes to survive?

Email: casting@skygreenproductions.com

'Skygreen Productions?' My voice sounds stupidly high.
Our phones ping in quick succession. The message
blurs in front of my eyes.

Hi guys.
I'm bored.
Wanna play Werewolf?

CONTACTS

If you have been affected by some of the issues touched upon in Isla's story, there is help out there and people to talk to (in confidence) – please don't be afraid to reach out.

Papyrus UK
Prevention of suicide in the young.
papyrus-uk.org
Helpline: 0800 068 4141

Samaritans
Suicide prevention charity.
samaritans.org
Helpline: 116 123 for free

Young Minds
Supporting young people's mental health.
youngminds.org.uk

ACKNOWLEDGEMENTS

I would like to thank Penny Thomas at Firefly Press for seeing the potential in my story. My fabulous editor, Hayley Fairhead, for all her editorial expertise; Becka Moor for the fantastic cover; Lucy Mohan and Grace Samuel for making my first YALC so much fun; and Graeme Williams for all his enthusiasm and fantastic ideas. Huge thanks to the whole Firefly team whose hard work, care and expertise have made my dream come true.

To my brilliant agent, Saskia Leach: huge thanks for believing in this project from the very start and for your unwavering support, enthusiasm and hard work in getting it to the right people. Thank you for calmly navigating me through the process – you're the best!

To my GEA 2019 Eggs, Imogen Cooper, Sara Grant, the Undiscovered Voices committee, my super-talented UV2022 cohort, Bryony Pearce, the Twitter Debut 2024 group, The Furies and all my SCBWI friends – thank you!

My crit group: Lucy Van Smit, Louise Roberts, Annette Caseley and Susan Sandercock, thank you for reading the very first sparks of this idea and encouraging me to apply to UV2022.

Special thanks to Tilda Johnson for always having my back and for your continued support long after I've flown the nest.

To the hugely talented Josie Jaffrey – thank you! I have learnt so much from you.

Sue Cunningham and Katja Kaine for critiques and evenings of wine and celebration, and to Rowan for her honest feedback – thank you. Cara Miller, I love our coffees at the Boathouse, your words of wisdom and hours of laughter.

To the best and most brilliant writers, Jan Dunning and Annette Caseley – thank you for always being there. You are the best critique partners ever – I couldn't have done this without you both.

To Orlando Capitanio, thank you for reading every single thing I have ever written and always believing in me. Your love and support mean the world.

To Mum and George for all your support over the years.

To my group of Mafia playing friends who gave me the inspiration for this book as we murdered each other over and over in the name of fun – still slightly bitter that I *never* picked that illusive Mafia card!

To all my friends and work colleagues at Fountain Television Studios – I loved working with you all and have so many fabulous memories.

Huge thanks to Dave Waterman and St Joseph's College Media and Drama departments and all the fantastically talented students that took part in creating our social media content – you are all stars in the making!

To Dimitry Davidoff for inventing the original game of Mafia. And to reality TV — our guilty pleasure, thanks for reminding us that no matter who we are or where we come from, we are all stars.

To the Clacks: what a team! To Tim, my biggest supporter and bestie, not to mention the very best reality TV editor – thank you for believing in this story from the very first words and helping me to make it shine. To Imi, my mini-Agent and advisor on all things scary; Ali, my very first and loudest cheerleader; Finn for always quietly supporting; and Cam for all your help creatively: your combined advice on all-things teenager is invaluable. Thanks for providing hugs, encouragement and chocolate whenever needed and for never letting me quit. You are my inspiration – I did this for you guys.

And finally to you, the reader. Thank you so much! If you haven't tried the game Mafia, grab a group of friends and give it a go, I promise you it won't be boring. A word of advice for those new to the game and a reminder for those seasoned players – never forget, no matter what – **Trust no one**.

A.J. Clack moved from a small village in South Wales to London, to pursue a career in television. She worked on a wide range of shows from *Teletubbies* to *Friends*, while also writing plays for the Edinburgh Fringe and development scripts/pilots for children's television. She now lives in Suffolk with a houseful of teenagers and can often be found freezing on the side of a rugby or football pitch.

Lie or Die was a SCWBI Undiscovered Voices 2022 winner.